THE ESCAPE

KAREN WOODS

HarperNorth
Windmill Green
24 Mount Street
Manchester M2 3NX

A division of
HarperCollins*Publishers*
1 London Bridge Street
London SE1 9GF

www.harpercollins.co.uk

HarperCollins*Publishers*
Macken House, 39/40 Mayor Street Upper
Dublin 1, D01 C9W8, Ireland

First published by HarperCollins*Publishers* Ltd 2025

1

A catalogue record for this book is available from the British Library.

ISBN: 978-0-00-870039-3

Printed and bound in the UK using 100% Renewable Electricity by
CPI Group (UK) Ltd

This book contains FSC™ certified paper and other controlled sources to ensure responsible forest management.

For more information visit: www.harpercollins.co.uk/green

In memory of my mother Margaret Price always missed
and my brother Darren Woods miss you always.

Also by Karen Woods

Tracks

Tease

Vice

The Deal

The Con

The Truth

The Watch

The Trade

Prologue

The setting sun glinted on the water, the lapping waves darkening and reflecting back the neon signs of the beach bars. The heavy gold bracelet on his wrist caught the light as he pushed the drink towards her.

'Go on, another won't hurt. You're a long way from Manchester now, darling, and I won't tell if you won't.'

PART ONE

Chapter One

Jane Morgan stood in front of the full-length mirror and smiled at herself. She looked mint and she knew it, but she made sure she always looked good. That's why all the men were all over her like a rash any time she was out in the pubs and clubs. A ten out of ten, anyone would say. She liked the fact people said she was a great catch, and she worked hard for the admiration. Her long honey-blonde hair looked like strands of spun silk and her tanned legs seemed to go on forever. Her friends told her she could have been a model, and on a good day she liked to think they were right. Get her on her good side, she was gorgeous. She applied her shimmering lip gloss and pouted her heart-shaped lips as she looked in the mirror one last time. She was ready.

Tommy Braxton came into the bedroom behind her and hooked his arm around her tiny waist, twisting her to face him. He was a good-looking man too, if you liked the rough-and-ready kind, and Jane knew all too well he had the women lining up.

'Bleeding hell, Tom, watch you don't smudge my make-up. Hours it's just taken me to look this hot. I'm going to have to learn to do it properly myself. I've been at the salon most of the day.'

Tommy rested one heavy hand on the nape of her neck, the cool of it making goosebumps rise on her tanned skin. Then, with his other hand he tickled her side, making her giggle. She felt her heart race, sensitive to his touch. 'Aw, Tom, stop pissing about, will you? The girls will be here soon and I'm still not bloody ready. I need to put my shoes on and all that. I'm always late for anything they arrange, and they'll have my hide if I'm not ready when they arrive.'

Tommy stood tall and pulled his shoulders back. 'You know what they say, Janey. You should always make time for your fella. Keep the romance alive and all that.' He smirked at her. 'What about a quickie before you go out? I'll be quick, I promise. In and out like a Ninja.'

Jane was unimpressed. She couldn't imagine anything worse at this moment in time. When she was going out-out with the girls, it took her nearly a full day to prepare: an age in the shower, then having her hair done, a full face of make-up professionally applied, lashes topped up, new nails, the list was endless. But he was still looking at her with hungry eyes. They'd not had sex for three days, and she knew what her fella was like. She had to come back with a reason to put him off. 'Tommy, babe, I don't want to rush it. Let's make a date for when I get home later on. I'll make it worth looking forward to.'

He was crestfallen. 'You'll be steaming when you get in, hun. You'll go straight to sleep like you always do. I'll sort myself out if you can't be bothered. Or how about a quick suck? Come on, I won't take long.' He looked pitifully at her, trying to convince her she was denying him his manly needs.

Jane stroked her slender fingers along the side of his face, letting her manicured nails skim down to his chest, and purred , 'Tom, I pinkie-promise you that, when I come in tonight, we will have a proper session together. I'm not really in the mood for getting drunk tonight, anyway. If it wasn't Lesley's birthday, I would have swerved it.'

Tommy smiled. He knew a pinkie-promise was nearly as good as a legally binding contract between him and his Mrs. He rubbed his hands together and nodded. 'Right you are, then. I'll only go for a few beers, then, while you're out. I'll grab us some food on the way home, too, and we can have a scran before we go to bed. You've not made me any dinner, I know. I always come second best when you're going out with your friends. Neglected yet again.'

Jane knew he was only half joking. 'Aw, is my little Tommy getting jealous? I told you from the start that my friends are like family to me, and we have a girl code that we all follow. Mates before dates and all that. Friends are important in this world – you need to know who's got your back.'

Tommy scoffed. 'If it was the other way around, you would be kicking off. If I was putting this much time into not just going out with the lads, but all bleeding day getting ready. Remember the other week when I said I was going to the match with our kid?' He raised his dark brows. 'You went ballistic, telling me I should go and move in with him if I wanted to put him before you.'

Jane sighed awkwardly. 'Yeah, that wasn't my finest hour. It was hormones. You know what I get like when I'm due on. I just wanted a bit of love and affection, that's all.'

'Well, same here, love. So when I ask for a bit of your time, don't give me the lecture about the girl code and the bond you all have and the rules you have to follow. If you're serious about us, then I have to come first.'

Jane could see he was getting agitated, his cheeks flushing.

'Bleeding hell, Tom, why do you always bring this stuff up when I'm in a rush? If you want, when I come in tonight, instead of having sex, we can talk about it.'

Tommy's eyes were wide now. She'd called his bluff and it was clear he wasn't willing to lose his night of passion for love nor money. Quickly, he backpedalled. 'You know what I mean. I just want to be as important to you as your girls. Anyway, I've booked you in for tonight, so don't be too late home. I've got work in the morning, unlike you, so I want a decent night's kip after you've tired me out.'

Jane grinned: it was game, set and match to her. She had her girls' night to look forward to and her fella ready and waiting for when she got home. Then, she could lie in while he got off to work the next morning. Tommy was a grafter, for sure. He lived for his work, and she loved that he was successful. His chain of gyms was flourishing, and it meant they were not short of a few quid. Their friends teased them, called them the Paris and Tyson of Manchester, but they weren't far wrong. Jane had everything a woman could have wished for: a beautiful house, several holidays a year, a smart car, and designer clothes bursting from her wardrobe. She even had a nice little earner – Tommy had invested some of the gym profits in a little salon that he'd put in her name. She liked being a business owner, even if she never went near the books and left the details to the girls that ran the place. But the one thing she craved wasn't happening: she still wasn't married.

Tommy had always said he would propose when the time was right but, up to now, she remained girlfriend not wife. He kissed her cheek and started to walk out of the bedroom. He grabbed his crotch and chuckled. 'You better be ready when you come in later, you dirty girl.'

Jane burst out laughing and bent to put her shoes on. 'You won't know what's hit you,' she grinned. One last twirl in the mirror, looking at her deep violet dress hugging her curves, and she was ready. She quickly checked her Rolex and headed down the stairs.

It was nearly eight o'clock and the girls had arrived at Jane's in a haze of perfume and anticipation. They'd been friends since school and, despite ups and downs and all of life's highs and lows, the four women still made time for one another. They were sitting in Jane's living room, enjoying a cold glass of wine before they headed into Manchester city centre. Lesley, Katie and Maxine had been her squad for years. Katie sipped her wine and kept her voice low. 'Where's Tommy, then, Janey? Is he in or out?'

'He went out about twenty minutes ago for a few beers with his boys. Dirty bleeder was after a legover before he went out, too. I had to smooth him over until later.'

The girls all laughed out loud as Katie continued, 'He might be a randy sod, but you've got a good one there, J. Did I tell you I've been talking to Jake Pritchard who we used to go to school with? He split up with his wife about six months ago, and he's been asking to take me out on a date ever since.'

Maxine pulled a sour expression. 'Oh my God, Katie, he was rotten in school, a right scruff, crater face. Rough, in fact.'

'Well, he's not anymore, he's decent. I think he might be after something serious, not just a shag.'

Jane shot a look over at Lesley and raised her eyes to the ceiling. Katie had never been lucky in love and, in her own words, she usually only attracted dickheads who never wanted anything more than a quick knee-trembler after the clubs had kicked out. She didn't mind that part but, as she told her friends, it would be nice if they wanted another date.

Lesley was the sensible one in the group, or so she claimed. But it meant she could never keep her mouth shut and said exactly what she was thinking, giving everyone her advice whether they asked for it or not. 'Katie, you need to stay single for a while and stop looking for a man. Protect yourself a bit. You fall in love too quickly. And, come on, if we're telling the truth here, once they've had your knickers off, you never normally see them for dust.'

Maxine nodded. 'I'll second that. You need to play harder to get. Look at that guy from the rugby club the other week. He was alright, but then you bombarded him with phone calls and texts, and he blocked you. He must have got the ick. No man wants a woman to be that available; they like the chase.'

Katie pulled a face like she was chewing on a wasp. She knew they were right, but she hated admitting it. 'I reckon he was gay, anyway. On my life, he wasn't even really into the sex that night. I invited him back to mine after the club. I'd bought all new sexy underwear and, when I walked out into the bedroom strutting my stuff, he carried on watching the footy on the tv and I barely got a second look.'

Jane could tell this was becoming a therapy session and closed the conversation down. 'Enough of this, ladies. It's Friday night, it's Les's birthday and we should be out painting the town red, so drink up and let's get pissed. Come on, neck those drinks, girls.'

Maxine downed her drink and started to collect the glasses the friends had used.

Jane shouted over. 'What are you doing, Max? Leave them there. The cleaner is here in the morning, as usual. She will shift them. I'm not paying her for nothing, you know.'

Lesley shot a look over at Maxine. 'We're not all as lucky as Jane, are we? A bloody cleaner who comes in every day and sorts her house out. Bloody hell, what I would give to have a rest and let someone else take over the cleaning duties even for a day.'

Jane burst out laughing. 'It's not my fault I'm successful, is it? Stop bloody moaning. After she's done a tidy-up here, I'll send her over to yours for a deep clean, my treat, so straighten your mush, Lesley, and let's go and party.'

Lesley hugged Jane. 'And that's why I love you...'

Maxine and Katie looked at each other, left out. 'And what about us? We're your friends too. Why does Lesley get a turn with your cleaner and we don't?'

Jane let out a laboured breath and picked up her Gucci handbag from the coffee table. True, she and Tommy paid a mint for a top-tier cleaning service, but it was nothing compared to the dough they both dropped on designer gear. She glanced at her mates, remembered when they were teenagers, trading make-up with each other or borrowing each other's clothes. When had they grown up, moved on to sharing cleaners and caring about how much sleep they got? 'For crying out loud, you can all have an hour or two with the cleaner tomorrow. I pay her top dollar to be at mine every day so I'm happy to share her.'

The four women left the house as they heard the taxi honk its horn outside. Now they knew that they could stay in bed tomorrow and nurse their hangovers in style, tonight was going to kick off. They piled into the cab, snapping selfies and laughing. Jane clambered into the middle seat, flanked by the others. She knew how lucky she was that she was the one with cash to spare and would treat them to all sorts. She'd take them away on spa weekends, bung them a few quid when they were skint, spread the luck that she and Tommy had. She loved to help the girls out – and she knew that, while they might not be able to pay her back in cash, they did so in something far more valuable: loyalty.

Chapter Two

Katie Dunstan opened her eyes and looked to her side. Who the hell was that next to her? She cringed and reached down onto the floor to find her knickers and something to shove on her top half. It was nearly ten o'clock already and she needed this guy gone before her daughter Jade came home. Jade had been away for the night with her friends in Blackpool and, if Katie knew her, she would want to get back home early to enjoy the rest of the day. Katie sat back down on the bed and smoothed down her bright red hair, pulling her pale legs up to her chest. She coughed a few times, eyes never leaving the man's back. He was well away, snoring. She reached over and gently tapped his shoulder. She couldn't even remember his name. She grimaced. She had been at the STD clinic twice this month already – any more and she'd get a loyalty card. She reached over and nudged her back-warmer. 'Erm, morning, love. Sorry but I've got to get ready and go to work, and my daughter is due home any minute so, if you want, I can make you a coffee or something quick, but then you have to leave.'

The man grunted and rolled onto his back. She could see him now, the night before coming flooding back into her mind. She cringed. She did remember his face now. It was that idiot who had been dancing next to her in the club all night long, hands all over her. She'd told herself she was going to stop doing this, but clearly she'd had her beer goggles on by the end of the night. His hand dug deep inside his black boxers. 'You were a right dirty cow last night,' he chuckled. 'I've not had a shag like that in ages. You made me graft, didn't you?'

Her eyes opened wide, and she felt bright red. What was this guy's name? For the life of her, she couldn't get a handle on it. Barney, Ben, Barry? She was sure it began with a B. 'I had a few too many last night, to be truthful. It was my friend's birthday, and we were drinking before we went out. I should have stayed away from the cocktails. I'm always the same when I mix my drinks. You're lucky you didn't have to carry me home.'

He nodded. 'Same here, love. I was drinking brandy. I never usually swap my drinks, but it was my mate, he was like, 'Come on, Brian, stop being miserable, get a few more drinks down you.'

There it was: Brian. That was his name, great. She knew it began with a B. She didn't feel as bad now the man had a name. She looked over at the time again. He clocked her and could tell she wanted him gone. His dark brown hair was stuck up and she could see the crease marks from the pillow striping his face. Still, at least he was moving now.

He pulled his jeans up and, struggling to fasten the button, he breathed in and sucked his stomach in. Katie was watching him from the corner of her eye, trying to avoid conversation: she just wanted him gone. He was still talking. 'So, what's the crack with us then, Katie? Are we on for another date or what? Because, if last night in this bedroom was anything to go by, then I'm defo up for a bit of that.'

Katie stood up and pulled her blue t-shirt as far down over her legs as it would go. She remembered what she'd told the girls last night, how she wanted a man who'd come back for more. But now it was a reality she just wanted peace and quiet, wanted her space. 'Brian, I want to be straight with you. Last night was a one-off. I've just come out of a relationship and I'm concentrating on myself at the moment. If I'm being honest, I've had enough of men to last me a lifetime.'

'Yeah, but that was them. And this is me. We had a good laugh last night, didn't we?'

She figured it was easier to agree with him to get him out of her house, so she nodded and led him to the bedroom door. She couldn't remember getting home, never mind laughing with him, but now wasn't the time to mention that. 'We did have fun, but I have a lot going on in my life and it wouldn't be fair on you. Honest, sometimes I think I'm damaged goods.'

'Maybe I should be the judge of that. Listen, I like you. It's not just the sex. Let's go out again, for food and maybe a couple of drinks, and see what happens. If it's not for you after a second date, at least you can say we tried.'

Katie clenched her jaw. Why did she have to finally bed the one guy who didn't cut and run? He'd put her on the spot now, and all she wanted was for him to leave her alone so she could get back in bed and sleep off this hangover from hell. 'Yeah, give me a ring, then. I have a busy lifestyle, so you have been warned.'

'Put your number in,' he urged, waving his phone at her. Katie typed hurriedly and passed it back, only thinking too late she could have put a false number in. Brian took it from her hands and leaned in for a kiss. Katie quickly moved away. There was no way she was kissing anyone in the morning until both she and they had brushed their teeth. Death breath was not what her hangover needed right now. He stood looking at her again.

'Brian, honest, I need to rush. I've got to get ready and be in work within the hour.' Katie dashed around making the bed to hurry him along.

'I'll wait, if you want, and I can drop you off in the taxi.'

'No, thanks,' she replied. Why could this guy not take the hint?

'Where do you work?' he asked as he finally started walking down the stairs, Katie following right behind him, to make sure he actually left.

'Asda, on the checkouts. I've been there for years. It's not for everyone, but I like the people I meet, and it pays the bills and that's what it's about, isn't it?'

Brian jerked his head forwards. 'It sure is. I think I told you I'm a taxi driver, so if you ever need a lift anywhere, give me a bell and I'll grab you. Here's my details.' He reached inside his black leather jacket and pulled out a business card.

Katie grabbed the card and held the door open with a forced smile. 'See you again, then.' Brian turned as he left, as if he was going to say something, but no sooner was he out of the front door than she slammed it shut. She stood with her back pressed against the hallway wall and let out a laboured breath. 'Christ,' she mumbled. Of course, she said she wanted a man in her life, she liked the idea of it, but not the reality, not Brian. He wasn't a bad bloke, she admitted, but he didn't make her pulse race. She ran back up the stairs, grabbed her phone from the side of the bed and hit 'call'.

'Bleeding hell, Lesley, how on earth did you let me go home with that guy? I woke up this morning and couldn't even remember his name. How bad is that?' Katie knew that, although her friends were straight talkers, they never judged her. They'd seen each other through first boyfriends and break-ups, dodgy hook-ups and wild nights. The men changed, but one thing never did – she could trust her friends to see the funny side in anything. Soon she was screaming laughing as she lay flat on the bed talking about the night before.

'Hold on, Les, someone's knocking at the front door.' She jumped up quickly and went to the bedroom window. If it was Brian who'd forgotten something, then he was getting blanked. Katie peeped from behind the cream-coloured blinds, still on the phone. 'I can't see who it is, Lesley. If it's him, I swear to you now, I'll one-bomb him.' Katie was listening and looking out of the window. 'Oh, it's the cleaner that Jane promised. Proper legend she is for doing that. My head's banging so much the thought of running the hoover round makes me want to die. Has she been to your house yet?'

Katie ran down the stairs and smiled as she let the woman in. She'd met Letty before at Jane's house and she was eager to let her inside to get cracking. She'd seen the miracles she worked at Jane's, ironing, changing beds, cleaning windows, cleaning the cooker. Jane never lifted a finger. 'Hiya, Letty. It's a bit of a mess, but I know you will work your magic on it all. Will you be able to change my beds, as well? What with one thing and another, I've not had a minute to do anything.' Katie had thought she might feel awkward having someone in her house, doing the jobs she usually did, but she was feeling so rough that the thought of help was a godsend.

Letty smiled at Katie, realising she had a call on hold. 'Yes, no worries. I'll do downstairs first, then I'll work my way up to the bedrooms.'

Katie held her phone to her ear, listening. 'Letty, Lesley says can you go to her next because she's going out and she wants to make sure you can get in.'

'Of course, Jane texted me all the addresses yesterday,' she replied. Katie had always thought she was such a friendly girl when she'd seen her at Jane's. She was probably being paid handsomely, she imagined. Decent money for her age. Letty must be around twenty, Katie guessed, and was pretty with it - dark features, raven black hair, olive skin. Katie smiled at her and headed up to bed again.

Once she was back in the feather, she folded her pillow under her head, keen to discuss the night before. 'Is it me, or was Maxine a miserable cow last night? On my life, she was moaning about everything.' Katie put the call on speaker and placed the phone on her chest.

'She's having a bit of a shit time with the hubby. Ian is up to his old tricks again, coming in late at night and giving Max a hundred and one excuses as to where he's been.'

Katie went quiet for a few seconds. 'Come on, he's always been a player, Lesley. I still can't look her straight in the eyes after what happened that time.'

'Oh my days, Katie, how many times have I told you to forget about that? It was years ago, and nobody needs to know. It was a mistake, and we all make them, don't we? The guy gives me the creeps, though. It's the way he looks at you, the way he feels the need to touch you when he talks to you. Maxine must see it, she's not blind. I mean, he was like that way back when, when we were all in school, and he's still not changed. Once a sleaze, always a sleaze, in my eyes.'

'But Maxine loves him, she always has. She should have left him when she found out he was cheating the first time, with that Donna Ramsey.'

'He feeds her buckets of shite, though, Katie. When it all came out, I was there with her, heard him denying ever sleeping with Donna, when we heard it straight from the horse's mouth. Maxine chose to turn a blind eye, if you ask me. You're right, she should have bin-bagged the wanker and got herself a new fella, and that would have showed him. He takes her for granted, always has done.'

Katie was fiddling with her hair next to her face. 'I wish I could turn back the clock, though, Lesley. It hurts me so much inside that I let myself down that night with Ian. I'd just split up with my fella and he took advantage of me, but I should have been stronger. I don't even like the guy when I'm sober. I'll tell you something for nothing: I might always be skint and single, but I would rather live my life than Maxine's. She's on eggshells with him all the time. Watch her the next time we're at her house. She's a bloody nervous wreck around him.'

Katie reached over for her vape and started sucking on it hard. She'd quit cigarettes over six months back, but by her own admission she barely ever had the vape out of her mouth. She felt more hooked on it than she had been with her ciggies. A cloud of heavily scented smoke blew from her mouth as she continued, 'So, are we all meeting at Jane's again Sunday night or what? Tommy is cooking she said, so it should be nice food.'

'Good, because as much as I love the bones of that woman, I wouldn't eat anything Jane had cooked. She's bobbins, she burns everything, even toast,' Lesley laughed. 'Even when we were all in school in the cookery lessons, she used to mess it up, and she's never had to learn since, has she? She's got the cash to never go near an oven.'

'Imagine that,' Katie went on. 'Someone cooking up a feast for you instead of my yellow-sticker ready meals for one!'

'Enough of that, K, your luck will change soon. I know you've had some hard times, but you're a fighter, you always bounce back.'

'So you keep telling me. But come on, out of us all, I've always been the one who has lagged behind – money, fellas, clobber. You lot always lend me stuff or pay for me to go anywhere. I am always like the poor relation.'

'That's what friends do for each other. That's why we are all still so close. We've all had our hard times, sure, but our friendship has always been something we can rely on.'

Katie went quiet for a few seconds, listening. 'Right, Jade's home. I can hear her talking downstairs. I'll bell you later. And do me a favour, please don't mention that bloody Brian to any of the girls. I'm ashamed already,' she chuckled.

Jade shouted up the stairs. Katie ended the call, pulled the duvet up and tucked it under her chin as Jade walked through the door and shot her eyes around the bedroom. 'Mam, why do we have someone cleaning downstairs? Have we won the lottery and you've not told me about it?'

Katie rolled onto her side and chuckled. 'Jane treated us all to a cleaner because we were out last night. So I'm staying in bed an extra hour, making the most of it. She's changing all the beds after, too, and doing all the jobs I can't bring myself to do, like cleaning them bloody windows.'

Jade plonked down on the edge of the bed and sighed. 'I'm knackered too, Mam. I've not slept a wink; the girls have been up all night laughing and joking. We had a top time but it's going to take me days to get over it. We never stopped drinking from landing there to coming home.'

'That's Blackpool for you, love. No one goes there for a quiet night in.' Katie peeled the duvet back and patted the empty space next to her. 'Jump in here with me and I'll put a film on. It's been ages since we had a duvet day.'

'I might just do that; I need a shower first and to sort myself out. I thought you were working today, anyway?'

'I was, but I've decided I'm ringing in sick.'

Jade rolled her eyes. 'Mam, you need to be careful they don't sack you. You have been off a lot lately and did you or did you not tell me that your line manager has had you in for a meeting?'

'Balls to them. That's what I say. And up to now, I've been genuinely ill when I've been off. You know I had Covid. I felt like I was dying, it took me weeks to get over it. And if I'm being honest, I'm still not right now. I'm tired all the time and get aches and pains in my body that I never used to get before.' She started coughing.

'It never stops you going out on the piss though, does it, Mother?'

Katie looked away. She knew her daughter was right. The number of times they'd argued about her going out on the town was untrue. It was meant to be mothers telling their kids not to go out on the lash all the time, but it was Jade who was the voice of reason in their relationship. Katie lived from hand to mouth, and it was Jade who was always left to pick up the pieces when Katie couldn't pay her bills. She winced as she thought of all the red notices that came through the post. She'd let the gas get into debt, had had bailiffs knocking at her front door for this, that and the other, and Jade had told her more than once recently that she was not bailing her out anymore.

Jade worked hard and already had a well-paid office job. While she chipped in for the house money, she had told Katie that didn't give her the right to think she would step in and pay all the bills when her mother had spent all her own money on going out with her friends. Jade was an only child and, although she had been young when her parents split up, she remembered the arguing, the sound of glass breaking, her mother's screams when her dad attacked her after a night out. It had been hard, but it had also made her determined to stand on her two feet as soon as she could. She wasn't rushing into any serious relationships. She was a career girl, and proudly independent. She'd started seeing a man from her office casually but was taking it slow. Maybe, Jade thought, she should fix her mam up with a guy who worked hard, had good family values, because she was well aware that, when left to her own devices, her mam picked deadbeats. The men she'd found on Tinder and Plenty of Fish looked like trouble from the start. The number of times Jade had to console her mother after yet another relationship failed was getting higher and higher. She recognised the signs well by now, knew when it was going to end in tears. Once Celine Dion was on the playlist at home, that was enough to let her know that her mother had hit yet another low. She knew her mam was always searching for 'the one', watching romantic films with fairytale endings, looking at other couples in love and craving what they seemed to have. She'd never said it to her mother, but she wasn't likely to find her Hollywood hero at kicking-out time after the pound-a-shot night at their local.

Jade yawned and stretched her arms over her head. 'Right, let me unpack my stuff and get washed and I'll be back. I'm not watching any soppy crap, though, Mam. I like to watch a good thriller, something with action in it, not women crying over some man who's cheated on them or running through an airport to declare undying love to some loser.'

Katie hunched her shoulders and sucked hard on her vape. 'Nothing wrong with a happy ending and being swept off your feet, is there?'

Jade scoffed and left the room dragging her cabin case behind her. 'No such thing, Mother. You make your own happiness in this life.'

Chapter Three

Maxine Bowen sat at her dressing table as she watched her husband Ian getting ready behind her in the reflection. He was handsome, his dark hair still as thick as ever, a tanned body that showed he spent more time on the sunbeds than most women. A lad's night out it was, he'd claimed, something that had been planned for months. He said he'd told her about it weeks ago, said she was a dopey cow and must have forgotten, but she knew he was lying.

Maxine opened her eyes wider and started to fan her eyelashes out with black mascara. 'So, where are you all heading to, then?'

Ian growled over at her, nostrils flaring, clearly hating the fact she was questioning him. If she pushed him, he'd say he was the man of the house and whatever he told her should be enough without her giving him the third degree. 'For fuck's sake, woman, I've not got a list of every pub and bar. How did I know I would get investigated? I'm going out with the lads, we'll see where the night takes us. If you don't believe me, then come with me. I'm sick of it, Maxine, sick of you quizzing me every time I'm going out. I've told you until I'm blue in the face that I'm not messing around with anyone. So, do yourself a favour and go back to whoever is filling you with all this bullshit and tell them that, too. I don't know how you can believe some nosey bastard over your own husband, anyway. We've been together forever. Do you think I would risk that for anything?'

Maxine stared at him through the mirror and sucked hard on her gums. The thought of him with another woman flashed through her mind, too much to bear. 'It's always the same story with you, Ian. You tell me you'd never mess around on me, but then the stories start. Why would somebody come up to me and tell me lies about you? And more than once. There's no smoke without fire, is there?'

'Bullshit, it's just jealous people trying to cause waves for us, that's all.'

'Waves like Donna Ramsey, you mean?'

He stuttered, 'How many times do we have to go over this? Yes, I knew her, yes, she wanted me, even tried to push herself on me, but I never slept with her. For crying out loud, woman, give your head a shake. Once again, you listened to your friends instead of your husband.'

'My friends have my back and when they smell a rat you can bet your last bleeding dollar that there is some truth in it.'

Ian walked over to where she was and spoke to her reflection. 'So, divorce me. Go on, file the papers and have done with me.'

Maxine swallowed hard and carried on applying her make-up. He knew her weaknesses and exactly how to play on them. He stood tall behind her and pulled his shoulders back, confident that his wife would never say it was over, couldn't stand the thought of being the one to call it quits first. Even when they'd been together back in school, she would do anything to keep him. All the girls wanted Ian Bowen back in the day and she'd fought so hard to get him. She'd never let him go, and he knew it. How could she ever admit that all that effort, all those years were for nothing? Ian was her prize, the one thing in her life she treasured more than anything.

She changed the subject. 'I've got four more perfumes to shift, if you can sell them, good ones, too: Creed and Jo Malone.'

Ian nodded, knowing she was back on side. 'I'll ask about to see who's after some.'

'I'm taking them to Jane's tonight, so hopefully she will buy them all, but just in case, ask around for me.'

Ian sprayed his own aftershave, Savage, all over himself and shot a look over at his wife, knowing she was still watching. 'I am allowed to put aftershave on, aren't I? Or is that another sign that I'm playing away? Mind you, I don't really need this stuff – the women are already like they're on heat round me. Fighting them off, I am, love, because I'm such a good husband.'

Ian was a cocky prick. He'd always been full of himself. Maxine stood up and snarled, 'I never said a word, did I? It must be your guilty conscience.'

Ian pulled his jacket from the wardrobe and shook his head. 'Anyway, I've told you to be careful at work. It's not that the extra cash doesn't come in handy, but you've been nicking a lot of top-quality stuff lately. If they figure out it's you, they won't give you any chances, they'll just sit back and let you walk right into their trap before they pounce. You've been warned. I know, before you start on me, that going on the take was my idea to begin with, but you've got to be smart about it. That's why you've got away with it for so long – they think you're as dumb as you look.'

Maxine was ready to wallop him, but Ian knew when to beat a retreat. 'Right, I'm getting off before you start again. I don't know what time I'll be in, but it will be late. You don't have a problem with that, do you? My mates have started calling me Cinderella because I always leave before twelve, do you know that?'

He was really winding her up now, and loving it. 'Do you mean your mates who don't have a wife and have nothing to go home to? They want to bleeding grow up and get a life.'

Ian chuckled and flicked invisible dust from the top of his shoulder. 'It's not my fault if some of the lads chose to be single, is it? Not a bad idea, if you ask me.'

Maxine's stomach churned like it always did when she thought about being alone. 'Just don't take the piss, that's all I'm saying. You don't see me staying out all night and arriving home the next morning, do you? No, because I respect you and my marriage. It's a shame you don't take a leaf out of my book.'

'Right, I'm out of here, I can't stand the earache.' Ian picked up his wallet and headed downstairs. Maxine tried to control her breathing, in and out, slow breaths – she knew she shouldn't let him see how much he got to her or he'd do it even more. The front door slammed shut and she stood at the window watching her husband getting into a taxi. Despite what he said, she had a gut feeling he was playing away from home again and this time she was going to catch him bang to rights, even if she had to catch the prick with his pants down. The thought of it made her feel panicked. She was never sure how she would react if the truth was right there in front of her. In her heart of hearts, she felt she'd never leave him, so perhaps it was better not to know? No, she told herself, she had to know for sure. And if she did catch him, and forgave him, then maybe he'd finally realise what he'd got with her and stop chasing every bit of tail.

It wasn't like she had eyes for anyone else. Ian had been her life, her soul mate. She'd never ever slept with anyone else, it had always been just the two of them, the dream team, she used to think before the rumours started. Even now, when her mates told her to give him a taste of his own medicine, get flirting with other blokes, it made her blood run cold. Another man touching her body, kissing her, taking her husband's place? The thought of it gave her the kind of anxiety that felt like a vice crushing her chest, too much to take in.

No, she'd show Ian that they could be the dream team again. That was partly why she'd let him talk her into nicking from work. She wanted to show him what she was made of. That and the fact that the little extra she made from selling on the perfume and make-up she lifted meant she could still get the dresses she wanted, or even underwear to try and catch Ian's eye. Not that he seemed to notice these days. She carried on getting ready. A fitted red dress that complemented her sandy blonde hair, red shoes to match the dress and now a final slash of red lipstick. She flicked her hair over her shoulder and gave a half-hearted smile to her reflection. It was time to go.

Chapter Four

Lesley Potter was sat watching the television as John her husband came back into the room eating a bag of crisps. He'd always had the appetite of a lion. He'd not long had his tea, and here he was munching on something else. No wonder he could never lose any weight – he'd pose and flex and complain in the mirror but never do anything about it. But he carried it well, she always said, forever in his designer gear. He liked the best of everything, he told her, and their house, although small, had all the latest kit. The huge tv dominated the room, a massive leather sofa taking up the opposite wall, and carefully chosen artwork setting it all off.

John spoke with his mouth full, licking his fingers. 'The footy is on at eight, love, just letting you know so you don't plan on watching anything else, not that *Married at First Sight* crap you like.'

Lesley scoffed. 'You can watch the football. I don't know why you always make out like I'm some crank who doesn't let you watch anything on the television. Six years we've been married, and I've never said a bloody word about you watching the football. I think you're confusing me with your ex.'

John rolled his eyes, knew she was telling the truth. His first wife was a piece of work. Angela Potter had moaned about everything and anything and then, when she found out her husband had started sleeping with Lesley, she'd hit another level and made their lives a misery for years. She said it was an affair, but John and Angela had been over for a long time, had stopped sleeping together and only lived together, or that was what John had always told Lesley. Angela didn't seem to see it like that, though. She'd ripped up all John's clothes, sprayed abuse on his car, smashed windows. John had two children, Kimberley and James, with Angela and over the last couple of years they'd both come to live full-time with Lesley and John. Lesley wasn't truly sure if it was because they'd had enough of their mum's antics, or if Angela hadn't been able to keep them in line.

Kimberley was a handful, Lesley admitted, and she couldn't stomach the sight of her dad's new wife. When John was there, she was all smiles, but as soon as he was gone, she gave Lesley a look that told her she couldn't stand the ground she walked on. James was easier. He liked doing his own thing, and never really seemed bothered about anything. If he was any more laid back, he'd be asleep, Lesley said. Recently, he'd taken to staying at his girlfriend's most nights. Lesley could go weeks without seeing him. And, even then, he only popped his head in to say hi.

As Kimberley came into the front room, Lesley wished it was her stepdaughter who'd decided to shack up with someone else. She eyeballed Lesley now and snuggled up next to her dad. The girl was obviously up to something. She spoke in the voice that Lesley couldn't stand, a baby voice designed to wrap her dad round her finger.

'Dad, all my friends are going out tonight into town for food and a few cocktails and I'm the only one who can't go.'

Lesley shook her head slightly and carried on watching the television, tracking Kimberley from the corner of her eye. She wanted to join in the conversation, tell this brat that she would be able to go for drinks if she got off her lazy arse and got a job instead of sponging from her old man, but she kept quiet. She couldn't face all the sniping that would follow.

John stroked his hand across the top of his daughter's head and smiled at her. 'Come on, cut the crap. How much do you need? The football's starting soon, and I don't want you chewing my ear off when United are playing.'

She fanned her long nails out and fluttered her long heavy eyelashes. 'Fifty quid should be enough,' she said.

Lesley couldn't hold it any longer. Money didn't grow on trees and John's money was her money too, so she had a right to know where the cash was going. 'Bloody fifty pounds for a few cocktails?'

Kimberley shot a look over at her and her voice changed. 'Lesley, I'm young and I want to go to the top bars, the classy ones where I know I'll be safe. Fifty quid isn't enough really, but I didn't want to be cheeky asking for any more.'

'And that's why you should get a job. When I was twenty-one, I was working flat out. I never asked anyone for anything. I stood on my own two feet, I did.'

Kimberley folded her arms tightly in front of her. 'Well, you've had nothing to deal with compared to what I have. My parents split up, are you forgetting that? Me and James were affected by the divorce, you know, and just because we don't say anything, it still hurts, we're both damaged inside. Come on, Lesley, my dad was your boss, and you were his secretary. The whole office knew about your sordid affair before my own mother did.'

Lesley was boiling with rage. This was totally uncalled for, completely out of the blue. John sat up now, bright red, clearly annoyed his daughter was even talking about the past, but Lesley knew he hated rocking the boat when it came to his first marriage. He reached inside his wallet and pulled out three twenty-pound notes. Why wasn't he shouting at her, telling her she wasn't getting a penny now?

'Here, go and get bloody ready, and stop talking to Lesley like that. How many times do you need telling that me and your mother were over a long time before Lesley came along? She's told you that many lies about what happened. Bullshit it is, complete bullshit. Your mother should sit you down and tell you the whole bloody truth, before I do.'

Kimberley's eyes were wide now, looking at her father then at Lesley. 'The truth about what?'

Lesley chirped in now, aware that it was getting heated. 'Kimberley, you only know what your mam has told you.

It's not my job to tell you, either, but as your dad says your mam is the one who should be honest with you, not him.'

And, here it was, the tears, her ultimate weapon in getting her dad to back down. 'Don't you say anything about my mam, Lesley. My parents were fine until you came along gold-digging. I've met girls like you and I know, once my dad gets older, you'll be on your way, looking for your next payday, and it will be left up to me to look after him then.'

There was no way Lesley was standing for this. She pulled her shoulders back. 'You need to bloody grow up. Get over it that your dad has found someone who treats him right. We fell in love; we couldn't help it. And, just for the record, I was single, so I have nobody to answer to, especially not you.'

'No one to answer to? What about my mam? They were married. Didn't that mean anything to you?'

'A wedding ring doesn't make a marriage.' Lesley's voice was shaking.

John dropped his head into his hands – he knew this was getting out of control. He was sick of it; he'd had enough of these two at loggerheads all the time. 'Girls,' he shouted. 'Just calm down, will you both?'

Kimberley stood up, heading for Lesley, but before she could reach her, her dad dragged her back. 'Stay where you are, Kim, and Lesley, why don't you go upstairs out of the way for a bit while this one here calms the hell down?'

Lesley was fuming, steam coming out of her ears. 'Are you having a laugh or what, John? You've heard how she just spoke to me, so send her up the bloody stairs not bleeding me. Like I would go and hide away, anyway. You can do one, if you think that's happening. We'll be having words later, me and you, don't you worry about that.'

Kimberley was still at it. 'You see. He's my dad, and you don't like it that I'll always come first with him. You'd like everyone to think he has no children, so everyone doesn't see you for who you really are: a homewrecker, a woman who stole a man from his children and his wife.'

John roared, 'Enough, Kimberley, bloody enough! Lesley's right, you have too much to say for yourself sometimes. This house belongs to me and Lesley, and if you don't like it then piss off back home to your mother.'

Kimberley stood with her hands on her hips, stamping her feet like an overgrown toddler. 'So, you're backing her over your own flesh and blood? Go on, tell me that.' Kimberley ran at Lesley, ready to scratch her eyes out. 'Bitch!' she screamed as she sank her long fingers into Lesley's hair.

John dragged his daughter back and flung her onto the sofa. 'How dare you cross the line, Kimberley? Get up the stairs and pack your stuff. You can go back to your mother's house, because you're just like her, delusional and toxic.'

Lesley stood straightening her clothes and her hair, relieved her husband had stood up for her.

'I'll go and get my stuff, Dad, but you better face facts. That one there will never amount to much. When she's bled you dry, you won't see her for dust, trust me, she'll be moving on to her next meal ticket then. Go on, Lesley, tell me I'm wrong?'

Lesley eyeballed her. 'Little girl, go upstairs and do what your dad has told you to do. You're a cheeky cow. We've put a roof over your head for how bloody long and you treat us like this? Your dad's right, you are like your mother. And for your information, I earn my own money; no man keeps me. So, when you keep asking for handouts, remember it's my money too, not just your father's.'

Kimberley looked wild. 'Yeah, like you make any decent cash in your own right. It's Dad's business. What do you actually do? If you've got any cash, I bet it's because you earn nice little extras on your back like the slag that you are.'

Anything that Lesley had been holding back was suddenly set free. 'Christ! If you want to know who's the slapper around here, ask your mam, go on, ask her about the man at the golf club and the guy who worked in the bank. I bet she's not told you about them, has she?'

John snapped. 'I'm fucking sick of all this. Every bastard day you two are gunning for each other. I'll tell you what, I'm pissing off down to the pub and watching the football in peace. I don't ask for a lot in life, just a bit of peace and quiet when I get home from work. You two can carry on with this if you want, but I'm not listening a second longer. Same shit, different day.'

Kimberley ran to her dad's side. 'I'll only leave if you tell me you really mean it, Dad. Go on, look me in the eyes and tell me you don't want me here anymore and you're picking her over me.'

John was already putting his coat on. 'I don't want you to go anywhere, but I can't live like this, none of us can.

It's a war zone every day and I'm not doing it any more. Lesley, give me a ring when you two have decided what's happening.'

John left the living room and they both listened as the front door slammed shut.

'It's your bleeding fault, this is. Your dad was all settled to watch the football and you couldn't give that mouth of yours a rest for one bloody night, could you? I'll be straight with you, Kimberley: I do want you to leave. I gave you a proper chance when you first moved in, but you've got your mother's evil mouth.'

Kimberley's fake tears had vanished, replaced by rage. 'Well, you talk to me like shit, too. I'm not some little kid who won't defend myself, you know.'

Lesley was right back at her. 'I've been nothing but nice to you, Kimberley. It's you who has the problem and, like your dad just said, if you can't hack it here then off you go back to your mam's. I'm not living my life with some toxic brat anymore. One day, when you've burnt every bridge, you'll find yourself alone and realise what you've done.'

Kimberley's eyes flooded with real tears at this. 'Fuck. It kills me to say this but you're half right. I'm messed up in the head, Lesley. But I've got reason. I was the one who sat with my mam when she was on all fours crying every night when my dad left her. I've never told you this before, but she tried ending it all, you know, had tablets ready to take. It was a good job I came home when I did, otherwise she would have been a goner. I sat for hours with her, making sure she was alright. I was a little kid and it's scarred me, screwed with my head.'

Lesley was unconvinced. 'I'm not saying you've not had some awful shit to deal with, Kimberley. But you never gave me a chance. I met your dad when I started at his company. We got close as colleagues before anything happened. When he told me his marriage was over in all but name and he was only living with your mother until he found somewhere else, well, in my eyes, he was fair game. If it wasn't me, it would have been someone else who'd have come along and fallen for your dad.'

'I know I've been a bitch, but watching your parents split is not something I would wish on my worst enemy. Do you know how hard it was for me and James? I've got fragile mental health, you know. I can't get a job. It's alright for you, you don't know pain like this since you're barren, don't know what it's like for a mother and daughter to have their bond ripped apart.'

Lesley bit her tongue and searched her handbag for her fags. She wasn't a big smoker, and it was only when she was properly stressed that she turned to nicotine for comfort. She took her lighter and headed for the back door, sick of hearing this one making excuses, thinking she knew it all. Once she was there, she pulled her light blue cardigan from the peg on the back of the door and stepped into the garden. It was a lovely garden, her thinking place. She sucked hard on her cigarette, her hand shaking. Her temper was still bubbling. She knew she needed to calm down and walk about a bit. Sure, the kid had been dealt some crappy cards in life – but she didn't help herself. And as for laying into her, if Kimberley had been a woman in the street, she would have ragged her all over the show, scratched her eyes out. She shuddered. The winter nights were kicking in and there was a chill in the air tonight. Usually there were birds in the trees singing, chirping at this time of the night, but not tonight, they were silent. They'd probably gone to roost in another garden where they could get some peace and quiet. Sometimes Lesley wished she could fly away as easily.

Lesley walked past Kimberley and went back into the living room. Bloody hell, what a night – how on earth would they move forward from this? She'd hoped Kimberley would have already been upstairs packing her stuff up, but, no, she was still sprawled over the sofa sniffing and sobbing like the drama queen she was. Lesley flicked the channel over and sat back on the sofa. There was no way this kid was spoiling the rest of her night. And, just for the record, when John got back home, he was getting a mouthful too. How dare he walk out on her when it was his daughter who was kicking up a fuss and disrespecting his wife?

Eventually Kimberley sat up, with her big black panda eyes, mascara still running down her cheeks. 'Lesley, can we sort this out? If not for us, then for my dad?'

Lesley tried her best not to get angry. A cunning cow she was, and Lesley knew how she worked. She could imagine her now talking to her dad later, telling him how hard she tried to make it right and how Lesley was the one who wouldn't let it go. 'I've heard it all before, Kimberley. You say you will change but, once my back is turned, you're throwing knives at it. How can we ever be happy when every day you set out to destroy us and our marriage? Your mam's doing well for herself, from what I hear, so I can't see what the problem is.'

'I'll back off. I know I've not been the best while I've been living here, but, come on, you're the woman who stole my father.' And there it was again, the allegation that Lesley was some kind of homewrecker.

'I'll tell you something for nothing, Kimberley. Your mother was the cheat, not your dad. She was the one playing away. Ask her yourself and see what she says. Your dad was a broken man when I met him and even though you say I'm only with him for his money, I'm not. I genuinely love him with all my heart. I would have loved you and James as my own children too, if you'd given me the chance.'

Kimberley sat playing with her fingers. 'Fine. I'll ask my mam about what you have told me. You sound all high and mighty, but up to now she's drummed it into me that you wrecked her marriage.'

'I don't want to get into this again. As far as I'm concerned, if you keep your nasty comments to yourself, then we can try to live together. But,' she stressed, 'one more thing out of your mouth about me being a gold-digger and I'll pack your bags myself.'

Kimberley stared at Lesley, digesting everything she said. 'That's fine by me. Will you ring my dad now and ask him for that money he was giving me?'

An hour later, John walked into the living room and threw his car keys onto the coffee table. Manchester United must have lost. He was always in a filthy mood when his beloved footy team let him down. He slipped his jacket off and slung it over the chair. 'Utter crap the football was, we got beat two nil.' John plonked down on the sofa next to her, reached over and grabbed her hands in his. 'It's freezing out tonight, there's a proper nip in the air.' He could tell by her reaction that she had something to say, and sat back looking at her. 'So go on, say what you have to, because I can tell you're angry by the way you're looking at me.'

Lesley spoke slowly. 'Angry is an understatement. How dare you walk out of here when *your* daughter is having a go at *your* wife? I know kids always have to come first, but you've got to draw a line somewhere. Kids need boundaries, you know that.'

'It was going on forever, you two at each other. I told her to pack her stuff, what more did you want from me?'

'A bit of bloody support, John, that's what I want. She was trying to physically attack me, have you forgotten? Are you not seeing this the same as I am or what?'

'Lesley, turn it down, love. Honest, I can't handle all this shit with you both. I love you and I love my daughter. I think she has got some serious mental health problems, you know. I always thought her mother was bipolar and I reckon our Kimberley is the apple that doesn't fall far from the tree.'

'Right now, I'm not talking about her issues. I'm on about you bailing on me and pissing off to the pub. I've had her down my ear all night – why should I have to listen to her crap when her own father can't be arsed? And, just for the record, if I see Angela when we're out, she's going to get a mouthful from me, too. Who the hell does she think she is, lying to Kimberley about us? Forget whether she's bipolar or not – the woman is a slapper. That's not down to her mental health, it's just who she damn well is. I thought all this was over years ago, thought she'd finally moved on, but it looks like her daughter is carrying it all on for her.'

John could see she was getting upset and the past came flooding into his mind. The endless phone calls, the death threats, the times Angela would turn up outside his work shouting and screaming. He reached over and cradled Lesley's face. 'Come on now, don't be getting upset. I'll have another word with her in the morning. You mean the world to me and, if she keeps on with her mouth, I will take her to her bloody mother's myself.'

Lesley looked deep into her husband's eyes and all the anger started to leave her body. He was a good man and had a heart of gold underneath it all. 'You can order me some food and I might forgive you. I fancy a curry, if you do?'

John smiled, relieved that the beef was over. 'I'll have whatever you want, my beautiful wife.'

She playfully punched him in the arm and the dramas of the evening seemed to be over.

Later that night Lesley watched John snoring next to her in bed. Every time he had a drink he'd snore like a donkey and tonight he was at his all-time best, the house was shaking. It wasn't just the noise that bothered her – more the fact that he could simply black out and go to sleep, while she went over and over the events of the evening, worrying. Lesley rolled on her side to get out of bed. She grabbed her mobile and her reading glasses. She'd hated to admit she needed them at night, and it had made her feel like a granny at first, but they did the job. She padded softly next door into James's empty room. Typical, they'd done his room up just before he shacked up with his new girlfriend. This was probably the most comfortable bed in the house and, whenever she got the chance to sleep in here, she would always get a good night's kip. She pulled the duvet over her body and snuggled down. She started to text the GIRLS GIRLS GIRLS WhatsApp group and hoped at least one or two of them were still awake. After Kimberley kicking off, she needed to vent. She started to type.

I've been this close to murder tonight with Kimberley. I swear that girl could test the patience of a saint. John wasn't much better, but we've made our peace now. I'll fill you all in tomorrow. Good night, girls, love yas Xxx

The message was sent, and Lesley placed her mobile phone on charge at the side of the bed. No reply: they must all be asleep. Lesley's eyes started to close slowly; all the arguing had taken its toll. Hopefully, after the latest chat with Kimberley, she might change her ways. One thing for sure was she wasn't holding her breath, though. Still, after all these years keeping quiet about the stuff Angela had got up to, it felt good to have let the cat out of the bag, even if Kimberley didn't quite believe it yet. Secrets were like acid – you could keep them bottled up but they burnt through everything in the end. She should know.

The black Merc at the end of the road didn't look out of place on Tommy Braxton's street. Nice motors were par for the course in this part of the city. It hadn't looked out of place when it was parked up outside one of the Braxton Athletic gyms earlier, either. Manchester was a big place, and normally Tommy would have clocked something like this. But tonight he had other things on his mind…

Chapter Five

Tommy Braxton was sweating cobs in the kitchen. He'd invited all the girls tonight, and their husbands. He loved hosting, and often thought if he could have gone down a different career path then he would have been a chef. But tonight was special, it had to be perfect, nothing could go wrong. Jane was out at the hairdressers having a curly-blow and her nails redone. He didn't mind – in fact, he liked her out of the way when he was cooking. She was a pain in the arse if she was hovering around him in the kitchen, tasting stuff, checking how long things had left in the oven. No, everything was going to plan. The duck and orange pâté was placed neatly next to the crispy toasts with a few sprigs of salad and a blob of chutney on the side of the plate. It looked mint too, just like something you would be served in a restaurant. For the main he'd made Jane's favourite, sirloin steak and all the trimmings. He only had the peppercorn sauce left to make. For dessert it was always chocolate cake. Tonight he was going all out: triple chocolate. Jane would love it. Tommy checked his watch, six forty-five. The guests should be arriving soon, and of course there was still no sign of Jane, always late. Seven o'clock he'd told them all to be here for. He ran upstairs and changed into fresh clothes with only minutes to spare. Jane would probably waltz in any second too. She was a princess by nature, never rushed for anyone.

Bang on seven, the guests started arriving – Jane rolling in as well, as if she was guest of honour at her own house. Katie nudged Maxine and kept her voice low. 'Tommy looks stressed, watch him, he's all over the place tonight. Is he alright? He's normally cool as a cucumber, loves showing off his fancy food.'

Maxine glanced at Tommy. Katie was right, he did seem edgy. Jane was laughing and joking with Lesley about old times and the other men were talking about football. Normally they could go on for hours about the weekend's match but tonight Tommy got everyone seated at the cream marble dining table promptly, music playing softly in the background, and he made sure everyone had their glasses filled.

The starter went down well, with everyone singing its praises, especially Katie, who'd had nothing to eat since she'd finished her shift at work. She'd arrived home barely ten minutes before Maxine and Ian picked her up. If she hadn't been going to Jane's for tea, she would have been on a cheap Whoops meal out of the fridges at work, so this was the lap of luxury. She took a long sip of her wine, letting the warmth unknot her tense muscles. When she'd been sat in the car with Maxine and Ian on the way over, she had felt a frosty atmosphere between them. Katie could usually read Maxine like a book and she could tell her friend was putting on the front that she always did whenever she was in company. That was typical Maxine, smoothing over the cracks, trying to paint a picture to the world that everything was hunky-dory in her marriage, when Katie knew it was a sham. She'd done everything she could to avoid meeting Ian's gaze. It gave her the creeps when she could feel his eyes on her through the rear-view mirror, lingering looks that made the hairs on the back of her neck stand on end.

Tommy had just tidied away the main course when he tapped the edge of his wine glass with a silver knife. Jane giggled to herself: Tommy always made speeches breaking bread with friends. Tommy wiped the sweat from his brow. He quickly swigged a mouthful of red wine and swallowed hard. 'As you know, me and Jane have been together for a lot of years.'

Jane chirped in, laughing. 'I'd get more for murder. I could have done him in and been out on parole by now.'

The girls chuckled as Tommy continued. 'I'm not going to lie to you all, Jane is hard work. I have never known anyone who likes everything just so, like this one does.'

Jane raised her eyebrows. 'I have high standards, that's all, baby. I appreciate the finer things in life, like you, love.'

Tommy nodded. 'And that's why I love you. You make me laugh and every day is different. You still excite me and shock me, and I love that about you. You're the only one for me.'

Maxine gave Ian a look that could kill. Katie was looking around for a full bottle of wine. Only Lesley had worked out what was about to happen. Tommy dug his hand in his pocket, pulled out a small black box and headed to where Jane was sitting. Lesley stretched her neck trying to get a butcher's at what exactly he had in his hand. He was down on bended knee. Jane had stopped laughing – serious now.

'I know you've waited a long time for this to happen and I always told you when I was ready I would ask you.'

Katie leant in. She was a hopeless romantic and she wanted to savour every second of this proposal. Ian and John grinned at each other, and Ian whispered so nobody else could hear him. 'Quick, stop him before he says it. It all changes when you get married, the ball-and-chain never stops bloody moaning.'

John nudged him to remind him where he was.

'Jane, will you marry me?' Tommy finally asked. He opened the small box, and everyone fell quiet, trying to get the first look at the rock. The princess-cut stone was a huge diamond, dwarfing Lesley's and Maxine's. Katie's hand instinctively went to her bare ring finger. No engagement or wedding band had ever touched her third finger. Jade's dad hadn't stuck around long enough to propose, and nor had anyone since.

Everyone seemed frozen for a moment, but suddenly Jane was screaming, jumping up, grinning. Tommy looked up at her, still waiting on an answer. 'Bleeding hell, Jane, I'm still knelt down here, you know, and my knee is killing me, so can you give me an answer before I keel over?'

She beamed. 'Yes, yes, a million times yes.' She let Tommy slide the white-gold diamond ring on her finger and helped him up from the floor. She swung her arms around him and kissed him with force. 'I can't believe you've finally done it. I thought you would never pop the question.' Jane had the ring on her finger now and her friends were gathered around her looking at the glittering jewel.

Ian watched them with a sour look. He nudged John and kept his voice low. 'I bet that cost a few quid, didn't it? More money than sense, these two. On my life, that's all I hear from Maxine – Jane's got this, and Jane's got that.'

John shook his head – he didn't see the harm in treating his wife when times were good. He didn't reply, but it didn't stop Ian. He was still going on.

'You see with you, John, you done the right thing and traded your ex-Mrs in for a newer model, whereas me, I'm still stuck with the dragon.'

John didn't like where this conversation was going and there was no way he was getting caught up in Ian's problems. He stood up and went to shake Tommy's hand. 'Well done, Tom, lad. Welcome to the married club. You've bagged a good one there, let me tell you.'

Jane overheard John's comment and shouted over to him, 'You tell him, John, tell him how lucky he is having me on his arm.'

Katie sat back down and filled her glass up again. So, it was official, Jane was getting married. She was the last single one in their girl gang of four. They all sat back down, Jane constantly fanning her fingers out, looking at her new ring. Lesley clapped her hands as an idea dawned. 'Oh my God, ladies, we need a hen party. A trip away with the girls. This is amazing, we can go to Dublin. My mate went there and said they all had a ball. Or what about Benidorm? At least there we can all get a tan, too. Wherever you want, J, it's going to be the hen do of the year!'

Tommy chimed in. 'Two can play at that game. I'm thinking a stag do to remember – or should that be forget? What do you say, John, Ian? We should jet off for a bit of sea and sunshine too.'

Ian whispered, 'A bit of something else too, you mean.'

Katie heard what he said and shot a look over at him. He was an out and out bastard and the sooner Maxine could see it the better.

But Jane was on cloud nine, not noticing any undercurrents between the group. She snuggled next to Tommy and whispered into his ear, 'I love you for now and forever and you have made me the happiest woman on this planet. I'm going to make you the best wife you have ever seen.'

Tommy leant in and kissed the top of her head. 'I know you will, baby. Sorry it's taken so long. I wanted to build the life you deserve. And we've done it, this is it – together we'll take on the world.'

Katie shouted from the end of the table. 'Let's celebrate with dessert then. Come on, I can't wait to see what the chef has hustled up for us all.'

Tommy stood up and took a bow for everyone. 'You're right, Katie, sweets for my sweet.' He nodded at Jane, who'd fallen quiet once more.

Her eyes clouded over. 'I just wish my mam could have been here to see me get married. She would have loved getting dolled up and wearing a big hat.'

Lesley rubbed her arm. 'Come on, love. Your mam will be looking down on you. She'd be so proud of you – and she'd have loved Tommy.'

Jane dabbed the white napkin against the corner of her eyes. 'And who's going to walk me down the aisle? I've not seen my dad in years. He's a waste of space and I don't know why I should tell him, let alone invite him when he's never been near me in years.'

Lesley could see the pain in her friend's eyes and knew this was a sore point. There was nothing as tricky as family – and she didn't want the pain in Jane's past trespassing on this happy time. 'Ah, don't waste your breathe on that lowlife, Janey. Sometimes the past is better left in the past, isn't it?'

That night, Jane cuddled next to Tommy in bed. 'I'm going to be Mrs Braxton. I can't believe it.'

'You better had believe it. It's happening, baby, you're going to be my wife.'

She stroked her fingers languidly along his hairy chest and looked deep into his eyes. 'You know what I'm going to say next. We can try for a baby properly now, and if I'm not up the duff soon, let's both get checked out and see why I haven't conceived.'

Tommy hated this subject, said it made him feel like less of a man. Jane hadn't been on regular contraception in years and she often joked that they put enough practice in. Tommy wriggled about awkwardly in the bed. He hated even talking about other people's babies. 'Come on, J. We have the wedding to plan now, so let's get that out of the way first before we even start talking about any bin-lids.'

'Well, let's not hang about. I'm thinking we get married as soon as possible. I can ring venues tomorrow and get some prices. We're not on a budget, are we?'

Tommy shook his head. 'Nothing but the best! I'm all up for getting the ball rolling. Let's find a place we love and get it booked.'

'You know me, babes. I know how to throw a party. In fact, didn't you say you'd be at the gym late tomorrow? I'll get the girls back around and we can dive in. Lesley is mint at planning stuff. She's got a good eye. Katie will be putting a playlist together already and Max might be able to get us some fancy gear with her staff discount. And we've got to get the hen sorted. Where are you thinking for your stag do?'

Tommy smirked and tapped the side of his nose. 'The less you know the better. What happens on tour stays on tour.'

She playfully punched him in the arm. 'Just you keep that snake in the cage, otherwise I will cut it off.'

Tommy hit her with a pillow. 'It's you girls I should be worrying about. I know what you lot are like when you're on one. I'm not bailing you lot out if you get done for drunk and disorderly!'

Jane prodded him. 'Don't you worry, Tommy boy, you won't have to hear a word about what we get up to. Sometimes silence is golden…'

Chapter Six

Jane opened her eyes and reached into the empty space next to her. Tommy had already gone to work. She didn't know how he did it. No matter how drunk he was, or late to bed, he always got up for work at the crack of dawn. He told her that's what being the boss meant. He'd gone from one gym to six in only a few years, and while Jane never knew exactly where he was, she knew he was always working hard for them and the life they wanted. Braxton Athletic was growing – people were noticing the sites, following the socials, liking the brand. She was even thinking she might start a clothing line to go with it. But first she had a wedding to plan. She reached over for her mobile phone and scrolled through the photographs from last night. The glow of happiness shone from the screen. This wedding was going to be top-notch, and everybody would be talking about it for forever and a day.

She found Lesley's number and rang her. She was singing as Lesley answered the call. 'Going to the chapel and we're going to get married.'

Lesley joined in. 'I'm so happy for you. John was saying last night how you and Tommy are the perfect couple.'

There was rustling outside the door and Jane lifted her head up as the cleaner walked past. 'Hold on a minute, Les,' she said. She sat up in the bed and shouted out. 'Letty, I know the kitchen is a mess, sorry. We had a celebration last night and we didn't have time to throw any of the rubbish out. I'll give you extra cash if it takes you longer than usual, don't worry.'

Letty stuck her head inside the bedroom and spoke, smiling. 'Thanks, Jane. I thought a bomb had hit last night when I walked in this morning.'

'Tommy proposed to me and let's say the party went on all night.' Jane waved her engagement-ring-laden hand at Letty.

'Amazing! Congratulations,' Letty said. Then she closed the bedroom door behind her.

'You're such a lucky cow, Jane, on my life,' Lesley said down the line. 'I've got to clean the full house today before I go anywhere. I've told Kimberley that she needs to start pulling her weight too. Bone idle she is, doesn't do a tap.'

'You were right to tell her straight. The more you don't, the more she will take advantage of you. You're not her slave, so get her told.'

'I will, I'm sick of her. I'll fill you in about her later on. I was going to tell you last night but after the proposal I put it on the backburner.'

Jane listened to Lesley's sorry tale then added, 'What the hell is up with Ian? He was in such a mood last night and don't think I couldn't hear some of the crap he was coming out with.'

'Tell me about it. I would have punched his lights out by now – a right arsehole he is.' Lesley agreed. 'Anyway, what's the plan, when are Bride Squad all meeting up?'

Jane grinned – she was going to be a bride. 'Let's seize the moment. Tommy's out working late tonight so the house is free. But first I've got something to ask – how do you feel about being my maid-of-honour?'

Lesley went quiet for a moment. 'I would love to, Jane. I'm touched. You stood right by me at my wedding. Now I'll be honoured to do the same for you.'

'Thanks, babes. Who'd have thought it when we were bunking off to meet the lads from the other school? We're both finally going to be married. I can't wait to see you all later and get cracking. I'll call the others and get a few bottles of bubbly in.'

This was it. It was really happening. Jane had waited years for this – had started to wonder if it was ever going to happen. She'd even wondered recently whether Tommy had lost interest, had another piece on the side somewhere, but she looked down at her ring finger again. It was true: diamonds were a girl's best friend.

Chapter Seven

Maxine stood behind the perfume counter in the department store where she worked and clocked her manager walking towards her. Shit. She needed to look busy. She grabbed a bottle of perfume and approached an old lady who was walking past. She was all smiles now. 'Would you like to try our new fragrance? It's floral with citrus top-notes and smells like a spring day…'

The old woman swerved her and pretended she'd not even seen her. Ros, Maxine's manager was at her side now. 'Your sales have been pretty low this month I've noticed. Have you been using all the latest offers?'

Maxine was on alert. Of course, she'd been doing her job. Okay, she'd not been on the ball this month as much as she usually was, but she had crap going on at home and her head wasn't with it at the moment. Remembering all the different gift sets and multibuys made her head spin. 'Ros, I try every day to sell as much as I humanly can. Young, old, fellas or women, I'm on them, spritzing and spraying. You try and have a go and see if you get a different result than me. Everyone's just window-shopping at the moment. Nobody seems to be buying much these days – with the cost of living going up, we're a luxury now.'

Ros looked unimpressed and stepped closer. 'Women will never stop shopping, Maxine, it's a well-known fact. Anyway, there's a staff meeting later on. I have a few concerns that I need to address, so if you stay behind for half an hour after work that would be great.'

Maxine winced and Ros could see she had something to say. 'I need to leave bang on time tonight. My friend is getting married, and we are all meeting up to plan it.'

Ros raised her eyebrows. 'May I suggest you prioritise what is more important in your life – your friends, or your income – because I've had head office on this morning down my ear. If you know who butters your bread, you'll make the right decision and turn up like everyone else.'

Maxine knew there was no point causing a scene arguing any more. Ros was a prize bitch and when she had a bee in her bonnet she would go above and beyond to prove she was right. Maxine flicked her hair over her shoulder and went back behind the counter. She forced a smile onto her face and went to help a woman who was looking at the array of bottles.

Maxine checked to see if Ros had left the shopfloor: she had to be quick. She used the distraction of the customer to do her usual swap with tester bottles and empty boxes and, quick as anything, she'd stashed two large boxes of Creed on the shelf below the counter. She waited a few more minutes, then checked behind her and walked to the stock room with the 'samples'. She couldn't deny there had been a thrill about stealing from work at first when Ian had put her up to it – it was a way of putting two fingers up to Ros. But now she took more than she admitted to her husband. It felt good to have a secret. Maybe it was to keep up with her friends, to buy new clothes each week, go on the weekends away. Or maybe, she admitted to herself, it was something to fill the void in her life. Ian used to be so romantic, buy her gifts, take her away on wild weekends. But those days were long gone. She'd seen the way he looked at other women when they were out, leering at them, laughing and joking when he thought she wasn't watching. He'd let all the blood rush from his brain to his penis and he was like a dog on heat. She knew well enough he'd always been a flirty guy and had the gift of the gab but, ever since the rumours started about Donna Ramsey, she'd admitted to herself he wasn't some great romantic hero – he was just one dirty bastard who was all over the women he looked at. Maxine had told herself she would curb her stealing, but the rush she got made her feel alive.

Maxine sat in the meeting room after her shift, looking at her manicure. Her glossy red nails were chipped. If Ros would get a move on, she might have chance to get home and paint them. Finally, Ros stood up and looked around the room at her team. 'Ladies, I hate to be the one to break this to you as it's embarrassing to admit. We have a thief working among us. There have been several stock-takes over the last few months that have all showed us down on stock. In fact, we have lost over two thousand pounds in products that have not been put through the till.'

Maxine could feel her face burning up, her eyes dropping low.

Ros continued. 'This isn't an accident – it's more than a smashed tester or a discount put through wrongly. This is theft and we will be pursuing every avenue available to us. So, if anyone has any information regarding this, please come and see me. Anything you tell me will be confidential and your name will never be shared. In all the time I've worked here, I've never worked with a thief on my shift before. Until we catch the culprit there will be new security measures I expect you all to follow.'

One of the newer girls was glaring. 'So are you calling all of us thieves? Because I've never stolen anything in my life and don't like being tarnished with the same brush as whoever is stealing.'

Ros changed her tone of voice, aware she was rubbing her staff up the wrong way. 'Don't shoot the messenger. I've had orders from the bigwigs to have this meeting. So, take it as a warning, this cannot continue. They will be caught and, when they are, they will have the book thrown at them.'

When Ros had finished, Maxine made herself stop staring at her feet, looked over at a workmate and rolled her eyes. 'She loves the sound of her own voice that one does. We should have been out of here half an hour ago. Do you think they will pay us overtime for this or what?'

Maxine grabbed her coat and went to her locker for her bag. She'd only just opened the door to it, hadn't even reached in, when Ros walked silently round the corner and stood behind her. Maxine's heartbeat doubled and she could feel she was sweating, knowing what was inside her bag. She pushed the locker door shut softly with the palm of her hand and stood with her back pressed gently against it.

'I'm just checking the rota for next week and wanted to know if you can work a late shift on Thursday evening?'

Maxine gulped and replied, 'Erm, maybe. Just let me check when I get home, because I have a few things on the calendar next week. I have to go for my smear at the doctor's.'

When in doubt, plead a gynie appointment, Max always thought. No woman would argue with you if you said you had lady problems. Maxine stared at her boss with her eyes wide open, hoping she would piss off and let her get her stuff out of her locker.

Finally, Ros turned on her heel and Maxine breathed out. She picked her bag up, careful not to let the bulges in the lining show, hoping these new security measures started tomorrow not tonight. She felt like she had guilt written all over her face.

Chapter Eight

'Hurry the fuck up if you want a lift to Jane's,' Ian shouted to Maxine.

She turned to face him, fuming, and snapped, 'Stop speaking to me like I'm a dollop of crap on the bottom of your shoe, will you?'

'I'll speak to you how I want when you have me waiting about for you. How long does it take to get bloody ready? I don't know why you bother anyway – what's the phrase – putting lipstick on a pig?'

Maxine slammed the hairbrush down on the dressing table and clenched her teeth. 'Listen, I've had enough of you and your so-called jokes. I'm sick of it. Give me some respect, for crying out loud. And don't think I didn't see your face last night at Jane's and hear your snide comments. I don't know what's up with you lately, but sort it out.'

Ian walked up to her and went nose to nose with her. 'If you don't like it, then fuck off. You know where the door is. Go to your mam's and give us all a bleeding break.'

'Me! Are you having a laugh? For months you've had a face like a smacked arse, grumpy, no time for nobody but your bloody self. Go on, when was the last time you did anything for me? You take me for granted and expect me to pick up after you every single day. I'm your wife, not a bleeding skivvy, or are you forgetting that?'

'For the record, it's you who's changed, not me. Always moaning, nothing is ever good enough for you. You're paranoid, Max – and it's not pretty.'

'And you think going out to the pub is the answer, do you? Maybe, sit down with me and talk about it, because that's what you do when you're married, you talk things through.'

'I'm sick of talking. Hurry up before I leave you here. I'm phoning the taxi now, so when it pulls up, if you're not ready, balls to you, you can make your own way to Jane's.'

Maxine was bright red, her temper rising. 'Fuck off, Ian. You go and do you, like you always do, and I'll look after myself as per normal.'

'Suits me,' he sneered as he left the bedroom. Maxine placed her hand on her neck and started to take long deep breaths to calm the pulse she could feel raging there. Her anxiety was bad at the moment, and she was popping herbal tablets like they were smarties. She needed something stronger – she knew where to get the pills, but she also knew so many women who were hooked on them. Was she strong enough to only have a few, take the edge off things?

Katie sat on the edge of her bed looking into her wardrobe. It was the same old story: sod all to wear again. Jade came into the bedroom and sat with her. 'Go on, what's up now?'

Katie let out a laboured breath. 'Everything I own is either falling apart or only fit for doing the cleaning in. Why can't I be rich and have a walk-in wardrobe, like Jane? Honest, lately, it's all getting on top of me. I get paid my wages, pay bills, go food shopping and never have a carrot left.'

'That's life, Mother. Maybe, if you cut back on a few things, you could save up for some new clothes.'

Katie dragged her fingers through her hair. 'You're going on like I splash out on luxuries all the time. I buy bloody food and that's it. The bills have gone up so much lately I'm scared of even turning the bleeding heating on. Why do you think I sit in my dressing gown every night and wear those big fluffy socks?'

Jade shook her head and touched her mother's warm hands. 'Mam, I know it's hard, but the tide will turn sooner or later. And sitting here worrying about it won't make it any better, will it? I'll have a look in my wardrobe and see if there is anything of mine you can wear. We're roughly the same size. What about the classic: a pair of jeans and a nice top?'

But Katie was in a dark place. 'Just leave me alone. I'll be fine. I'm having a bad day – wondering how life's got me here – and on top of all that, work is pissing me off. They're always adding more jobs onto me for the same money. They're lucky I never told them to shove their poxy job up their arse today.'

'Now, Mam, that would be silly, wouldn't it? And, what then? You'd be unemployed and have no money.'

'Ever since we got the new supervisor, I dread it every day. That line manager of mine is a dickhead. All the staff hate her. She doesn't care about anything but herself. Go on, leave me be to get ready. I'm already late and God knows I need a drink tonight.'

Jade stood up. 'Do you think I'm daft or what? It's not just tonight you need a drink is it, Mam? I've seen the credit cards, the extra bottles of wine you're buying each week, and I've heard the bullshit you tell the loan sharks when they knock on the door. I'm only trying to help you, but it's your life – you do it your way.' Jade marched out.

Katie turned up her music to block out having to think about what her daughter had said. She knew she was in a self-destruct spiral, but couldn't pull herself out. She needed her mates tonight. She pulled a white pair of jeans out of her wardrobe and flung them behind her on the bed. She always looked okay in them and, once she put her red top on with them and her red heels, she would look half decent. She scooped her hair back and put it in a scrunchie. There was just a bit of time to put a slap on and then she would have to leave to go to Jane's to talk about the wedding and how much it was all costing. She knew she'd be full of envy, but at least it would take her mind off things.

Lesley was ready when Kimberley came into the room and looked her up and down. 'Off out again, are we?'

'I sure am. Why, do you have a problem with that?'

'Not really, but you and my dad were out last night too, and I had to make my own tea.'

Lesley let out a sarcastic laugh. 'And what's the problem with that? You can cook, can't you? Some women have families of their own by your age.'

'It's not the point. I would like to spend some time with my dad, you know, instead of you dragging him out all the time.'

Lesley shook her head at Kimberley. 'Are we really going down that road again? I thought, the last time we spoke, you were going to try and play nice. Anyway, your luck's in – I'm going out with the girls, not your dad, so you can have him to yourself this evening. But if you start chatting shit about me, don't kid yourself it won't get back to me.' Lesley could hear a car honking its horn outside and pulled the blind back to check if it was her taxi. She picked up her grey leather clutch, hooked her coat over her shoulder and left the room. She could hear Kimberley shouting something after her. She rammed two fingers up behind her as she opened the front door. 'Bye,' she shouted.

Kimberley stood at the front window glowering at Lesley as she got into the taxi. 'I'll show you, bitch, just you watch.' She went upstairs and straight into Lesley's bedroom. She walked over to the dressing table and the bottles of perfumes all neatly displayed there. Lesley loved perfume and seemed to always be bringing home a new bottle of something or other. Her mate worked on one of the fragrance counters at a shop in town – well, she could go begging to get more from her. Kimberley picked up a bottle of perfume and sprayed it all over her. Then she grabbed a few more bottles and took them into the bathroom. Wrenching off the lids in turn, she emptied the contents into the sink. She went back into the bedroom and did the same with every single bottle of perfume until they were all empty. This was war and, if this was how Lesley wanted to play it, Kimberley was ready for her. This was hers and her father's home, not Lesley's. If her plan worked, her father's hussy would be packing her bags and leaving before the month was over. Kimberley walked over to the large white wardrobes now and opened the double doors. She picked out one of Lesley's favourite blouses. Using all her strength, she yanked at it, causing it to rip. She let out a menacing laugh and placed it back neatly on the coat hanger. 'Let's see your face when you find this,' she muttered as she closed the wardrobe door.

Chapter Nine

Jane already had the music pumping and was dancing and singing when the girls arrived. She'd put on a 'Hen Party Classics' playlist and Abba's 'Dancing Queen' had just hit. In life, Jane thought, there was always one song that, when you heard it, took you right back to a time when you were happy and carefree, dancing like nobody was watching. This was their feel-good song, a tune that put smiles on their faces and took all their worries away for a few minutes.

They'd all had their worries in the past, had times when they'd been on their knees crying for help, but there was something about getting hitched that made Jane feel like she was wiping the slate clean. After all, it had worked for some of the girls. She thought back to what Lesley had told them years back when she'd broken down one night and shared a secret that all of them would take to the grave. Yet she and John had gone on to a happy life.

As 'Dancing Queen' reached a crescendo, Katie walked into the front room, followed by Lesley and Maxine, who held Jane's hand, singing as she spun her around. It was a long time since any of them were seventeen, but for a few moments they were like schoolgirls again.

Jane plonked down on the sofa as the song changed and grabbed her glass of red wine from the coffee table. 'So, any ideas for my hen party or what? I've asked Lesley to be my maid-of-honour so, if you have anything you want to add, please go through her.'

Katie looked at Maxine. Jane and Lesley were always sneaking off for lunch, just the two of them. It was easy for them – both of them sleeping with the boss meant no work rotas to rearrange, days off whenever they wanted.

'Now don't be put out, you two. I asked Les because we all know she's the more sensible one out of all of us. I love you all the same, but Lesley has good organising skills, and she will make this hen do a belter.'

'If you say so,' Katie muttered.

Lesley was aware that jealousy was in the air and tried to smooth it over. 'Bloody hell, this should be a happy time, and look at your faces. Come on, girls, we need to make this a holiday to remember.'

Katie was already thinking about the cost of the holiday, and anything she threw into the mix was going to be cheap and cheerful. What was wrong with Blackpool? she asked.

'Katie, this is Jane's hen party. We want sunshine, music, good nightlife.'

'And where do you think I'm going to get sunshine money from? I can't even afford a sunbed down the precinct at the moment, never mind jetting off somewhere.'

Jane jumped in like she always did. 'Katie, you just save some spending money and I'll pay for the rest of it.'

Katie shook her head, always the charity case. 'I don't want you to have to do that, Jane. I'll see if I can get any extra shifts at work. When are we talking?'

Lesley looked at Jane for the answer. 'So, I've earmarked the church and the reception venue already. I spoke with them this morning. I'm getting married in six weeks. I've been waiting for years – I'm not hanging around any longer than I have to!'

'Crikey,' Maxine said. 'Well, we better get our arses in gear then and get this holiday booked. Who do you want there, Jane?'

'Just us girls for the proper one, I think. I'll do a local thing for everyone else.'

'Great,' Lesley said, waving a pen and pad she'd brought with her. 'For that, I'm thinking of asking the girls from the salon, the ladies from Zumba and any of your relatives you want to invite too. Is there anybody I've missed?'

Jane looked at Lesley and sat thinking for a few seconds. 'No, that should be fine. I'm glad it's just us for the weekend. I'm not inviting my family to any holiday. Our Tracy is bloody lethal. Do you remember her at my last birthday party? She's lucky she never got arrested.'

Lesley coughed. 'Right, you said Tommy had suggested Benidorm, Jane. Might even chuck in some cash to help us celebrate in style. He's class, your fella. Sorry, fiancé! But I think he's on to something. It's a quick flight, we'll have sunshine there, nightlife, and cracking food. Who's in agreement?'

Katie rubbed her hands together. She loved Benidorm. The last time she was there, she met a guy who she spent most of her holiday with. She hadn't told Jade, but she'd just taken out a new credit card – that'd have to cover it. She wasn't proud of this, but she'd used Jade's details to get the card. She'd clear it all before her daughter found out – she just needed a bit of sun to get herself sorted. 'Yep, I'm up for that. I've got all my summer clothes and bikinis from the last holiday I went on.'

Maxine nodded too. A weekend away from Ian sounded like heaven right now.

'Jane?' Lesley asked.

'Yes, go for it. Benners it is.'

Maxine was running her finger around her glass, tipsy now; and her worries were there for everyone to see. 'Are you alright, Max?' Jane asked in a soft voice.

Katie and Lesley looked over at Maxine too now.

'No, I'm not. I know what you all think: that Ian is a twat and you think I should have left him long ago.'

Jane sat back in her chair and sucked hard on her Cherry Cola-flavoured vape. 'I can be honest with you, Maxine, but do you want to hear what I have to say without going on the turn?'

'Of course, I want to know. You three are my best friends in the whole wide world and if I can't hear it from you then who can I hear it from? Do you think Ian is still knocking about on me?'

Lesley sat back with her arms folded tightly. This was going to be uncomfortable.

Katie gulped; she was not going to voice her opinion. People who live in glass houses shouldn't throw stones, should they?

There was silence, none of them wanted to go first.

'I'll start, then,' Lesley said. 'It's well known on the estate that Ian will fill any hole that's on offer. I heard he was banging the barmaid from down the pub. I haven't got proof, and it was just hearsay, but, come on, Max, there is no smoke without fire, is there? You should have carted him when you had the chance. Donna Ramsey was more or less shouting it from the rooftops when he was seeing her, but you never said a word. Why?'

'Because my head was all over the place and I reckon I was scared of what she would tell me. If she'd have said she was sleeping with him, then what? Ditch Ian? I thought I wasn't strong enough to go through it all, to end up alone, but I can't go on like I am doing now. He's leading me a dog's life and I can't hack it anymore.'

Lesley chirped in. 'You need to catch the sly fucker. Get all your ducks in line first though because, once you have outed him, he will want half of everything. Start clearing the accounts. Anything of value, start moving it. Log everything down so, when you go to the solicitors about a divorce, you'll have dates and times.'

'A divorce,' Maxine snivelled. 'A bleeding divorce,' she repeated. 'We came here to plan your wedding and here I am talking about walking away from my marriage.'

Jane patted her shoulder and spoke in a softer voice. 'He broke those vows first, Max. You deserve better than Ian, love. If you're being honest with yourself, if this was any of us, you would be telling us to walk and never bloody look back. You are stronger than you think, Max. We're all behind you.'

'It's just so ruddy hard when I've only ever known Ian all my life. No other man has touched me like that, if you know what I mean. I don't think I will ever move on. I will be a lonely old woman with twenty bleeding cats keeping me company.'

'Alone doesn't need to mean lonely. Ian knows your biggest fear is being without him, and that's why he's been doing the things he's been doing. We're all here to support you. Look at Katie – she's been single for like forever.'

Katie smirked. 'Exactly – just because I'm single doesn't mean I don't get my needs looked after. You talk about only ever having slept with Ian, but I've got to tell you girl, sometimes sex is just sex.'

Maxine looked horrified. 'No disrespect to you, Katie, because, if you're happy, then fair enough. But I would die a thousand deaths if another man touched me like that. The thought of it makes me ill.'

Jane had another blast from her vape. 'Well Benidorm could change all that. Let's go, have the time of our life, and get you trained up for some wild, passionate sex. Katie can be your mentor.'

Katie burst out laughing. 'Bloody hell, I don't even remember their names. Sometimes, I just lie there and let them do all the work. Maybe I should care more about the men I'm sleeping with but, when I've had a few too many, all best intentions go out of the window. I'm there to scratch an itch, not be their agony aunt. Perhaps, that's the reason I'm still single. But I live in hope that my Mr Right is right around the corner waiting to meet me. Eh, I might find my true love in Benidorm.'

The girls laughed and Jane said, 'So that's settled – Katie and Maxine, you go get 'em. Les and I will be on our best behaviour, so you two have got to have enough fun for the four of us when it comes to blokes. And you know the code – your secrets are safe with us!'

Lesley made sure everyone's glasses were filled. 'Jane, this is it. Are you ready to settle down? Or will it be one last fling before you get hitched?'

Jane twiddled her hair. 'I'm not going to lie. You lot know I've always wanted to get married but, now I've been granted my wish, it scares me a bit.'

Lesley delved deeper. 'In what way?'

'I mean, I love Tommy with all my heart but, come on, girls, the same willy for the rest of my life?' Jane giggled. Then her face fell and she looked serious. 'Am I ready? I've never cheated on Tommy, but getting engaged has really made me look at things in a different light. You know me, I've always hated following rules and being told I can't do something. I always want the one thing I can't have. And now that one thing is another man's hot body against mine…'

Katie laughed. 'I know I've never been married but…' she paused, thinking. 'How can I put this? Right, we all like steak, don't we?'

The others nodded, eager for her to get to the point.

'So, imagine having steak every bloody night for your tea. No matter if it has a sauce with it, if it's cooked differently, it's still steak. I say it doesn't matter how much you love it, it'll taste bland after a bit. The flavour's dull, there's no excitement anymore about eating it.'

Katie always made them laugh. Jane's eyes opened wide, the thought unsettling her. 'I can't imagine that, Katie. Tommy's prime fillet. I'm going to make sure we keep it fresh. I'll dress up, role-play, anything to stop our sex life going stale.'

Lesley looked sceptical. John was older than she was and already sex was on the backburner for them. Now that the girls were speaking about it, she worked out they'd not had sex for over a month. She'd have to do something about that. Lesley had always made the effort until now, but it had crept up on her and, if she was being honest, these days she would rather have a bag of crisps, a bar of chocolate and a glass of wine than a session with her hubby. She no longer trussed herself up in sexy knickers like back in the early days, preferring what she called the passion-killers – proper cover-it-all-up granny pants that she yanked up over her stomach. Maybe this was what she needed: a wake-up call and some time to find the spark with John again. Maybe eyeing up the fellas in Benidorm would get her in the mood. After all, nobody would ever find out and it would be strictly look-but-don't-touch.

Maxine looked determined. 'Will you help me catch him, then? I'm ready to see what that arsehole is really up to. I don't buy that he's got endless late-night meetings and catch-up pints with the lads three times a week. All the signs are there and he's forever checking his body out in the mirror or guarding his phone like he's got state secrets. He's even signed up to Tommy's gym, so what does that tell you? Because we all know he hates any kind of exercise. He moans when I send him upstairs for anything, yet suddenly he tells me he's training for a 5k.'

Jane slammed her flat palm on the arm of the chair. 'So, let's take him down. He doesn't know who he's messing with. Let's get the hen do done, then you can be our next project. If we do this right, in a few months' time, you'll be a free agent.'

Maxine started smiling – she had a look in her eye that her friends had never seen before. A woman on a mission, a woman who would not stand for any more crap from her abusive husband. Ian's days were numbered, and the clock was ticking.

PART TWO

The man looked at the pile of money. Funny how a small fortune came down to just a few wads of notes. People lived and loved and worked all their days for this kind of cash, he thought, as he slammed the safe door shut after checking the handgun he kept for insurance was still there. Yes, he thought, this kind of money changed lives – and ended them too.

Chapter Ten

Jane was rushing about the house getting the last few things ready: passport – check; money – check; sun-cream – check. She was almost ready to go. Letty was cleaning the kitchen while she dashed around – Jane hated the thought of coming back to a messy house. 'Right, Letty, I'm off in a moment. It will only be Tommy at home for a few days, so you shouldn't have much to do – he'll probably be working all hours while I'm away.'

Letty carried on wiping the sides as she spoke. 'No worries. I hope you have a fantastic hen party too. I'll look after Tommy, don't you fret. If I know him, he'll probably be moping about until you are back home. That's what he did last time.'

Jane chuckled. 'You know him so well, don't you? He's like a big baby. I've been shopping for him too, but he'll probably eat out or get takeaways. He hates cooking when there's no one to impress.'

'I'll keep my eye on him, don't worry.'

Jane looked at her phone. 'Bloody hell, that's my lift. I better move my arse otherwise I'll miss my flight. Any problems, give me a ring.' Jane rushed out of the kitchen, grabbed her leather jacket from the peg in the hallway and pulled the handle up on her white suitcase. '*Adios!*' she shouted behind her.

Katie opened the minibus door and immediately passed her a pink t-shirt with 'Girls on Tour' written in silver across it. 'Get that on. Your hen party starts now, girlie.'

Jane looked inside the minibus: her friends were dressed the same too. She was passed a white veil and a diamante tiara, and she'd barely sat down before the girls shouted that they were doing shots. Maxine was keeping a close eye on Katie – the last time they all went away, she got rat-arsed in the airport bars and only just made it on the flight. They'd had to hide her away from the cabin crew because they would never have allowed her to fly if they'd clocked the state she was in, almost paralytic.

Lesley cuddled up to Jane after she'd put her t-shirt on and whispered into her ear, 'This is going to be amazing. Be prepared for the days that lie ahead. Go big or go home, that's what I say.'

Jane felt apprehensive and shook her head. Lesley was known for great surprises and, now they had free rein and no partners were here with them, the world was their oyster.

The girls landed at Alicante airport at six o'clock that night. They could feel the sultry heat as soon as they stepped off the plane. Lesley made sure the coach taking them to the hotel was the right one so they could start this holiday in earnest. It had been planned in a hurry, with Jane's insistence on a quick wedding, so the hen do had come round fast. But Lesley had been glad of the distraction. She'd had enough of life at home – after Kimberley's stunt with her perfume, she didn't feel welcome in her own house. A weekend of girl power was just what she needed.

The plan was to check into the hotel, throw their suitcases in their rooms, and get straight on it after a quick outfit change. Tonight, the girls were hitting the town dressed as nurses. 'Young Hearts Run Free' by Candi Staton was blaring from Maxine's phone as they wound their way towards the hotel. The friends were loud, and a few of the other holidaymakers were eyeballing each other and even hiding their children away from the rowdy crew, obviously praying this lot wouldn't end up in the same hotel as them. Katie didn't care. She stood up and made sure she had everyone's attention. 'So it begins, girls. Let's have the time of our lives. And forget "chicks before dicks" – I'm here to find love.'

Maxine winced. Was this the single life she had to look forward to if she walked away from Ian?

Jane stood back, looked up at the Ambassador Hotel and nodded. 'You've done well, Lesley. I'm glad we haven't ended up in some dodgy joint like that one in Greece we stayed at. Do you remember, we had massive cockroaches in the bathroom? This looks lovely.'

Lesley sighed with relief. Jane was hard to please at the best of times. 'It's all inclusive, so we can eat and drink whatever we want.'

Katie was happy not to be spending any more money than she had to. She'd not told the girls, but she'd not paid her bills for the last few weeks and, when she got back home, she would have to beg, borrow and steal the money to pay for the gas and the electric that was well overdue. Anyway, that was then, and this was now. Forget everything else: she was here to party and hopefully grab a man.

Jane double-checked plans as they headed to their rooms, a suite with doors to link their rooms so they could make sure getting ready was a pre-party to remember. 'So, we're all dressing up as nurses tonight, Les?'

'Yep, we sure are. Army girls tomorrow night and sailor girls the following night. Don't worry, I've got everything planned, so you can move your arse and start getting ready.'

Maxine and Katie headed into their room, while Lesley unlocked the adjoining room for her and Jane.

'We've got an hour, and then let's hit the town. It's going to be good tonight. I've already found the bars where we're going. I've got all sorts of places to try – even that place Tommy recommended. He's got us on the VIP list. I didn't know he knew people out here. Your Tommy is a dark horse, J.'

Jane smiled. She loved how even when she was away Tommy was thinking about her. When she'd told him they were definitely going to Benidorm like he'd suggested, he'd sprung into action and got them a private table at one of the best places in town. She was lucky, she knew that. So why was there still a tremor of doubt in her mind?

'Am I doing the right thing getting married, Lesley, or should I stay as I am? I know I've always wanted a ring on my finger but now it's happened I worry my heart's not in it. I've got this nagging feeling in my tummy.'

Lesley was right at her side, comforting her. 'Tommy is a lovely man. The best. And look, I know you're superstitious and don't like to mention it, but is it the kids thing? You're still young – you can go see a doctor, or adopt, even? You two would make great parents. And look at the bigger picture of what he brings to the table; he's funny, rich, he cooks,' she eyeballed Jane. 'And you're always telling me he's like a porn star in the bedroom, so it's all gravy baby, isn't it?'

Jane struggled to raise a smile and inhaled deeply. 'I know, I know, it's only me getting cold feet, I think. You're right, Tommy is a mint guy, but I feel like there's a side to him he never shares. I think he thinks it makes him less of a man for not knocking me up. Anyway, I don't mean to be a misery. Not after all the work you've put into planning this. Let's get this party started and do what we do best: having some well-deserved fun.'

Lesley was putting her make-up on and spoke to Jane with her mouth half open as she fanned her lashes out with black mascara. 'We can do a few songs tonight; I've got a karaoke bar on the list for later. Do you remember in school when we spent all our breaks practising songs? We thought we were going to be the next big girl band.'

Jane grinned. 'God, that huge fight we had when we said Melissa Myers couldn't be in our band, and we picked Katie instead.' Jane was brushing her hair as she carried on. 'Imagine, if we could go back to school knowing what we know now, what would you change?'

Lesley went beetroot, her bottom lip trembled, and her eyes clouded over. 'I think you know what I would change.'

Jane realised what she meant and quickly went to hug her. 'Come on, now, no tears tonight. You did what you had to do, and we all stuck by you.'

Lesley snivelled and looked up at Jane. 'You girls all got me through it. I could never have done it without you guys.'

Jane quickly checked her watch. 'Right, come on, enough talking and let's get our arses ready. These are my last few nights as an unmarried woman, so move it.'

The girls were in high spirits as the night took hold. Men buzzed around them like flies, gawping at their sexy outfits and trying to work out which of the women might put out later that evening. They'd been to two bars already by the time they hit Neptune's for karaoke. The atmosphere was amazing – a sense of freedom, pleasure and no rules flowed through the crowd. Katie was on form already. Party was her middle name – she never let the side down. She'd already flashed her knickers to a man who was wolf-whistling at her and now she went straight up to the karaoke and spoke with the man there before returning to her friends with a tray of shots. 'Voddies!' she yelled as the women downed the drinks.

Before they could get another round in, Jane's name was called over the PA system. Katie punched her clenched fist into the air as she dragged the girls along with her. Lesley, Jane, Katie and Maxine all got onto the stage, each of them knowing exactly where they should be before the song started. They'd been singing this tune for twenty years and each knew their part by heart. The bright lights shone on them, and Jane held the microphone in her hand, no nerves whatsoever. The first sweeping bars of 'I Will Survive' began and the crowd went wild. Once they started singing, the girls had the full club behind them, holidaymakers and partygoers joining in, singing and dancing too. For the three minutes of the song, anything felt possible.

No one noticed the man in the navy jacket and white shirt watching the girls with a shark-like attention. By the time the music faded, he was gone.

The evening had felt like a blur, but finally they reached El Dorados, the club Tommy had suggested. He'd given Jane a letter for the club owner and, when she asked for him, the bouncers had ushered them in straight away and a hostess led them to a table behind a velvet rope.

They'd barely sat down before a tall, dark, handsome man approached, flanked by two bouncers. He made his way to Jane and whispered something into her ear. Jane burst out laughing and fluttered her eyelashes at him. 'Maybe, maybe not,' she replied as she handed over Tommy's letter, which he tucked into the inner pocket of his navy blazer promising to give it to his boss, the owner. He waved his friends over and soon they were all chatting and flirting. Katie was on fire, and it must have been only ten minutes before she had her tongue stuck down one of the men's neck.

'Can I get you a drink? I mean, all of you?' the man asked. Katie was straight back at him, her radar for a free drink never failing her, 'I'll have a Black Russian and so will she,' she said as Maxine smiled at him.

Jane was a lot cooler than Katie and she knew that no man liked a woman who was easy prey. 'Not for me,' she purred. 'I think my friend has already got one coming for me.' She walked over to Lesley at the other side of the table. She looked back over her shoulder and could see the man was not used to getting blown out by any woman. True enough, a minute or two later he appeared at her side again.

'So, Jane, can I be your Tarzan?'

She chuckled and flicked her hair. This guy had game and a great sense of humour. Maybe she would give him a bit of her time after all.

'Come on, let me get you a drink. It's a drink, not a marriage contract.' The man waved to a bartender who scurried over immediately.

She smiled as she looked at him in more detail. Big blue saucer eyes, slight tan set off by his crisp white shirt that revealed a hint of the body of a Greek god. Yep, he ticked all her boxes.

'My name is Francis, by the way, in case you were asking. My close friends call me Frankie.' He didn't take his eyes off her as he spoke. 'Your Tommy asked the boss to give you all the VIP treatment, and I can see now that it will be my pleasure.'

Jane had half-expected to hear a European accent but, despite a hint of Spanish, this man sounded like he came from her part of the world. Maybe he knew Tommy through the fitness world. It certainly looked like he worked out – his biceps strained against his jacket sleeves. He looked like he'd be able to pick her up with one hand.

'In that case, Francis, can I have a vodka and coke, please?'

The guy grinned like he knew it was game on. He disappeared to the other end of the bar and Lesley, Katie and Maxine were by her side straight away. Katie was looking over at this fresh piece of meat. 'If you don't shag his brains out, then I'm definitely having a go at him myself. Jane, he is so handsome. He's like a superhero.'

Even Maxine was practically drooling as she watched him too. 'Forget what I said about Ian being the only man for me. I hope he has a brother for me or a good-looking friend.'

Lesley knew it was time to take her usual role as the voice of reason, and she placed her hand on Jane's shoulder. 'No judgement from me if you fancy a harmless flirt. The girls are right: I wouldn't kick him out of bed.'

Francis was back now with a tray of drinks.

'Cheers,' Katie said as she took hers. The others followed. Katie slammed her empty drink on the table as a new song came on. She dragged Lesley and Maxine with her. 'Come on, girls, let's shake our arses.'

Alone with Francis, Jane ran her finger around her glass and looked at this guy. She could feel the heat between them. What exactly had he meant when he said he'd give her the full VIP treatment?

The time sped by. Jane hadn't realised how fast the night was slipping by in Frankie's company. It was past midnight now and he made sure he'd kept her glass full. They were getting on like a house on fire. It turned out Francis had a place in Manchester too, not far from where Jane lived. He spent half the year out here, he told her, helping run the club and building up a property business, but when he was back in Manny they'd been in the same bars, eaten in the same restaurants and, yes, he'd met Tommy at one of his gyms. How weird was that? Maybe it was fate that they were going to meet at some point in their lives.

Francis leaned in nearer. She could smell his Halfeti aftershave, knew the fragrance well as Tommy wore it, too. 'So, now you've seen the best of Benidorm night life, I've got a suggestion. This place, mint as it is, always feels like work to me. How about a walk on the beach? That's the real magic of this place. You can't come to Benny and not feel the sand between your toes.'

Jane looked around for her girls. Katie was snogging the face off some guy, and Maxine was chewing someone's ear off in the corner of the room, probably telling him how unhappy she was at home. Lesley was propped up next to her on a stool, sipping on a fishbowl cocktail that looked like it was meant for a whole tableful, and making the thumbs-up sign at her friend.

Jane knew she was getting on to dangerous territory. But a moonlit walk on the beach: how romantic did that sound? Tommy was a lot of things, but he was never a big romantic. He showed his love with gifts rather than experiences. Maybe one moonlit walk on a beach before she got hitched? She nodded and stood up. She hooked her handbag over her shoulder and felt Frankie's strong hand warm at the base of her back as he led her out.

The night sky was glittering. The sea breeze just enough to cool them both down. Francis kicked his shoes off and held them in his hand. 'This feels like a little patch of heaven, the sand is so smooth.'

Jane yanked her shoes off too. He was right, the sand felt good underneath her feet. As she sank into the uneven surface, she stumbled. Francis reached over and held her hand in his. He oozed confidence, and it felt so natural to be here with him. They walked a short way in silence, until Francis pulled his jacket off and placed it on the sand. 'Come on. Let's have a sit down for a bit. Listen to the sea, how calming is that? Such raw power when it wants, then so gentle.'

Jane sat down and looked out at the dark mirror of the sea, trying like anything not to look at Frankie in case she got lost in his eyes. She breathed in a mouthful of cool air and lay back on the jacket, looking up at the sky. How stunning was this? Nothing else seemed to matter to her right now. She would savour this moment forever. Francis lay back and joined her.

'Makes you feel small, doesn't it?' Jane scanned the sky for constellations. 'They say you can see patterns in the stars; bears and women, and all that? We barely see the stars in Manchester, do we? I never bother looking up.'

'It's amazing what you can miss, even when it's right under your nose.' Frankie had turned on his side now, one hand on the bare skin of her shoulder. The other lay between them, not touching her but she could feel it millimetres from her where her skimpy pants showed below the garish costume the girls had dressed her in earlier. Suddenly she wished she was in her own clothes, all natural and alone on the beach with this guy.

She felt his warm hand trace down her arm to clasp hers and she turned to face him. The whites of his eyes looked brighter than ever, and she was drawn towards him like a magnet. His lips touched hers and she felt electric sparks between them as they kissed. He dug his large hands into her hair and kissed her again. It felt like all the film kisses she'd ever seen. The ones where she'd turn to Tommy and say, 'Why don't you ever kiss me like that?'

Jane pulled away from him as she realised what she was doing. But, before she could protest, he kissed her again and again. She heard the lapping of the waves almost in tune with her thudding heart. She was lost in the moment and before long they were having sex. Suddenly, she had no inhibitions. Their hot sweaty bodies connected and, as he flipped her and manipulated her, she came again and again. Tommy was a good lover, but he was more of a wham-bam-thank-you-mam kind of guy. He didn't worship her body like this man was doing; he was more of a joker in the bedroom. This was hot, hard, sex. The kind every woman wished for, if they were lucky enough to know it could be like this. The kind that would always leave you hungry for more.

Jane was gasping for breath when the sex was over. He was still kissing every inch of her, though, still making her tingle from head to toe. She searched in her handbag and pulled out her vape. She needed to calm down, before she passed out. Frankie lay next to her and tickled his fingers along her stomach. 'That was beautiful, Jane, the best I've ever had.'

She smiled at him. She had no words yet, nothing to say. She was still seeing stars, and not just in the sky.

Finally, she started to brush the sand from herself, and tried to put her clothes back on. He pulled her back. 'Don't get ready yet. There is plenty more where that come from,' he chuckled. 'Let's stay here together and watch the sun come up. Have you ever seen it before?'

Jane shook her head. 'No, not like this, anyway.'

He moved closer to her and kissed her breast slowly. 'So, let's stay and watch the sun rise together.'

Suddenly reality came rushing in. What had Jane been thinking? Her first night here and she was having sex with a guy she'd only known for a few hours. She was meant to be here to celebrate the fact she was getting wed to the love of her life, yet here she was, screwing not even a stranger, but someone who knew Tommy. She felt the first wave of guilt rising up and making panic blossom in her stomach. But before she could stand up, Frankie's powerful grip held her by the waist.

Katie had been missing for over an hour from the club. Lesley and Maxine had tried phoning her but got no answer, and now they were heading back to the hotel. They were finding it hard to stand up and even the alcohol wasn't numbing the pain their heels were causing. Stumbling, they took two steps forward and two steps back. It was going to be a long walk back to their room. Maxine was slurring her words. 'I kissed another man, Lesley. I'm a cheat now, just like Ian is. My marriage is over and I'm just as bad as him.'

Lesley growled and pulled her friend closer. 'It was a peck on the cheek, for crying out loud. You need to sleep with someone else for it to count. And I'm not being funny, but I bet Ian has kissed hundreds of girls. He's a cheeky bastard, that one is. I'm glad you can finally see him in a different light. Put yourself first on this holiday and, when we get back home, we can sort everything out to make sure when you divorce him you get everything you're entitled to.'

Maxine was sobbing now as she wobbled along the grey gravel path. 'I've been a good wife, why wasn't I good enough for him? I know sex has been a bit stale, but we could have worked on it, sorted it out.'

'Men like Ian never change, Max. We've all seen you struggling for years with that twat. Honest, I've wanted to punch his lights out a right few times, when I've heard the way he's spoken to you. He was always gobby when we were at school; thought he was God's gift to women.'

'I've been caught up in it for so long that I never really saw what was right under my nose, did I?'

'It happens to the best of us, love. Sometimes we fall in love with what we want to see rather than who is actually there in front of us. We're taught all this nonsense about "love conquers all", but life is hard and sometimes it's not enough. Look at how Kimberley is drawing a wedge between me and John at the moment. Anyway, enough talk about the misery at home. I'm sure it will be waiting for us both when we land.'

Maxine burst out laughing, still wiping the tears from her eyes. 'What are we like? Still, at least Katie will be having the time of her life. You know, sometimes I wish I had her happy-go-lucky outlook on life.'

Lesley sighed. 'It's all a show, Max. She's never got a penny to spare and she's always dodging the loan men. I couldn't live like that, no bloody way. At least we have partners behind us. She never has nobody to support her.'

Maxine nodded. 'Let me try calling her one more time.'

This time, the call connected. 'Katie, mate, where are you?' Lesley shouted over the noise of a busy bar in the background.

'I'm fine, girls!' Katie slurred back. 'I'm with this mint guy, Pete. He seems lovely, says he's going to take care of me. Don't wait up – he's just bought me another drink. See you later, ladies.' The call disconnected.

'Maybe, that's where I've gone wrong. I've never put myself or my needs first. Never been strong where Ian is concerned. He says jump, and I say how high. I've never really been able to say no to him.'

'And that's the problem. Maybe, if you'd given him a piece of your mind every now and then, he would have fell back into line. But he won't change his ways now, Max.' Lesley sat down on a wall and kicked her shoes off, rubbing at her feet.

Maxine perched next to her. 'I can feel myself getting stronger, you know. That feeling in my stomach that I always felt when I thought he was going to leave me has eased off. That song was right earlier – I will survive. I'm going to make him pay, Lesley, make him wish he had never been born.'

Lesley stood up and hooked her shoes over her shoulder. 'We're all here right behind you, Max. Remember: you fight, we all fight.'

But Maxine wasn't listening. She was tottering down the street singing 'Show me the way to go home. I'm tired and I want to go to bed. I had a little drink about an hour ago and it's gone right to my head.'

Chapter Eleven

Lesley opened her eyes and winced at the bright sunlight. She'd crashed with Maxine last night and no one had thought to draw the blinds. Her voice was croaky. 'Water, I need water and gallons of it. My mouth is like a flip-flop.'

Maxine's eyes were still closed, but she blearily reached over to the bedside cabinet, trying to locate the bottle of water she had stashed there, false eyelashes hanging on by a bit of glue, mascara smeared under her eyes, more bronzer on the pillow than was left on her face. Eventually, she found it and threw it over to the bed next to her.

After gulping some down, Lesley let out a laboured breath and looked around the suite they'd booked so they could all share together. She dug her knuckles into her eyes and looked again. 'Where the hell are Jane and Katie?'

Maxine lifted her head up slightly and peered at the empty beds through the adjoining door. 'Big girls, they are, Lesley. Go back to sleep and stop worrying. They'll come home when they are ready.'

Lesley was like a mother hen. 'How can I stop bloody worrying when we didn't even see Jane leave the club and Katie could be dead in a gutter somewhere?'

Maxine smirked and folded the pillow under her head. 'You told me Jane left with that minted guy. And, from what I could see, she was loving the attention.'

'And Katie?'

'Katie was chewing the face off that man all night long, so I will bet my life on it that she's in his bed.'

'I hope so, Max. You know I'm a worrier. Bleeding hell, what is Jane doing staying out all night with that guy? I never thought she would cheat on Tommy.'

'Nobody has said she cheated. Wait until she comes back and I'm sure she'll fill us in. Probably just having a bit of fun, no harm in that, is there? Jane is no slapper and she'd want a diamond ring or a new car before she dropped her kecks. Whereas Katie, we all know what Yo-yo Knickers is like. She's had more nob-ends than weekends, that one. A bloody kebab and a few voddies, and she's anyone's. You know she'll have us in stitches when she tells the tale.'

They both started laughing their heads off and sat up in bed, discussing the night before. 'This holiday has really opened my eyes,' said Maxine. 'I mean, I've still got game, men still find me attractive, don't they?'

Lesley nodded. 'I think, once you've carted Ian and slept with someone new, the rest won't be a problem. Like I always say, if you can't beat them, then bloody join them.'

The door handle moved slowly as the door creaked open. Jane stuck her head inside and looked surprised to see the girls were both awake. She closed the door behind her. Maxine hugged her knees, ready for the gossip. Jane kicked her shoes off and flopped down flat on Maxine's bed. Max shuffled up to make space for her.

'Girls, don't even ask where I have been. Although, hang on, where's Katie? Dirty stopout? Wow, what a night! I feel like Sandy from *Grease*.

Jane rolled on her side and dragged the duvet around her. 'It's been one of the most romantic nights that I've ever spent in my life. We walked on the beach, looked at the stars, and watched the sunrise together.'

Maxine opened her eyes wider. She was listening eagerly to every word. 'Cut the small talk, Jane. Did you shag him or what?' Maxine was waiting on the answer to her question, looking at Lesley and then Jane.

Jane blushed. 'Girls, it wasn't just a shag. He rocked my world. He kissed me in places I have never been kissed before and let's just say he played me like an instrument. The guy made mad passionate love to me all night long. I swear, I've never had sex like it. And I've got sand where no woman should ever get sand, let me tell you that.'

Lesley's mouth opened wide, gobsmacked. 'So, are you seeing him again? What is this, some wild final fling?'

'Oh, God, I don't know what I'm doing but, yes, he's meeting me again this afternoon. I know I shouldn't, but I can't say no. In for a penny, in for a pound.'

Lesley was quiet – she'd seen something in Jane's eyes that unnerved her. She was all up for having a bit of fun, expected Katie to have a quick knee-trembler, thought Jane might even go as far as a sly snog with some of the lads on holiday out here, but this seemed so much more. 'You can't go swanning off with this man, Jane. You barely know him, plus me and the girls have things planned for you. It's your hen do, remember?'

'By the time you find Katie, and you've all recovered, I'll be back with you. But I've got to see him again. You said yourself that this could be the last time I ever sleep with another man, because once that ring is on my finger, I'm snookered, aren't I?'

Maxine nodded slowly, her own marriage springing to mind. 'You know what, men fuck us over every single day, so it's about time we returned the favour. You go out with him and have a blast, girl. Like you say, it could be your last chance. Call us when you're done and we'll have the Prosecco ready and waiting.'

Lesley hesitated then slowly agreed. She'd only ever seen Jane with this look in her eyes when she first met Tommy, and she had a gut feeling this would come back to bite them. But before she could warn Jane any further, there was a knock at the door and in staggered Katie.

'Bleeding hell, look what the cat dragged in,' Lesley chuckled. Katie stood with her hand resting on the doorframe. 'I feel like I've been at a rodeo all night, girls. I can barely walk. On my life, he ruined me.' Katie kicked her shoes off and dived on the bed next to Lesley, wincing slightly. 'I'm a good-time girl and I know it, so don't give me them eyes, Lesley. Remember, I'm single and I answer to nobody. I just wish I could remember the end of the night.'

Lesley looked sour. 'I never said a word.'

'Yeah, but I can tell by your face that you're not happy.' Katie was looking at some purple marks on her arm.

Lesley rolled her eyes over at the others. 'Katie, you can sleep with a hundred men and it's none of my business. I just want to know that you're safe and happy. So, if you tell me you are, then that's that.' She paused and looked at her friend. 'It's just those bruises look a lot like finger marks to me. You've got them on your neck, too. I'm not judging what you get up to or what gets you off – each to their own, I say – but just take care, that's all.'

'I'm a big girl, I can look after myself, Les,' Katie replied, her voice quieter than before. 'I mean, like I said, it all gets a bit hazy towards the end of the night. I remember the guy, Pete I think he was called, kept buying me drinks – a proper high-roller – then we had a walk on one of the jetties, but after that it's a blank. I knew I should have stayed off those Pina Coladas. Lethal, they are. Still, what happens in Beni, stays in Beni, right, girls?'

Lesley laughed. 'Well, I'm glad you're having a good time, because that's what this holiday is all about. So get showered, get your bikinis on and let's get ready to get some sun. We can have breakfast and then see what happens from there, because I bet everyone is done in from last night.'

Katie shot a look over at Jane and saw she too was still dressed in the clothes from the night before. 'Oi, tramp, don't tell me you just got in, as well?'

Jane sniggered and stretched her arms above her head. 'I sure did, Katie. I've been on the dirty girl boat with you.'

Katie scoffed. There was no way she could be judged now when Jane was just as bad as her. She swapped beds and lay next to Jane, eager to find out more. 'Please tell me it was that fanny magnet you were talking to, because he was drop-dead gorgeous.' Jane fluttered her long dark lashes and nodded. 'You would have been a fool to let him walk by.'

'His name is Francis Vance. He lives in Manchester too for half the year, and it's funny because, when we got talking, he's been to all the bars and places we go to, so he's probably been inches away from me when I've been out in town. I think it's fate, you know. I was destined to meet this guy one way or another.'

Katie shot a look over at Maxine. Yes, she could see it too: Jane was smitten with this guy. Katie playfully pushed Jane. 'Right, if that's the way you want your hen do to go, who are we going to pull tonight?'

Jane shook her head at Katie. Her tone changed. 'Katie, it's not like that. I know it's wrong, but I think I might have been making a huge mistake rushing the wedding. I'm seeing Frankie again today. He wants to take me out for lunch – we're going to get to know each other properly, sober, in the daylight. I'm going to have a shower and get my slap on and I'm right back out. He's lovely, he makes my stomach flip, you know, butterflies.'

Lesley had heard enough. The sun was out and there was no way she was lying in bed all day when she wanted to get a tan. She sprang up from the bed and stretched her arms over her head. 'Right, I'm getting my bikini on and getting a lounger saved for after breakfast.

If you two dirty stop-outs want to do something else, that's fine.'

Katie had already turned over to sleep off the night before and muttered, 'I'll be down later. I need some sleep first, then I'll be back in action. Do me a favour: if anyone comes looking for me, especially that guy from last night, tell him I've gone home,' she giggled.

But Jane was too excited to sleep. She was love-struck; it was written all over her face. Cupid had shot his arrow and it had hit her right smack-bang in her heart.

Maxine and Lesley were getting ready when Jane's phone started ringing, Tommy's name flashing across the screen. The four friends froze until Jane picked it up like it was a hot coal and shoved a pillow over it. Out of sight, out of mind.

Lesley rubbed carrot oil on her pale legs and over her body. The sun was scorching already, and small beads of sweat were forming in her cleavage. It was probably best Katie wouldn't be down for an hour or two – she was known to burn very easily, and the girls had already warned her to make sure she had enough sunblock with her. The last time they were away, Katie had fallen asleep on the sun lounger and woke up like a lobster. The tan lines didn't fade for weeks. This time, Lesley worried they'd be coming home from their weekend with far more lasting problems than tan lines.

Lesley had just finished a call with her John. He really seemed to be missing her. She could tell something was happening at home that he was not telling her, and it didn't take a mind-reader to work out it was something to do with Kimberley. He was edgy, avoiding any conversation about his daughter. Lesley sat thinking before she reached down for her drink and took a large mouthful. There was no point letting the call get the better of her. Any problems would still be waiting for her when she got home, but this was her time, time to relax.

Maxine had her shades on next to her and already she was complaining about how hot it was, tossing and turning, restless. 'At least John has called you. That bastard Ian hasn't even rung me, Lesley. I heard you speaking with John and thought to myself: why has my husband not sent so much as a text to see if I'm alright?' She paused. 'I'll tell you why, should I? Because he doesn't bloody care. He's probably out with one of his tarts. Do you know what, Lesley? You girls were right. This holiday has been more than an eye-opener for me. I can see that prick for all he is. He only cares about himself, and he doesn't give me a second thought. Well, that's all changing. Fool me once, shame on you; fool me twice, shame on me.'

Across town, Jane could see Francis as she walked slowly up the beach front. He was dressed in crisp white shorts and a pink t-shirt. Just the sight of him made her skin prickle. Her legs felt like jelly, her heartbeat doubled and, all of a sudden, her mouth went dry. It was part lust, part fear. She knew last night had happened in a whirl of booze and adrenaline, animal attraction moving faster than her mind could. But in the cold light of day, what would they say? Would he judge her? Was he going to tell Tommy? She didn't even know what she wanted to happen, she just knew she couldn't look away.

'Good afternoon gorgeous,' Francis said as he wrapped his arms around her and kissed her on the cheek. 'I've booked us on a boat trip. Hope you don't get seasick.'

Jane was still trying to find her voice and smiled gently back at him. He held her hand and they started walking up the beach front. 'I don't know about you, but I'm knackered today. Mind you, we didn't get much sleep, did we?' he chuckled as he ran his fingers over her hips. She'd imagined their first words to be awkward, embarrassed even, but Francis oozed confidence. Anybody looking at them would have thought they had been together for years. He was at ease with her, not scared to show affection towards her in public. Tommy was never one for that. Even when they were out together on a date night, he never held her hand, never kissed her when anyone else was there, nothing. Any blokes he saw acting like that he called pussies. Francis's easy way of draping his arm round her shoulder was a revelation. She felt he was proud to have her on his arm. This was what Jane needed in her life, something she hadn't even realised had been missing from her relationship. Maybe she didn't know until now what affection meant – touch that didn't have to mean sex. It was something she was enjoying. Francis looked at his chunky watch. 'Shall we have lunch first? We have about an hour before we have to get on the boat. I've not had anything to eat yet, have you?' Even this innocent question sounded like a come-on.

'No, I just about had enough time to get ready, never mind anything else.'

He kissed her cheeks and stroked her hair. 'Well, my poor little lady needs some food then, doesn't she?'

Suddenly, she was ravenous. 'Sounds great. I missed breakfast in the hotel.'

Francis stood thinking. 'I know just the place. Me and the lads went there the other day, and the breakfast was banging. I hope you're not one of those girls who only eats lettuce all the time.'

Jane chuckled. 'You must be joking. I'm a proper foodie.' She had to stop herself mentioning Tommy. 'I love trying all new stuff. I'm in your hands.'

'That will do for me, then, kiddo,' he grinned as he held her hand again and turned towards a quieter part of town.

At the beachfront café, Francis watched Jane eating. She could feel his eyes on her. He reached over with his white napkin and dabbed it around the corners of her mouth. How embarrassing. 'I'm a messy eater, aren't I?'

Francis smiled over at her and carried on demolishing his food. Now she'd felt the force of his muscles, she understood how much it must take to keep a body like that. Three pieces of toast he demolished with his breakfast. Jane placed her knife and fork down neatly on her plate and sat back, rubbing her stomach. 'I'm so full now. I will eat properly later. I only usually find my appetite later on.'

Francis grinned. 'Don't you just! I can't get anything done without a good breakfast inside me. It sets me up for the day. I'm at the gym so often I need to keep my strength up.'

Jane flicked her hair back over her shoulder. She felt uncomfortable in case the conversation turned to Tommy. 'I like the gym too. I prefer lifting weights to cardio, though.'

'I can tell you work out. You have a great body, there's proper strength there.'

Jane blushed and stared right back at him. Tommy never commented on her body. He always seemed glad to get his hands on it – but he never put it into words like this guy. 'I'm here for one last day then I fly home on the late flight tonight.'

Jane was disheartened but acted cool. 'And what then? Is it back to the real world?'

Francis finished eating his last mouthful of food and took a quick swig from his coffee. 'I don't think I'm ever coming back down to earth after last night. I'll be straight with you. I'll be getting back, waiting on you to come home, and then we can see what happens. I'm not mucking around. From the moment I set eyes on you I wanted you. I know we've got some stuff to work out...' he glanced at the engagement ring on Jane's finger, and she moved her hand out of sight onto her lap. 'But when you feel something as powerful as this, the normal rules don't apply. And I know we've basically just met, but I think you feel it too.'

His eyes bored into her and Jane felt her insides melt. Usually, she would have kept her cards close to her chest and never told a man what she was thinking, but here she was opening up and saying what she felt in her heart. 'Frankie, I feel the same. It's sounds wild, I know. I wasn't here to pull, you know that. In only a few weeks' time, I'm meant to be a married woman, and yet there was something about you that instantly attracted me to you. I would never, ever, normally let someone I'd just met lay a finger on me. Sex would have been two or three months down the line.'

He reached over and touched her hand. 'It's like I said, Jane. This is the real deal. I don't want to hurt anyone, most of all you, but you deserve to know what you've done to me.'

Jane simply sat there, drinking him in, desperate to stay in this moment rather than face up to the almighty decision she'd have to make once she got home.

'So, what do we do once you're back at home, then?' Francis was cutting to the chase.

Jane began to fidget, no eye contact. 'We can swap numbers and see where we go from there. I think this is pretty much the definition of "It's complicated".'

He knew a brush-off when he heard one. 'So, this is a holiday fling for you, is it? I'm not lying – I'll take as much of you as you'll give me. If it's only twenty-four hours, then fine, but I would have liked to have something more.'

Jane had decided that sometimes silence was safest. But it was as if she had no control over the words coming out of her mouth. 'I want more, too. It's just… well, you know...' She didn't want to mention Tommy's name in case it broke the spell. She was a scarlet woman and felt like his name in Frankie's mouth would turn her from goddess to whore.

'Look. I know what I'm getting into. I know you've got a rock on your finger, and I know who put it there. I'm only saying you're not Mrs Braxton yet. And if I didn't say this to you now, I might be regretting it for years to come. I'm not pushing you into anything – we can simply enjoy today. But know that I'm serious, Jane. Deadly serious.'

Francis checked his watch and stood up quickly. 'Come on, gorgeous. We have ten minutes to get to the boat.'

Jane had a last sip from her coffee and off they went, hand in hand.

Anyone watching would have thought they were a fairytale couple; anyone, that is, apart from the guy on the moped Jane hadn't clocked. Not when he recced the street, nor when he parked across the street from the café, and not when he pointed his phone in the direction of the couple and started filming.

Chapter Twelve

Jane sat with the girls on their last night in Benidorm and ran her finger around her wine glass. 'He's not stopped texting me since he landed.'

Lesley rolled her eyes and nudged Maxine who was sat next to her. They were all aware Jane was a wild woman – the kind who might have been expected to have a final fling before she got married – but this was getting out of hand. They needed to tell her a few home truths, get her head back in the game.

Lesley was the spokesperson. 'Jane, don't you think you should kerb it now? I mean, we go home tomorrow, and what then? Don't tell me you're going to carry on seeing him?'

The girls moved in closer and heard the tremor in Jane's voice. 'I really like him, though; I've never been like this before. He could be my happy ever after.'

Maxine jumped into the conversation. 'I thought Tommy was that. You have always said what a good guy he is and, let's be honest here, you could do a lot worse.'

Jane snapped, her voice getting louder. 'Are you not listening? I said I really like him. I could be making the biggest mistake of my life by marrying Tommy because, let's face it, if I was that in love with Tommy, I would never have slept with Francis, would I?'

Katie stubbed her fag out. 'Jane, take it from someone who has been around the block a few times. Tommy provides everything for you. You will never want for anything while you're by his side. You've just got a bit sidetracked, that's all. A bit of holiday madness. But what counts is back home. I would give my kidney to have a man like your Tommy.'

Jane dipped her head low. 'Look, this sounds harsh, but it's not only the sex with Frankie, or the connection we've both felt. It's about who I want to be. Tommy doesn't think he can have kids, does he? And yet he keeps putting off going for the tests. Worst thing is, I know it's him because, when I was with Graham, I had a miscarriage, so I know it's not me. You girls helped me through that – helped me pick myself up when I thought my heart was breaking when I lost that pregnancy when I wasn't even twenty-one. I've never told Tommy about the miscarriage because it would do him in to know he was firing blanks. You all know what he's like.'

Lesley picked up her glass of wine and she could feel Maxine's and Katie's eyes on her. 'Jane, like Katie said, take this for what it is. A holiday romance. You and

Tommy are a strong couple and any problems you have, you can overcome them together. I want you to be happy more than anyone here, but I have to make you see sense. Francis might be different when you get home, who knows? When you're on holiday you're all happy and laid back, but in his normal day he might not be like that. Just be mindful, that's all. We all love you and will stand by you no matter what, but I'm saying look before you leap.'

Katie coughed to clear her throat. 'Girls, while we are being honest here, I have to tell you something. You know I said I booked holidays from work? Well, I actually told them I was sick, and I've just had an email from them telling me I have a meeting with the big-wigs when I get back home. I think they will sack me.'

Jane reached over, glad the heat was off her for a moment. 'Bleeding hell, Katie, why didn't you follow procedure like you should have?'

'Because I knew two other staff were on holiday and they would have said no to me. I'll have to start looking for a new job. To tell you the truth, I was ready for a change. But it's alright for you lot – you've got blokes who'll bail you out if you're skint or have jobs that do more than barely cover the bills. Now it looks like I've lost that – what am I going to do?'

'Katie, bloody hell, just breathe for a minute, will you?' Jane jumped in. 'You're a survivor. If you do need another job, you'll find one. I thought you said you applied to the betting shop on Rochdale Road?'

Katie realised she was getting angry and inhaled a few times to calm down, long deep breaths. 'I haven't heard anything back from them. The closing date is in two weeks, though, so I still might be in with a shout.'

'See, there you go. We don't have problems, we only have solutions waiting to happen.' Lesley made it sound so easy.

Maxine shivered suddenly despite the heat of the day. The reality of going back home tomorrow was lying heavy on her mind, too. 'We've all got shit to deal with back home, Katie. We'll stand by each other and find a way through, though. Like we've always done.'

At that moment, Jane's phone rang, Tommy's name flashing across her screen. She'd spoken to him a few times while she'd been away, but she wasn't in the mood for an audience this time. She stood up, answered the call and walked away from the table.

Katie watched until she was gone. 'Forget about us. The shit's going to really hit the fan with that one, let me tell you. I can see it in her eyes that she's fallen for Francis. Tommy's not daft, you know, and if she's acting like she is now when she gets home, he'll be on to her straight away. If he even senses she's got doubts, he'll be out of there before she can say a word.'

Lesley looked over at Jane in the distance and lowered her voice. 'So, what we need to do is get this wedding day all sorted as soon as we get back. You know, make her excited about it, tell her how special the day is going to be. She needs to see she can't throw her life away for a bloke from Benidorm – no matter the size of his biceps, his dick or his wallet.'

'You're right,' said Maxine. 'It's our only hope, Lesley. They say love conquers everything, but will she realise too late who she really loves?'

Two men watched the grainy CCTV footage of the club's front door. There she was – the British woman they'd been told to watch out for. She looked so happy that for a split-second something like guilt flickered between them. Still, it was the innocent ones that made the best targets and here was fresh meat.

PART THREE

Chapter Thirteen

Lesley had been relieved to get home, but worried that John would ask her how it had all gone and she'd spill the truth about Jane. From the moment she stepped foot back in the house, she realised he was distracted. Something wasn't right and he was hiding something.

'Where's Kimberley?'

John fidgeted and gave her no eye contact. 'She's been a bit upset, love. Her mam is not in a good place, and she's been spending a lot of time with her.'

Lesley couldn't summon any sympathy. 'Like I care if that woman is going through a bad time or not. Karma, isn't it, for the way she's treated us over the years?'

John swallowed hard. 'I never keep anything from you, so I need to tell you something.'

Lesley could see the concern in her husband's eyes and sat back with her arms folded tightly in front of her. 'Go on, then, spit it out.'

John sat back and sighed. 'Before I tell you, I want to say how much I love you and how important you are to me.'

Lesley tried to stop herself from jumping to conclusions, but a hot flush filtered over her body.

John stuttered as he began. 'Angela came here with Kimberley and stayed for two nights. The woman was a mess and honestly, if she hadn't stayed here, God knows what would have happened to her. She'd been drinking and Kimberley said she'd took some pills. She said her relationship with her man had fell apart and that she was in a state. I told Kimberley she shouldn't have brought her here, but what else could she have done? It's her mother.'

Silence. Lesley felt a stifled scream filling her throat, her words trapped behind her teeth. 'She should have taken her to bloody hospital, that's what she should have done. I despise that woman, and I thought you did too?'

'Lesley, listen, will you? I did it for Kimberley, not bloody Angela. The woman means nothing to me. It's you I love, nobody else. And when she arrived, the woman wasn't suicidal – she was pissed and furious. You might as well know, she made a pass at me.'

Lesley stood up. 'You're not a bad man, John Potter, but you are a bloody idiot. Kimberley has played you. It's probably all part of her plan to get you two back together. But I can tell you something for nothing, I won't be sticking around to watch it. I'm going to stay somewhere else until I can think straight.'

'Lesley, just listen to me, love. I didn't know what to do. I'm sorry.'

Lesley made her way to the door and turned back. 'You will be sorry, because I'm gone from here while I decide what to do. Where did she sleep? It's enough to think that woman has been in my house, touching my stuff, my belongings, without imagining she's been sleeping in my bed.'

'She was in James's room, but after she'd tried it on with me, I stayed downstairs. Honest.'

Lesley pulled the handle up on her suitcase. 'I'm not even going to unpack.'

'I slept on the couch, love, I swear – nothing happened.' John was pleading now. 'Please Lesley, don't go. Let's talk for a bit, let me say my piece.'

'Are you having a laugh or what? You've said enough. I go away for one weekend and suddenly you and Ange are back playing happy families,' she snapped. She dragged the suitcase behind her, flustered and sweating as she searched for her car keys.

John sat on the bottom stair with his head held in his hands. 'I'll sort this out – on my life I will.'

Lesley opened the front door and snarled at him. 'Grow a bloody set. That's what you should have done and told Angela to crawl back under whichever rock she came from.' The front door slammed shut.

Lesley's mind was still racing when she got to Jane's house. She'd rung her on the way there and asked if she could stay for a night or two.

Jane opened the front door and escorted her friend inside, dragging the suitcase behind her.

'Go straight into the front room. Tommy's just nipped out to get some food and I've told him to get a couple bottles of wine while he's out, too.'

Lesley shrugged her coat off. 'I'm sorry to land myself with you. Tommy was probably looking forward to having you all to himself. I need a breather to work out if John's spinning me a line and, well, I thought you might need a friend in your corner, too, J.'

'Don't, Les, honest I feel like I'm torn in two.' Jane had been distracted all day as they travelled back. She'd vanished off early from the hotel and showed up late to breakfast, saying Frankie had messaged to say he'd forgotten his briefcase and, if she could pick it up from the club, they could meet up in Manchester and take it from there. The only time Jane hadn't been glued to her phone waiting for WhatsApps from either Frankie or Tommy was the short time they were in the air on the flight home.

'Come on, we're back home now. Real world. Benidorm was great but I don't know why you agreed to bring Francis's stuff back. I think you were looking for an excuse to see him again. You're playing with fire, Jane. Don't get burnt.'

Jane was at her best friend's side now. 'Don't worry about me, Les. I'll sort it out. Focus on you and John. You've done the best thing by coming here. It will make John realise what he's done and how serious it is. He worships you – he'd never risk losing you by going back to a crazy bitch like Angela. Just give it twenty-four hours and you'll both calm down. Time's a good healer, love, trust me, I know. Like I said, chill for now. I'll pop the kettle on, and we can have a nice hot cup of tea before Tommy comes back.'

Lesley struggled to raise a smile. She was terrified Tommy would be able to see on her face that something was up. But Jane was back with two steaming hot cups of tea. 'Bleeding hell, hurry up and grab one of these cups. They're burning my fingers,' she shrieked. She gave a cup to Lesley. 'I'm not used to brewing up. It's Tommy's job, not mine. In fact, most things are Tommy's job in this place,' she said, thoughtfully.

Tommy was back. They could hear him arriving. 'Jane, I'll plate up. You and Lesley sit at the table, and I'll bring it in. I've got us a lovely Ruby, not too hot, and some starters. We're on the full shebang tonight, babes. Fuck the diet, I'm starving. And, if I know you girls, you'll have been living off cocktails in Spain, no proper grub.' And here he was, popping his head in through the door, smiling from cheek to cheek, blissfully unaware that it wasn't only Lesley who was weighing up her life choices. 'Cheer up, Les. John's a daft bugger, but he'd never cheat on you. That's lower than a snake's belly to screw around on the one you love, he wouldn't do that.'

Jane was glad she didn't have to look him in the eye just then, busying herself with the curry. Tommy continued, 'Right nutjob, the first Mrs Potter was. John won't go back, trust me. Why would he have hamburger when he's got prime steak with you, Lesley? Anyway, one woman's enough bother – what guy wants double trouble by keeping two on the go?!'

Jane had regained her composure now and glared at Tommy, hinting he keep his big trap shut. Lesley knew he was only joking and tried to raise a smile, not meeting Jane's eyes, aware of the bitter irony of Tommy's words.

The three of them sat eating the curry, but Lesley and Jane were only picking at the food. Neither woman could summon much of an appetite. Tommy spoke with his mouth full as he sat there, trying to get the full story of what had gone on in Spain. 'So, I hope my girl had a great time on her hen party, Lesley. She didn't give much away on the phone, if I'm being honest.

Jane blushed, not giving Lesley time to answer. 'Wouldn't you like to know, eh? I can't dob my girls in – you've got to let us have a few secrets. After all, I bet your stag will be on don't-ask-don't-tell rules… unless you're planning a night of tea and board games?'

Tommy burst out laughing and didn't see Jane shoot a look over at Lesley that meant, don't get into any conversation about the holiday whatsoever. Jane was glad when her phone beeped, giving her the chance to change the conversation.

'So, brace yourself, guys. Katie has been sacked from work. She's just texted to say there was a letter waiting for her on her doormat telling her that her employment has been terminated due to unauthorised time off.'

'Poor Katie. What's she going to do for a job? It's not like she can walk into another checkout job. She's already lost jobs at every supermarket in town, hasn't she?'

Tommy let out a laugh. 'She's her own worst enemy, that one. Has she always been a liability?'

Jane shook her head: this was her friend he was slagging off. 'Tom, she's got a heart of gold. She's just not cut out for the nine-to-five. She's a free spirit and likes to move about. She'll have another job soon enough, just you watch. She said she might have a chance of a job down at the betting shop, so fingers crossed she gets in there. Or maybe you could see if you've got a receptionist job going at any of the gyms?'

'You must be kidding!' Tommy looked horrified. 'I've heard you lot cackling away and sharing stories – she'd be the first one to admit she'd be trying to pull half the customers. It's a gym, not a knocking shop. She's not finding love on my time and money!'

Lesley looked distracted. 'I don't know if I can face work this week, either. I'm going to take an extra couple of days of leave. Working with John used to be a dream, but I won't be able to sit across the office from him and not be reminded what he's done, having that woman paw him, stay over, try and worm her way back in.'

'You two will smooth it over.' Tommy tried to calm the situation. 'It's not like he's shagging around. You can stay here in the spare room as long as you want, you know that. Anyway, it's company for Janie with me working away this week. It's nice to know she won't be on her tod. And you two will be busy – I hope you've not got so caught up in the hen do that you've forgotten there's a wedding to plan. I want it to be a day to remember.'

Chapter Fourteen

Tommy was up early and left the house to go to London. Jane was up next, relieved not to have to act normal in front of her fiancé. She was poring over her phone when Lesley came into the front room, looking bleary and stressed.

'I've not slept a bloody wink; I tossed and turned all night long. I don't know what to do for the best.'

Jane patted the space next to her. 'You and me both, Les. I never thought I'd be the one to be thinking of leaving Tommy. I always said I was the one who'd tamed the bad boy. I've wanted to be his wife for so long and now—' Jane stopped abruptly, and they both looked up as they heard a key in the front door. 'Morning Letty, just ignore us,' Jane shouted. 'We'll stay out of your way. Can you give the windows a clean today, if you get a chance?'

Letty stood in the doorway, clocked all the dirty plates from the night before, and for a moment her face clouded, before she returned to her usual happy self. 'I will do, Jane. Anything else you need doing?'

'The beds can wait until tomorrow. No, just do your normal.'

Jane and Lesley were alone again. Jane pulled her mobile out and showed a text message to her friend. Lesley sat back. 'Jane, I don't know what to say. Francis was a holiday fling. If you go and meet him, then it's something more, isn't it? *I'll* drop his bleeding luggage wherever it needs to go, if it saves you running back into his arms and losing your head.'

'I can't get him out of my mind. Since I got home, he's all I think about.'

'You're playing with fire, if you ask me, and you know what happens next, don't you?' She held her head to one side and spoke slowly. 'You. Get. Burnt.'

'Look. He wants to meet me in the Midland Hotel today for lunch. I've already decided I'm going, so don't start giving me a lecture. I might look at him today and think, no, he's not all that, it was just the sun and cocktails. But I need to know. I can't go into marriage thinking "What If…"'

'But what if you look at him and your heart skips a beat, and you like him even more? Some things are better left in the past. By you going today, he might think he's in with a chance and start chasing you. He could ruin everything for you. Just look around at the life you have.

Tommy has his faults, sure, but don't we all? And he idolises you.'

Jane's head drooped. 'But is Tommy the one who will make me happy forever? I have my own money, thanks to the salon, and I could survive on my own, you know.'

'I'm not saying that you couldn't. I'm saying be careful, because if you're spotted today, the shit would hit the fan. And I can tell you now, having a secret eats you up inside – look at me.'

Jane played with her fingers, digging the sharp points of her manicured nails into herself. 'I told you: you should have told John you'd a kid years ago. Bleeding hell, Lesley, you were barely more than a child yourself and had no other choice than to have her adopted. It's nothing to be ashamed of – you were giving that baby the chance of a life you couldn't offer it at that point.'

'It is still a secret, though, isn't it? It's like I'm always carrying a weight around with me. And now I can't tell John because I've given him all this grief about the shit his kids are causing between us. Honestly, J, you've got a chance to nip this in the bud. No one knows what happened in Spain, but if you start wining and dining another fella right here in Manchester, it's going to get back to Tommy. Plus, let's talk straight here, Tommy would leather Francis if he ever got wind of this. Jesus, the two of them would probably kill each other. He might forgive you, he might not, but is that a chance you want to take?'

Chapter Fifteen

It was pouring with rain as Jane parked her car. She got out and dipped her head low, umbrella held tightly over her, to hide her face as much as to protect her from the rain. She pulled her candy-pink gloss from her handbag and struggled to top up her silky-smooth lips with one hand. The pavements were heaving, everyone in a hurry to get out of the rain. They barged past her, bumping into her, and by the time she reached the Midland she was beginning to doubt what she was doing. Maybe Lesley was right – she could still walk away. She was wind-swept, hot and bothered, dressed in her black leather pants and her bright green jumper covered by a long cream fur coat.

Then Jane spotted Francis at the entrance of the hotel and a smile filled her face. He was as hot as she remembered. All her anxiety about meeting him seemed to disappear. She ran her fingers through her hair and shook it about in hope the bounce would come back.

'Hello, gorgeous. You look beautiful.' He wrapped his arms around her and kissed her forehead. They walked into the hotel together and Jane's face dropped as she clocked a blast from the past.

Melissa Myers. Jane carried on walking towards the restaurant. She turned her head back one more time and they locked eyes. 'Fuck, fuck,' she whispered under her breath. She hadn't seen her for years. She tried to look around subtly. She was gone. But what did it matter, anyway? Francis could have been anyone: a friend, a work colleague, a relation. Jane was seated facing Francis. She handed over her coat and Francis's briefcase, but kept her own handbag clutched in her lap like some kind of shield. The waiter took their orders for drinks.

Francis stared over at her. 'I've not stopped thinking about you. On my life, you are my last thought at night and my first thought as soon as I open my eyes in the morning.'

Jane was floored by his honesty. He wore his heart on his sleeve – she'd never known a man do that. Maybe these were sweet nothings, but she loved every second of them.

'I feel the same. I didn't know if it was holiday madness, but I've had butterflies just thinking about you.' Jane couldn't believe how easily the words came. This was so out of character for her. Usually she was a closed book, kept her cards close to her chest. But with Francis, she'd changed; she was vulnerable.

'Same here. I don't know what you've done to me. My head's in bits with you.' Francis swallowed hard, reached over and touched her fingertips. 'You said on your message Tommy's away. Let's stay the night together. I'll get us a room here tonight, and we can go out on the town and pretend life isn't as complicated as it is.'

Jane stuttered, 'But it *is* complicated, Frankie. You knew from the first moment that I was engaged. You've got to believe I've never done anything like this before. I've never played away, never even been tempted.'

Francis sat back in his chair. His tone changed, with a look in his eyes that didn't sit right with her. 'Is it just that, though? I've put myself on the line for you – I know that sometimes lightning strikes between two people. I wouldn't normally go for another man's woman – but this is too powerful. Instead of thinking we're unlucky we didn't meet when we were both single, you've got to think we were lucky to find each other before you got a wedding band on your finger. If you feel how I feel, you'll know I'm right. I get that you need to let Tommy down gently, I just get the feeling that you're holding back. Don't be playing mind games with me, Jane, I don't roll like that. You can't have us both. Or is this all just an act because you feel bad about dropping your knickers in Benidorm?'

Jane sat up straight and flicked her hair over her shoulders. She wasn't being spoken to like this. 'Like I've told you before, what happened in Spain was a one-off. Anyway, sort your attitude out, speaking to me like that. I'm in deep, Frankie. Whatever I do, someone's going to get hurt.'

Francis nodded. 'I had to ask to make sure. I don't want to put all my time and effort into you for you to think it's all a game.'

Jane leant in, touched her hand to the side of his face, and under the table, slid off her shoe and ran her stockinged foot up his leg. 'Does this feel like a game to you? You were right, Frankie. Let's take today and pretend it's all simple. I've got decisions to make and conversations to have when Tommy's back, but until then, let's imagine we're still on holiday.' Even as she spoke the words, her heart was hammering, and not only out of lust. The cold chill of danger was running down her spine. For crying out loud, she was out in full view where anyone could have seen her. What did she expect? It was only a matter of time before someone bubbled her.

'So, is that a yes for turning this into a full night date?'

Jane nodded. There were at least twenty missed calls from Lesley on her phone, but she'd placed it on silent. She didn't want disturbing. Who knew what lay ahead, but a lot could happen in a night.

Chapter Sixteen

Maxine sat biting her fingernails as she watched Ian getting ready to go out again. Usually, she would be asking where he was going, who he was going with, a long list of questions. But not tonight, she kept schtum. This was operation 'Catch your cheating husband' and she was sticking to the rules and not losing her rag.

Ian walked over to the bed. 'Don't be waiting up for me. It's going to be a late one tonight. It's Arnie's birthday and the lads have got a lap-dancing bar planned for him.'

Maxine was fuming, knowing her husband would have his hands all over the dancing girls, sliding his money in their bras and knickers, drooling over them. He knocked her sick. She had to hold it together, though, not say a word. Ian repeated what he'd just said and stood looking at her with confusion. It was as if he was waiting for her fury. 'I said. It's Arnie's birthday and I'm going to a lap-dancing bar.'

Maxine yawned and felt around the bed for the remote control, pretended she'd not been listening to him. 'Yeah, whatever. Keep the noise down when you come in.'

Ian bent down to kiss his wife, but she turned her cheek away from him. 'I was hoping you'd sold some of your perfumes and you could bung me a few quid. Brassic, I am.'

That was it, she couldn't keep her mouth shut any longer. 'What, you think I would give you my money to shove in some girl's thong? Like that will ever happen. I've told you before, you do you and I'll do me. Any extra money I get is being spent on me from now on and not on you to piss it up the wall. I must have daft cow written all over my face. Here's me working all the hours God sends and then coughing it up to you. It's not happening anymore.'

Ian backed off. 'Wow, don't get your knickers in a twist. I only asked for a bit of money, not a bleeding kidney.'

'So, save your breath in future, because the answer is no. Find your own money for your dancing girls. And don't come running back here with the clap.'

'Sweet,' he hissed at her. 'Maybe I'll stay out tonight.'

'Suits me fine.' Maxine sat up in the bed now, face of a thousand cuts. 'Do one and leave me the hell alone. If you can stay on Archie's sofa tonight, then do it, because I don't want any pissed-up man laying next to me, waffling on all night or pawing at me for a quickie.'

Ian's ears pinned back. How dare his wife speak to him like that? He'd given her a crack in the past and he'd do it again if he needed to. In his book, women were meant to stay at home and let the man of the house make the decisions. If they got mouthy, then he saw nothing wrong with a slap to show them who was boss. He bent down and gripped Maxine by the throat, his eyes bulging out of their sockets. 'Listen, you cheeky bitch, who the hell do you think you're getting lippy with? If I want more money, then I'll fucking take it. Your money is mine, remember that.'

Her heartbeat doubled and she wriggled about trying to get out of his grip. 'Get your hands off me, you wanker. How dare you think you can man-handle me like this? I'll tell you what, I'll give our Tony a ring, shall I, and tell him what's going on here? Yes, let's see what you're like when he's got you pinned up against the wall, shall we? Not so bold when you're picking on someone your own size, are you?'

Ian loosened his grip. Tony was Maxine's eldest brother, and, in the past, he'd had run-ins. One night, when they were all out celebrating their mother's birthday, he'd watched Ian leering at some other woman in the pub. He'd pulled Max to one side, couldn't believe his eyes, gobsmacked that she was sitting there while her husband was all over another woman like a rash. 'How can you sit there and let that prick be all over her over there. Nah, sack that, he's getting told. Does he think you're some kind of a muppet or what?'

And that's what he'd done. He marched over to Ian and dragged him outside by the scruff of his neck. Ian never told his wife what had happened when they were outside the boozer but, whatever was said, when Ian came back inside the pub he sat down next to his wife, and he never moved a muscle for the rest of the night. Tony had told her time and time again that, if Ian stepped out of line again, he was only ever a phone call away. But, up to now, she pretended that everything was still rosy in the garden whenever they saw him. But Maxine knew she needed the big guns on her side now.

Ian pulled his shoulders back and stood over her, making his mind up what his next move would be. He let out a menacing laugh. 'I've shat bigger than your Tony. He's lucky I've not put him on his arse before now. He's a dickhead, and me and the lads have all said he's too big for his boots. I've only not dropped him because he's your brother.'

Maxine reached over for her mobile phone. 'So, you'll be alright me ringing him, then, won't you?'

Ian quickly grabbed the phone out of her hand. He panicked. 'I'm not having that twat in my house. You're my wife and you live by my rules, remember that.'

Maxine backed off to the corner of the bed. Ian grabbed his coat from his wardrobe and stormed out of the bedroom. 'Bitch,' he shouted behind him. The front door slammed shut and shook the whole house.

Maxine jumped up to the bedroom window and pulled the curtains back. She started crying and threw an ornament from the window ledge across the bedroom, smashing it into a hundred fragments on the floor. It felt like her heart. 'I'll show you, Ian, mark my words. For every tear I've cried, you will cry a river.'

Maxine knew what she had to do. Before she called her brother, it was time to text the girls. She clicked into their WhatsApp group and tapped out a message.

`It's on. Arnie Mac's birthday. Lap-dancing. See if you know any of the fellas he's going with. I want pictures. Let's nail the bastard.`

She bent down, pulled a bag from under the bed and pulled out three bottles of perfume. At least she had some extra money now, cash to plan her freedom. She looked at the bottles she'd grabbed. Envy. Escape. Poison.

Chapter Seventeen

Lesley parked up outside her house. John had been ringing her endlessly and she'd agreed to have a chat with him. She turned the engine off and reached over to the passenger seat to grab her handbag. She looked haggard in the rear-view, her skin pale, hair shoved back in a ponytail. She'd not slept properly for days. Taking a few deep breaths, she got out of the car and crossed the road. Grey clouds hung low in the dark sky, like a blanket of misery over her head. John must have seen her pull up and was stood waiting at the front door for her as she walked down the garden path. She did a double-take – he looked as rough as she felt, dark circles under his eyes, hair stuck up, creased clothes.

'I'm so glad you came, Lesley. Come on, get in out of the cold and I'll put the kettle on. Do you want a hot drink or a cold one?'

Lesley felt strange – like a guest walking into her own home. The house was cold, no lights on. As she looked closer, she could see everything was out of place, her lovely home going to pot. John stood at the kitchen door, fidgeting, not sure of what to do next. 'Shall I make us a coffee?'

'Yes, I'll have a small one. Can you turn the heating on, too? It's brass monkeys in here.'

'Yes, course. I don't function without you, Lesley. On my life, I've tried to clean the place up, but I don't even know where to start.'

Lesley couldn't resist. 'You should have got Angela in to give you a hand. I'm sure she would have jumped at the chance to get back in here again.'

John went bright red and disappeared into the kitchen. He had no comeback and didn't want to make matters worse than what they were already. Lesley sat quiet and still. John came into the room carrying two white mugs. He passed one to Lesley. 'There you go, nice and milky, just how you like it.'

She raised a half-hearted smile, still not sure if she wanted to launch the hot drink at his face, make him feel pain like she did in her heart. John sat facing her and took a small sip from his drink. 'Do you want a biscuit or anything? Something to eat, a sandwich?'

Lesley shrugged. 'I'm here to talk, not for coffee and biscuits, John. I only agreed to come here so you would stop belling my phone out, so say what you have to and then I can get going.'

His face changed, a sadness in his eyes that told her this was not what he wanted to hear. 'I'm so sorry. I never thought it would turn out like this, otherwise I would have told Angela to piss off home. It was Kimberley pulling at my heart strings, on my life. She was sobbing and begging me to let her mother stay. What else could I have done? I genuinely thought she was having a crisis, not hatching a plan to stick her tongue down my throat.'

Lesley had heard enough. 'It was a big set-up, John. Take your head from out of your arse and smell the coffee beans, man. Kimberley wants you and that witch back together and she was probably the one who put this plan together. What is it, eh? Has Angela's new man seen right through her and, now she's back on her own, she needs a new victim? No man will ever stay with that destructive cow for long. She's tapped in the head.'

'I would never look at another woman like I look at you, Lesley. I've already told Kimberley what trouble all this has caused and told her straight that she can go back and live with her mam if she cares about her that much.'

'And what did she say to that?'

John stared over at her, mouth moving but no words coming out, thinking for a few seconds before he answered. 'She said she is staying here, but she won't invite her mam here again. I've told her, from now on, what you say goes.'

Lesley's eyes widened and she pulled her shoulders back. 'It should have been that way, anyway. Come on, you're not daft, are you. You've seen Kimberley and the way she acts around me. It's all false and I don't trust her as far as I can throw her. I'm sorry to say this, John, and I know she's your daughter, but the girl is messed up in her head. She relies on you for everything, and she needs to stand on her own two feet instead of bumming from us all the time.'

John knew what she was saying was true and he nodded slowly. 'These last few days without you have been hell. I can't think straight, and I've not even been in work. Without you in my life, I can't do it. I may as well not be here. My heart is broken, Lesley, smashed into a million pieces.'

Lesley sat forward in her seat. 'How do you think I feel? Angela has been a problem for us for years, and finally we get her out of our life, and I turn my back for two bloody minutes and she's in my house, playing Goldilocks.'

John could tell she was ready to up and leave. 'It won't ever happen again. I have no feelings for that woman whatsoever, you're the one that I love. Me and Angela were over years before you walked into my life, and I told you that, didn't I?' He was looking at her for an answer.

'You did, so why does she think the door is always open?'

John moved over and sat next to his wife. He took her cold hands in his. 'Lesley, look deep into my eyes and you will see how much I love you. I messed up, I know, but I'll do anything for my kids, regardless of their mother. And I believed Kim when she said her mum was in a bad place mentally. I hardly even spoke to her – she arrived off her head and barely said a word before she started groping me and trying it on.'

Lesley rubbed at her arms as a cold chill passed over her body. She knew she had to make a decision – she had to either leave for good, or let it go. And if she chose the former, she knew she'd be walking out of her life. And at least John had been open with her. Somewhere inside, she knew she was putting him through the wringer because of her own guilt. Perhaps she was looking for a reason to walk away rather than admit she'd had a child she'd given away. Maybe it was time to accept that everyone had sins and secrets.

'Go and put the heating on and flick the lamp on, will you? It's like a bloody morgue in here. If I'm staying, I don't want to freeze to death.'

John dropped his head on his wife's shoulder. He was mentally and physically drained. 'I can't tell you how good it feels to know you'll be back here tonight, love.' He stayed silent for a moment, but Lesley could tell he was feeling better. 'Do you fancy ordering a pizza or something?'

Lesley smiled. If he was thinking with his stomach, he was back to himself again. 'Yes, I'm the same as you. I've not eaten proper for days, either. Don't get me wrong, Tommy and Jane have been cooking for me, but I've not had any appetite.'

John leaned over and kissed her softly on the lips. 'I never want to be without you again. I swear to you, I'll never hurt you again. You're my number one from now on. What you say goes, and that goes for Kimberley too. I've had a lot of thinking time over these last few days, and it's hit home exactly what you have had to put up with. Kimberley has been disrespectful to you, and I see that now. Honest, my hand on my heart, I'll stand by your side in whatever you say with her in the future.'

Kimberley came into the front room as Lesley and her dad were eating their food. She slowly peeled her coat off. 'I'm starving, I hope you ordered me something, Dad?'

John lifted his eyes and spoke with a mouthful of food. 'No, I didn't know you were home tonight, so I ordered enough for me and Lesley. If you want something, get on the blower and order it, or go and cook something. The freezer is full of stuff to make.'

She looked furious. 'How can I do that when I don't have any money?' she hissed.

'Not my problem, because, from today, if you don't get a job then you won't be getting a penny from me. You're a bright girl, Kim, it's time you put that brain of yours to use.'

Kimberley scoffed at her dad's words and flicked the tv on. John finished eating and went upstairs to get a shower. Lesley could feel Kimberley's eyes burning into her.

'Do you have something to say?'

Kimberley checked they were still alone and kept her voice low. 'I can't believe you acted the way you did just because my mam stayed here for a few nights. Are you that insecure that you needed to kick up a fuss?'

Lesley felt calmer than she'd done in days. She stared at Kimberley for a few seconds before she spoke. 'I know your dad loves me more than anything and, if I was you, I would keep that big mouth shut before you're flung out of here like your mum. You brought your mother here knowing I was away on holiday, probably hoping Mummy and Daddy would get back together. But your plan failed so it's my rules now.'

Kimberley had nothing to come back with. She waited a few minutes, then got up and left the living room in a strop.

Upstairs, Kimberley rummaged in her jewellery box and found the hoop earrings her mother had given her. They were her mother's trademark – far more dramatic than the gold studs Lesley wore. Kimberley held them tightly in her hand and crept along the landing to her father's bedroom. Quickly, she nipped inside and pulled the duvet back, placing her mother's earring bang in the middle of the bed. Revenge was sweet.

It was nearly midnight, and Lesley and John had been sat on the sofa all night talking. He reached over and held her hand in his. 'Shall we go to bed? I don't know about you, but I could do with a good night's sleep.'

Lesley nodded, her eyes heavy.

'Come on, sleepy head, let's get you in bed.' John put his arm around her.

Lesley felt the madness of the last few days fade away as she snuggled into her own bed. All the chaos of Benidorm – Katie going missing, Jane risking everything for a fling – she could handle anything now she was back where she belonged. This could be a fresh start – maybe even re-ignite their spark. She reached out to John, only to feel a pain in her side. She flicked the bedside lamp on and dug her hand under the duvet. Slowly she pulled out a gold earring. She shoved it in John's face.

'Where the hell has this come from? And don't insult my intelligence by giving me some cock-and-bull story.'

John swallowed hard, eyes wide open. 'I've never seen it before in my life. Give it here, let me have a closer look. Are you sure it's not Kimberley's?'

Lesley went nose to nose. 'Why would Kimberley's earring be in our bed? Come on, let's hear what bullshit you're going to tell me to get away with this one.'

John sat up in the bed. 'I'm not feeding you any bullshit. I've never seen this earring in my life.'

Lesley jumped up from the bed. 'Own your shit, John. Man up and tell me the truth. You owe me that much. Go on, tell me the bleeding truth because, if I don't hear it, I'm gone from here and I won't be coming back, ever.'

John jumped out of the bed frantically. In his grey boxer shorts, he paced one way then the other. 'Lesley, I'm not telling lies. I don't know how to prove to you that I'm telling the truth. And, sleeping with Angela? Come on, love, give me some bleeding credit. Been there, done that, worn the t-shirt and would never do that again. Like I said, I told her to sleep in James's room, but I stayed on the sofa so God knows what she did up here.'

Lesley stared at him and couldn't make her mind up what to believe anymore. 'In that case, I'm taking a leaf out of your book. I'm going to the sleep on the sofa tonight, and don't,' she stressed, 'don't be following me because, I swear to God, I will ring a taxi and go and stay in a hotel.' Her words were firm, and she meant every word she said. She grabbed the grey fluffy blanket from the bottom of the bed and stomped down the stairs.

Kimberley held her ear to the wall. Once she heard Lesley going down the stairs, she walked along the landing to her father's bedroom. 'Dad, are you alright? I heard you arguing.' She edged into the bedroom and patted her father's shoulder. 'Dad, come on. I don't like seeing you upset. What's gone on? I thought you two were sorted.'

John held the gold earring out. 'Is this yours?' She took the earring from her dad's hand, twisting it one way then the other, giving a performance any leading actress would have been proud of. 'Never seen it before in my life, Dad. Are you sure it's not my mam's?'

John panicked. 'For crying out loud, don't be saying that. How on earth would it have got here, because she never came into my room, did she?'

He stared at his daughter until she replied. 'No, not that I know about, unless you two had a few cuddles for old times' sake. Because it happens, Dad, doesn't it? You'd both had a drink, I know that much.'

John went white. 'I hope this is not you playing silly buggers because, if it is, I will not see the funny side of it.'

'Don't even go there trying to blame me. At the end of the day, Lesley is a mard arse, always moaning. My mam needed a bed for a few days to sort her head out and she's kicked off over that. The woman is insecure, and you know it.'

John was deflated and sat staring at the bedroom window. 'Go back to bed, Kimberley. I need some time on my own to clear my head and try and sort this mess out.'

Chapter Eighteen

Jane lay awake wondering how one night could feel so long and lonely, and how Tommy could sleep so soundly inches from her. As she stared at the bedside clock, it was the clock in her head counting down to the wedding that terrified her more. It wasn't long to the big day and yet she felt frozen. She needed to make some big decisions – the biggest – but whatever she did, whoever she chose, someone was going to get hurt. All the anxiety was making her ill. There was a cold slick of sweat forming on her skin. She jumped up and ran to the toilet. With her head hanging over the bowl, she was sick until she felt hollowed out. She'd told Tommy she didn't want any curry last night, but he forced her to have some of his homemade chicken madras. Tommy had always been a feeder, told her that when he cooked for her it was because he loved her. He probably hadn't cooked the chicken properly. She sat huddled on the tiled floor and swept her hair back from her face. Footsteps outside the bathroom.

The door opened and Tommy rubbed his knuckles into the corners of his eyes.

'Bloody hell, have you been spewing? I heard you from the bedroom. I've had belly ache all night, too. I think that curry was dodgy, if I'm being honest.'

Jane lifted her head slowly, white as a ghost. 'It just come over me all of a sudden. I told you I didn't want any. I feel like death now.' She was teary-eyed, and her emotions took over as she stood up. 'I'm supposed to be going with the girls to try my wedding dress on. It's the first fitting.' She stood up and walked to the double mirror, pulling her eyelids down. 'I look like I've been dragged through a hedge backwards. I'm trying to lose a bit of weight for the wedding – but not like this. I want to look nice in my dress, but I'll look like a zombie bride if I still feel like this.'

Tommy offered her a hand. 'You go and lie down for a bit, and I'll make you a bacon buttie.'

Jane felt nauseous at even the thought of a sandwich. 'I'm not eating a single thing, so don't be trying to feed me again. The girls will be here in a few hours, so let me have a lie-down for a bit and I'll probably feel better.'

Tommy started to walk down the stairs but stopped and turned back. 'I don't suppose there's any chance of me joining you in bed, then? I've got an hour before I have to go out, if you're up to it?'

Jane gave him a death stare.

'That was a no then,' Tommy chuckled after her.

Back in bed and shivering, Jane reached for her mobile phone and quickly scanned the messages. There were two from Lesley and four from her Frankie. She'd put his number in as 'Wedding Planner'. She'd felt like dirt doing it, but it was the only way she thought Tommy wouldn't get suspicious about all the messages if he saw her screen. She read them as fast as she could, glancing at the bedroom door. She opened Lesley's message and sighed.

Tommy was back in the bedroom now, looking for his watch. 'What's up with your mush?' Jane shook her head slowly. 'Lesley has found an earring in her bed. She's only been back with John for two minutes and it's kicking off again.'

'Dodgy, that is. I bet he's been banging the ex-Mrs while you lot was on holiday. You know I think cheaters are the scum of the earth – I thought John was better than that.' Tommy sneered.

Jane wriggled about in the bed awkwardly. 'Me too. John and Angela have been over for years. He can't stand the sight of her anymore, or that's what he's told us all.'

'You don't look at the mantelpiece when you're poking the fire, Jane,' he chuckled.

'If it's true, what is Lesley going to do now? Because there is no coming back from this, is there?'

Tommy sat on the edge of the bed. 'No, once you've slept with someone else, there's no going back. Who wants damaged goods?'

Jane pulled the duvet around herself even tighter. 'Mistakes happen, Tom. Let's just say he was weak and he ended up with Angela in the feather. If it was a one-off and he swears it'll never happen again, maybe all their good years together outweigh one screw-up?'

Tommy looked unconvinced. 'Jane, if you so much as thought I had my eye on someone else, you would bin-bag me and kick me out on the street, so what's with this it-could-have-been-a-mistake malarkey.'

Jane realised he was right and replied straight away. 'Dead right, you would be gone. But this is Lesley and John, not us. I don't know what's happening to us all lately. Maxine and Ian are on the rocks. She had someone spying on him at a strip club the other night, and Maxine has had the patience of a saint with him, so if she's had enough, he must really be treating her like dirt. I mean, Katie has always been single and I'm starting to think she made the right choice.'

Tommy leaned towards Jane. 'You won't say that once you've got that wedding ring on your finger. I can't wait to tell everyone in the church how I feel about you.'

Jane raised a half-hearted smile. 'Me too,' she whispered under her breath.

'Tell Lesley she can come back here again, if she wants. I know you like having the girls around you, anyway. Maybe have a girlie night tonight and I'll piss off down the pub, if you want. The footie is on and, well,' he chuckled again, 'You know me, I'll have a few cold ones with the lads.'

Jane agreed almost straight away. This meant she could speak to Francis all night long and text him without worrying about Tommy looking over her shoulder. 'That's a great idea, Tom, and like you said, Lesley will need some support now this has gone on. I'll send them a WhatsApp to make sure they can all come back here after the fitting. If I've stopped spewing by then.'

Jane didn't know what was worse – the food poisoning or the guilt. Either way, she just wanted to be left alone. She had lost all energy recently – she should have been checking on the salon, preparing for the wedding, but she hadn't even unpacked her holiday case. Tommy was still searching about the bedroom for the things he needed to get ready. Before he finally left, he shot a look over at his beloved and whispered, 'Love you, babes, I don't deserve you.' And then Tommy was gone.

Chapter Nineteen

Katie was the first at Jane's house and, as soon as she got there, she cracked open a bottle from the fridge full of Prosecco that Jane had got prepped for all their wedding planning sessions. It should have meant long lunches and gossipy nights, mates reminiscing, planning and partying – yet suddenly the fizz was there to drown out all their sorrows rather than to celebrate.

Jane still looked haunted. She'd had to cancel her wedding dress fitting until she felt better and had only dragged herself up an hour ago. She'd paid Letty extra to do overtime and stay on until the girls arrived, so at least the house looked good, even if Jane felt like she was falling apart. She held her flat palm out in front of her as Katie tried to fill her glass up with wine. 'No, not for me, Katie. I've had a dickie stomach all day and I'm not chancing anything. On my life, I've been burning up, hurling all day. Tommy thinks it's the curry we ate last night, and I bet he's right.'

Katie filled her own glass and kicked her shoes off. 'Well, I'll have a drink for you. The day I've had, I need it. I went for the interview at the bookies, and they said they would let me know by the end of the week. They asked for references, though, and I had to put that moody cow's name down from Asda, so I'm not holding my breath. One thing for sure, though, is that I need a job and fast. Our Jade's not spoken to me for days because I've lost my job, but she'll come around if she sees I'm looking. She's a hot-head sometimes. I'm so skint the ducks will be throwing bread at me soon.'

Jane smiled at Katie, feeling her pain, knowing the bite of poverty was no joke, despite her friend's effort to see the funny side. 'Something will turn up for you, Katie. I would say I'd give Letty the boot and you could be my cleaner, but I don't want you grafting for me. I'm a funny cow and we would end up falling out over daft stuff regarding the cleaning, so I'm not risking our friendship.'

Katie agreed. 'Yes, I get what you mean. You *are* a fussy cow and like everything tip-top. I'm clean myself, but you're on another level, and you probably wouldn't want me cleaning your karzy.'

Jane nodded and watched as Letty walked past the doorway to open the front door. 'Here's the girls now.'

Maxine and Lesley came walking into the front room as Katie was quizzing Jane about her symptoms. 'So, you were sick this morning and you went all hot?'

Jane nodded. Katie gulped a mouthful of wine and started laughing. 'I bet you're preggers. As soon as I was sick in the mornings, I knew I was tubbed. You better check.' Katie saw Jane's thunderstruck expression and backtracked. 'But Tommy's firing blanks isn't he, so ignore me, I'm just kidding around. Like you said, it must have been that curry you ate. There is nothing worse than the ring of fire after eating a curry.'

Lesley looked confused. 'Who thinks they're pregnant? I only caught the last bit of the conversation.'

Katie filled her in as she swigged more Prosecco. 'False alarm. Jane was telling me how she's been sick this morning and she keeps getting these hot flushes. I told her that was one of the first signs when I was in the pudding club, but then I remembered Tom doesn't have strong swimmers, or so we think.'

Jane was grey now, looking worse every minute. 'Girls don't be saying that. I know we think Tommy is firing blanks, but are you forgetting that I've slept with Francis, too?'

Maxine covered her mouth with both hands. Lesley looked at them all and tried to calm this situation over. 'Let's not jump to any conclusions. So, when was your last period? I bet you're just a bit stressed with the wedding getting nearer, that's all.'

Jane got her mobile phone out and started to look at the calendar. She stared at the screen and looked up at her friends. 'I'm two weeks overdue.'

'Christ, Jane. You've done it now,' Katie blurted out. 'You play with fire, and you get burnt.' Lesley glared at her to keep her big trap shut.

Maxine grabbed her handbag. 'I'll nip to the shops and grab a pregnancy test. There is no point in sitting here all night worrying about it, is there? I need some lemonade, anyway.'

Jane pulled her cardigan tighter around her body, panic filling every inch of her. 'Katie, why the hell did you even mention being pregnant? Now you've got me all paranoid. Lesley is probably right, it's all the stress that's caused me to be late.'

'The stress of the wedding or the stress of sneaking around behind Tommy's back?' Katie asked, her tongue loosened by the booze.

'I won't be long,' Maxine shouted behind her as she left the room.

Jane sat down next to Lesley. 'Enough of my dramas – have you and John sorted things yet?'

Katie chimed in again. 'It will be something to do with that daughter of his. She's a canny bitch, that one is. I bet, if you searched her bedroom, you would find the matching earring. You're giving her everything she wants by leaving the house again. I'll tell you something for nothing, shall I? I would piss on her parade: go back home and act like nothing has happened.'

Jane tilted her head to the side. 'For once, Katie, you might be speaking sense!'

Katie continued, 'I can spot a womaniser a mile off and John has no game whatsoever. He is a one-man woman and he's not the sort who plays away from home. Trust me on this, because I know.' Katie checked the door was closed and kept her voice low. 'Lesley, how many times did I tell you that Ian was a player? Even before Maxine married him, even before… you know, I could tell he would always be one of those guys who played away from home, and am I right about that?'

Lesley stared over at Katie, reminding her that she was one of the women Ian had slept with, and she went bright red. But she continued. 'All I'm saying is John does not strike me as a cheater. I could lie in a bed with him naked and he would not lay a finger on me.'

Jane had to agree. 'I think Katie is right, you know, Lesley. It's got to be Kimberley playing head games. I think you should play her at her own game and see what she does then. Tell John you want to make it work and you're coming back home. That's the way to really show Kimberley she can't mess with you.'

'Amen,' Katie preached. 'I wish I could have met a man like John instead of the wankers who I keep meeting. I've given up on men, anyway. Just for the record, I'm staying single now and concentrating on finding a job and sorting my finances out.'

Jane raised her eyebrows high and smiled at Lesley. If they had a pound for every time Katie had said she was staying single, they would have been rich women.

Maxine arrived back and stood reading the box she was brandishing. 'It says wee on it and leave for two minutes. One blue line is negative and two red lines is positive. Two minutes to find out your future – it's better than Mystic Meg.' Maxine held a white stick up at Jane. She could see she was hesitating and gave her some support. 'Once you've done it, you can put your mind at rest then, and get on with enjoying the night. Otherwise, you can sit there and be a nervous wreck all night not knowing if you are or not.'

Jane took the test from her and left the room. Katie was tipsy now and louder than ever. 'Men only have to hang a pair of pants on my bed and I'm pregnant. That's why I had Jade so young and why I've always had the coil fitted since, no mither.'

Lesley and Maxine filled their glasses. Katie quickly necked the last bit of wine from her glass and shouted, 'Fill me up, girls. I will drink free wine all night long, I will.' Lesley passed the bottle over to Katie. Maxine was rummaging in her handbag and pulled out three bottles of perfumes. 'Hopefully, Jane will have these,' she said as she placed them on the table in front of her.

Katie was always too broke to buy any, and Maxine knew Lesley hated her nicking stuff from work. Maxine had tried to explain that, although it was Ian who had talked her into it, she'd got used to it – and now it was the only way she was building up her escape fund for leaving Ian.

Katie picked up one of the perfumes and examined it. 'One hundred and ten pounds for that little bottle; are they having a joke or what? I could get a big shop with the money you would pay for that perfume, I could. A big shop and a trip to Iceland for my frozen stuff. How the other half live, eh.'

Maxine chuckled and threw a small sample bottle over to Katie. 'Here, get some of that sprayed on you. That one is free.' Katie caught the small bottle, pulled the lid from it and sprayed it all over. She inhaled deeply and closed her eyes. 'I can smell lemons, spice fragrances and maybe a bit of Oud. Oh, and top-notes of Prosecco and pizza!' Lesley and Maxine burst out laughing at Katie, always the joker.

Jane came back and closed the living room door behind her. The girls fell silent. Jane stood with her back against the door and slowly her legs buckled from underneath her. She slid down the door like butter dripping from hot toast. Lesley was first up, followed closely by the other two. 'Jane, what was the result?' As if she needed to ask.

Jane lifted her head, eyes red raw from crying. She snivelled as she handed the test over to her friends. 'Have a look.'

Katie examined every inch of the test. 'For crying out loud. A bun in the oven. It's not what you need just before you're getting married, is it?'

'No, it's bloody not, Katie, but I don't need you telling me that. Fuck me – all I ever wanted was to get married and have babies, and now I'm getting both and yet I feel like I've ruined my life.' Jane was sobbing now and the girls were all on the floor, supporting her. 'I can't have it, can I? I've always wanted a baby. Could I tell Tommy this is some kind of miracle? This could be my only chance at having a baby.'

Lesley found her vape from her bag and sat down chugging hard on it.

Jane was a mess, strands of hair stuck to her wet cheeks like rats' tails. 'I've messed everything up, haven't I? I should have been happy with what I had and told Francis thanks but no thanks. I've always wanted more than what

I already have. The grass has always been greener. What an idiot I've been. Go on, girls, tell me I'm wrong.'

Katie was about to say something when Maxine jabbed her in the leg.

Katie snarled back and rubbed at her thigh, refusing to be silenced. 'Well, at least this way, you're going to have to make some decisions. You can bullshit through most things in life but not birth and death. Imagine what everyone will say when they find out.'

Jane made a strangled noise and the girls thought she might faint.

Lesley tried to calm her. 'You are going too much into this, Jane. As I see it, you have a few options here. One: you choose not to have the baby; two, tell Tommy it's his, because, let's face it, it could well be, sack off Frankie and get wed; or three, tell Francis you think he's the father and see what he's saying. But this stays in this room, okay, ladies? We tell nobody – not our kids, not our fellas, nobody, until Jane has made her mind up. It might take you days or weeks before you know what you want to do, but think it through or you could regret it forever.' Lesley's eyes clouded over, her emotions getting the better of her. 'I was going to say another option could be adoption – but you know I'm telling you from the heart when I say giving up a baby isn't easy. It's the greatest gift you can give someone – but it's the hardest thing to do. And that's without thinking what Tommy or Frankie might say. My advice is to do what feels right for you. At least you can rely on one thing – whatever you do, you've got us.'

Katie was bubbling to say something, and Jane gave her the nod, readying herself for a pearl of wisdom.

'I know this might not be the time or the place, but if you decide you are going through with the pregnancy, can I have your old clothes, J, because they won't fit you in a few months' time, will they?'

Jane knew Katie was only trying to make her laugh and she tried to see the funny side of things, but she was finding it hard. She sat back on the sofa and checked her phone.

'It's Frankie. He wants to take me out again tomorrow night. What do I do?' Jane looked like she had the weight of the world on her. There was a particular kind of agony that came with knowing she'd got herself into this mess. She looked around the room at these girls who'd been with her through thick and thin. She considered how they'd survived all kinds of things – heartbreak and gaslighting, abuse and adultery. They had kept her secrets safe. Surely together they'd get through this, whatever she chose to do. The problem was, how did you make a choice like this?

Chapter Twenty

Lesley didn't envy her friend – but Jane's suffering had at least made her realise how lucky she was. She had a chance to make things right with John, a chance to not get played by Kimberley. Life was about learning when to stay and fight your ground and when to walk away. And Lesley knew that she might not be the loudest, she might not be the flashiest or the mouthiest… but she knew she had fight in her, and after staying the night at Jane's, she went home with her head held high. John had just gone to work, and Kimberley had stayed over at her friend's house. Lesley was going to work herself too, but she was in no rush; being married to the boss had to come with some perks. Instead, she savoured the chance to be home alone. Lesley took her time doing a few chores. She pushed the bedroom door open and looked at Kimberley's dirty washing scattered about the floor; she rolled her eyes. 'Scruffy cow, how hard is it to pick some washing up and put it in the bloody washing basket?' she moaned under her breath. Lesley walked about the bedroom scooping clothes up from the floor. She went over to the window and straightened the blinds. She looked out of the window and could see the postman on the street, walking in and out of people's gardens. The wind sent leaves circling in the air, throwing them up like a circus juggler. She held the clothes in her arms and made her way downstairs into the kitchen. Once she got there, she flung them on the floor near the washer. As she threw them down, a glint of light caught her attention. She bent down and picked up the gold earring, examining it. The twin of the one she'd found in her bed. Bingo! It was Kimberley all along. With haste she grabbed a sheaf of black bags from under the sink and sprinted up the stairs. She walked straight into Kimberley's bedroom. She was done with treating Kimberley like a child. She was legally an adult, even if she refused to act like one. There was no way Kimberley was getting the better of her. This was her house, her rules. She started pulling clothes from the wardrobe and tossing them in the bin-liners. 'We'll see who's laughing now, shall we?' She looked around the bedroom: she'd packed every item that Kimberley owned. She dragged them down the stairs and placed them in the hallway. Once everything was downstairs, she sat in the living room and sent a text message.

The letterbox rapped several times. Lesley marched to the front door and yanked it open. Angela was stood there, hands on her hips. 'So, what is that important you demand I come and see you? You've dragged me out of work – this better be good.' She started to barge her way in, but Lesley didn't want her trampling over the mail, so blocked her way to pick up the post from the doormat and place the letters on the side table. One of them caught her eye – gilt-edged. It must be Jane and Tommy's wedding invitation. There was no way she was opening that in front of Angela.

'I've texted you to come and pick up Kimberley's stuff, because as from today she's no longer welcome in this house. She's poisonous, just like you. What, did you think just because I was on holiday that you could have another crack at John and try and get back in his bed? He told you then and I'm telling you now that he does not love you anymore. If I'm honest, he can't stand you. You broke his heart when you started sleeping around, and it's me that's healed that wound. Get over it.'

Angela threw her head back and let out a sarcastic laugh. 'Listen, you stuck up bitch, John will always want me. I'm the mother of his kids. It's something you wouldn't understand – you can't break that bond. You're forgetting when you were away with your slaggy mates I was here in your home. Do you think me and John didn't sit reminiscing about old times, about the way we were? If I wanted to, I could have bedded him. I'd only have to click my fingers and he'd come running. I can see it in his eyes when he speaks to me that he still feels the attraction between us from our first time. I don't need to tell you if I slept with him or not. I owe you nothing, John is your husband now. But I will always be his first love.'

Lesley kept her cool. 'Your daughter put an earring in my bed. Did she think I would think it was yours and walk out on my husband? Don't get me wrong, I know you'd love to be back in his bed now your latest fella has ditched you, but then I remembered what a nasty skank you really are and how John would not give you the time of the day. He's a good guy – when Kim told him you were vulnerable, he let you in out of love for her, not you. All these years, I've said I'll never come between John and the kids. But they're not kids anymore. James, he's practically moved in with his girlfriend. And he's a nice lad – there's a lot of his dad in him. But your daughter, well, she's cut from your cloth, isn't she? Anyway, Kimberley can come and live with you now and you can be the mother to her that you should have been all those years ago. I mean, come on; what kind of woman walks out on her husband and young kids so she can go swanning around the country with some man she's just met? And, for the record, I will make sure Kimberley knows the truth about you if she turns up here tonight, because, let's face it, she deserves to know.'

Lesley dragged the bin-liners to the front door, dropping them in front of Angela.

'Daft cow. Her dad won't allow anyone to fling his own flesh and blood out on the streets, you bloody idiot. He's your boss at work, and he's still the boss here so you should know where you stand. Plus, I have no room at my house. I'm renting a one-bedroom flat.'

'So, she will have to get her own place then, won't she, because she's out on her arse from here. I've got nothing more to say to you.'

Lesley was about to slam the door in her face when Angela stuck her foot inside the door and shoulder-barged it back open. Angela gripped her hair, wrenching clumps from her scalp. Something in Lesley roared into life and she broke Angela's grip. Angela stumbled, clearly not expecting her victim to have fought back with such force. She staggered back into the wall and fell to the floor, hitting her head on the way down.

Lesley hauled her up. 'I feel sorry for you. You've got nothing good in your life apart from the memories of the things you broke. You and Kimberley deserve each other. If you ever darken my doorway again, I'll go town on you. I'll call the dibble, I'll take you to court, get a restraining order, make sure Kimberley knows the kind of woman her mother really is. Do you hear me?' Angela had thick red blood dripping from her nose and already her eye was starting to swell. Lesley turned and walked back into the house.

Angela never took her eyes from Lesley as she dragged her daughter's clothes from the garden. By the time she was at the gate, her courage was returning and she shouted back at Lesley. 'Watch now, just you watch. You can act all high and mighty, but I tell you this for nothing – everyone's got something to hide, something to be ashamed of – even you.'

Lesley slammed the front door shut and stood with her back pressed firmly against it. She was finding it hard to catch her breath.

Not long after, John pulled up outside the house. It was in darkness, yet Lesley's car was parked on the drive. John pushed his key into the front door and turned it. 'Lesley?' he shouted. He closed the front door behind him, walked into the living room and flicked the main light on. 'Lesley, what are you doing sat in the dark? I was so pleased to see you were home, but you had me worried for a few seconds then when I pulled up. You never turned up at work either, and now you're here sitting in the pitch black.'

Lesley squeezed her eyes against the bright light. John knew she'd been crying and rushed to her side. 'Baby, what's up?'

Lesley reached for her vape and sucked on it hard. 'It's been a nightmare of a day, John. I was going to come into work, but it all happened so fast.' She told him the story of the morning – showing him the bald patch where Angela had torn hair from her scalp.

John dragged his coat off and threw it over the back of the chair. 'And, Kimberley, where is she?'

'She texted me to say she was staying with her mum tonight – the two of them deserve each other, in my book. I'm sorry, love. She's your daughter and I never want to come between you two, but she's a grown woman and, if she put even half the energy she puts into trying to split us up into finding a job, I'd be happy.'

'I know, love. I'll always want what's best for her, and I'll always be on the end of the phone, but for now she needs to step up and start being an adult. And that means accepting you and me. Right, I'm going to get changed, then let's try to have a normal evening – no more dramas, eh?' John passed her the post he'd picked up on the way in. 'Probably more bills to pay.' He headed upstairs.

Lesley opened the first piece of junk mail and scanned it. Nothing of real importance. She clocked the gold envelope again; her name and address had been written by hand. She sat up, slid her long fingernail under the flap and pulled out the card, thinking it was odd Jane hadn't mentioned she'd sent out invitations. She'd assumed Jane was still thinking about cancelling the wedding and swanning off with Frankie. Maybe this was a good thing – something to make the wedding seem more real. As she slid the card out, small silver heart confetti fell out of it onto her chest. But as she read the words inside the card Lesley's face changed.

Her name was written at the top of the card in black ink and below it, it read:

'Secrets, secrets. You can run with a lie. But you can't hide from the truth. It will always catch you.'

Lesley read over the words again and again. She shoved the card back into the envelope and rammed it into her handbag. Who would send something like this? Was it just guesswork? After all, everyone had secrets, didn't they? But who knew her darkest moments and ugliest truths – and what did they want by sending this?

Chapter Twenty-One

Ever since the night Ian had attacked Maxine, she'd felt something change inside her. That night had finally broken her marriage beyond repair, but it hadn't broken her. She'd spent the days and weeks in between planning, saving and constantly sending WhatsApp messages to the girls. She still hadn't told them he'd half-strangled her – they'd have been on to the cop shop immediately. No, she needed to have him branded as a cheat before she took him down as a coward and a bully too.

Tonight was the night that Maxine and her friends were going to make that first piece happen. They'd been trying to catch him, and had come close before – they had pictures of him at lap-dancing clubs, leering at barmaids, chatting up strangers – but nothing that proved he was more than a lech. Tonight was different – they'd double-checked via all their sources. Ian's so-called 'lad's night out' had to be a cover. All the mates he usually went out with were busy or doing something else. It was the red flag they'd been waiting for. It had been a long time coming and something Maxine was finally ready to see with her own two eyes. Jane and Lesley were in Lesley's car outside, facing Maxine's house, and Katie was parked up at the top of the street waiting to pick Maxine up. The girls were going to be with her all the way – it wasn't just about catching Ian, it was about helping Maxine face the sordid truth about the man she'd spent all her adult life with. They were ready – now they just needed Ian to leave the house.

Ian walked over to the dressing table, not a stitch on, straight from the shower, and sprayed his Mancera Cedrat Boise all over his body. He even sprayed some on his crotch. Maxine cringed as she watched him. She'd got him that aftershave a few months ago. It was a lovely fragrance, fresh and clean, smelt like a summer's day, and here he was freshening up for some other tart with the gift she'd bought him. She should have jumped up and smashed the bloody bottle right over his head. She was looking at him differently tonight, he was knocking her sick. Maybe because she knew in her heart of hearts that this would probably be the last time Ian would be in her bedroom with her. She examined every inch of his body, remembering how that same body had lain next to hers and how she'd kissed every inch of him, his lips, his chest. She watched him put on his crisp white Calvin Klein boxer shorts. He was whistling a tune, happy as Larry, full of confidence. The same confidence he'd drained from his wife over the years. He never let her speak for herself, he always kept her in the shadows, did all the talking. When they were younger, she hadn't minded, hadn't known any better, but as she got older, she realised how much Ian was controlling her by doing this. He'd ridicule her if she did try to speak up, call her thick or ugly so many times that she'd started to believe him.

Ian was ready. He spun around in the mirror and even did a few dance moves before he turned to face her. He loved rubbing salt in the wound. 'Well, that's me ready for a night on the town – I'll leave you to your brain-rot telly. And make sure you tidy the place up as well. I'm not having a messy gaff. If anyone comes round, they'll think you're a slob.'

Maxine was used to him and never reacted. As far as he knew, she would be asleep by ten and he wouldn't see her until the next day – if he decided to even come home. Maxine's phone was on silent mode, and she could feel it vibrating at the side of her leg. She didn't look at it once until he left the room. Her fingers trembled as she typed the message to Lesley.

`Get ready, he's coming out soon.`

Ian shouted up to her from downstairs. 'I'm gone, taxi's here. See you later.'

Maxine didn't reply. She'd told herself she was ready – imagined what she would say and what she would do when the moment finally came and she confronted Ian. Maybe she would be calm and simply shake her head, perhaps she would make a scene, she wasn't sure, and she was playing this by ear. She looked over at their wedding picture on the wall, slightly faded now. Maxine wondered when it had gone so wrong – how two people could love each other so much and pledge to love each other until their dying breath and then end up moving farther and farther apart until either they gave up on their relationship, hating the sight of each other, or the relationship blew up and went down in flames. Was there a moment when they could have saved it, or was Ian a bad apple all along? Maybe, before the first time he belittled her, or threatened her or belted her, they could have had marriage guidance or found a way back to each other. Marriage was hard work, Maxine had known that, and you only got out what you put in. But she'd thought it was about the little things, that you had to spice things up – sexy underwear, date nights, surprise each other, talk and laugh together, kiss each other. Maxine knew all these things and in her own way, as soon as she'd sensed Ian getting distant, years ago now, she'd tried everything in the book to make her husband want her again, find her attractive, want to have sex with her, but nothing worked. She should have known then he'd probably had a roving eye from the beginning. It had gone on so long that it had started to feel normal – and Maxine had thought for a while that she could bear it, knowing Ian was out there putting it around, as long as she didn't have proof, have to see it or hear about it. That way, she'd been able to keep her head in the sand and carry on. She'd even saved up last year and taken them both to Paris for a weekend getaway, thinking that was what couples did. He'd spent most of the time on his phone, the rest of it slagging off the food. But the weekend had had its uses – it had shown her once and for all that this marriage wasn't hers to save. If Ian wasn't trying, there was no point in her running around after him. She'd pulled back since then, and although Ian hadn't said anything, he must have noticed as that was when he started getting physical. She shuddered now to think she'd put up with it for so long, but he'd been in her head, made her feel worthless, glad to accept the scraps of his time he gave her. Well, no more, the end was nigh.

She slipped her dressing gown off. Underneath she was already dressed in faded jeans and a white t-shirt. Quickly she shoved her shoes on, and she ran down the stairs and out of the front door. Katie came skidding towards her and she dived in the passenger side. Katie didn't wait for Maxine to put her seat belt on, she pulled straight back onto the road. 'Get Lesley on the blower and see where we need to go. We need to keep them on the phone so they can give us directions. Hurry up, I don't have a clue where we're heading.'

Maxine dialled the number and put the call on loudspeaker. 'Where are you?'

It was Jane who answered. 'Get on Rochdale Road. We're stuck at the lights, and you should catch up with us if you hurry. We can still see the taxi so it's all good.' Katie was a fearless driver and swerved in and out of the traffic. She had her head in the game, and she was nearly on the road where Jane said they were. Maxine was sat forward in her seat, chewing on her fingernails. 'He must be heading into the city centre. I bet he's going to the Northern Quarter. He's mentioned The Millstone pub to me before, said it's buzzing in there. So, I bet your life he goes there.'

Katie's eyes were on the road, and she yelled when she clocked them. 'Eyes to the left, I can see the girls.'

Jane stayed on the call as they tailed the cab. 'You were right. The taxi is pulling over at The Millstone.' Park up where you can and we'll meet you at the end of the street. We'll make sure he doesn't come straight back out if it's heaving in there.' Jane ended the call as Katie looked for somewhere to park.

Once they'd pulled up, Katie reached over to the back seat and pulled out a furry hat and a couple of colourful wigs, bright pink, blue, neon green. 'Left over from the hen do. Knew they'd come in handy. We'll look like any other bunch of party girls. Ian'll never clock us in this get-up. Here, get that on and straighten that mush, will you? You've wanted this for months so don't start backing down now.'

'I know I have but just give me a few seconds, bleeding hell. We don't have to go rushing in straight away. Let the prick get a drink and get settled.'

Katie straightened her wig in the rear-view mirror and sat back until her friend was ready. After a few deep breaths, Katie and Maxine made their way to the bar across the road from The Millstone. Lesley and Jane were loitering outside also in full fancy dress – vaping, but mainly as an excuse to keep an eye on The Millstone.

Katie grinned and Maxine winced as they went into the bar. It was rocking in there, music blasting and they saw it was advertised as an '80s night' on the colourful posters stuck on the windows. No one batted an eyelid at the friends in their get-up as 'Girls Just Wanna Have Fun' belted over the speakers. 'Get that table near the window there and I'll get the drinks in,' Katie shouted.

Maxine trudged to the corner of the room while Katie peeled off to the bar. Jane came in and joined Katie, keeping her voice down. 'Bleeding hell, Maxine looks like death warmed up, even in this get-up. I hope she's going to be alright after she finds what we've come for. I've no doubt we're going to go in there and see him with another woman.'

Jane ordered the drinks and got them a double vodka each. Dutch courage was needed tonight. Then she looked at hers and froze. She tipped her drink into Maxine's and ordered a lemonade instead. It wasn't just Maxine who was facing some huge life choices. Jane rubbed her belly, glad that Katie was distracted, keeping her eyes on the window.

They joined Maxine at the table who grabbed her vodka gratefully. Even when she took a sip, her eyes were on The Millstone across the narrow road. Satisfied they were near enough to spot Ian if he decided to leave, Katie waved Lesley in. She looked distracted too.

Lesley made sure they were all listening and placed her tan-coloured leather bag on the table and pulled out the gold envelope.

'Have a look at this that came through the post today. I've been waiting until we were all together so I could show it you. I think this has Kimberley's stamp all over it, but it spooked me out.' She passed the card over to Jane first.

Jane frowned as she read it. She passed it over to Maxine and then Katie.

'Bleeding hell, what's all that about?' Katie asked as she shot her eyes back to the window.

Lesley rubbed at her arms and spoke slowly. 'It can only be Kimberley playing daft buggers, can't it?'

Katie nodded. 'Leave them to it. They must lead very boring lives if this is all they can think about all bloody day.'

Lesley looked relieved, convinced she had been worrying for nothing.

As she downed the last of her drink, Katie stood up from the table. 'Right, you lot, wait here. I'll have a quick butcher's over the road and see what lover boy is up to. Is my wig on straight?'

Maxine tried to raise a smile as she sat looking at her friends all dressed up, all for her sake, and her eyes filled up. 'Girls, thanks for this.'

Jane could see she was getting ready to blub. 'You'd do the same for us. No judgment, no bitching, no backstabbing – that's why we're still mates after all these years. I'm going through my own shit, as you know, Maxine, but as long as I know I have you lot by my side I know I can get through anything. Come on, we're not little girls any more, we're women with battle scars; we fall down, we get back up again. We make mistakes, sure, but we keep going. And that's the way it'll always be.'

Katie was gone and Maxine was necking the vodka like it was nobody's business. With each swig she took, she was getting angrier. 'I can't wait to see his cocky face. He'll shit a brick when I confront him. He probably thinks I'm tucked up in bed, the loser. But I'll tell you something for nothing: after tonight I'm going to be living my best life. Your hen party has opened my eyes to another world out there for me.'

Jane dropped her head, her emotions all over the place. 'Well don't take a leaf out my book. The hen do has taught me a lesson I'll never forget, that's for sure. I've still got to tell Francis I'm pregnant. I'm sure he knows something is up because he keeps asking me if I am alright. I've got to admit I've not been sending him the same kind of sexy messages I was. I don't feel like sending him a pic of my knockers when every time I look down I ask myself if I'll be needing a maternity bra next rather than my usual lacy stuff.'

Maxine nodded. 'I know I've got my troubles, Jane, but I would be on the floor now if I was dealing with what you are. I'm not going to lie to you, I thought you were mad for cheating on Tommy – and I know what it's like to be the one cheated on – but I've got to admit this whole shit-storm with Ian is easier to face without kids in the mix. I always wanted a baby but now I think at least I'm not tied to Ian by anything more than a piece of paper and my own stupidity for putting up with his BS for so long.'

Jane ran a single finger around the edge of her glass. 'God, Max. I know. In Benidorm it seemed like an unstoppable force was pulling me to Frankie, just as I was worrying that I rushed into booking a wedding date with Tommy. I wonder if he's got his doubts as well – he seems distant too, if I'm being honest, or it could just be me being paranoid. Maybe he can sense something is wrong with me, or perhaps it's because he's been working all hours – been round all the gyms dawn til late. I told him I'm stressed out with the wedding and all that, so he's probably just leaving me to it.'

The doors next to them swung open and Katie stood there gagging for breath, her wig askew. She inhaled deeply and stood in front of them with hands on her hips.

'What's up?' Jane asked.

Maxine folded her arms tightly in front of her and sat back in her seat as if to brace herself. 'He's sat over there like he's God's gift. He never noticed me but, on my life, I was inches from him at one point, could hear him talking all his weasel words. He's all over her, kissing her, groping her arse. It made me feel sick to the bottom of my stomach. I swear I wanted to punch his lights out right there and then.'

Maxine pulled her shoulders back and her nostrils flared. 'Is she pretty, thin, long legs? Because that's the type he goes for. I bet she's young, too; young enough to believe his shit.'

Katie paused before she spoke again. She reached over and swigged the last mouthful from her glass and plonked down next to Maxine and looked her directly in the eyes. 'Sorry, Max. You know the woman, we all do.'

The women huddled closer together. 'It's Donna Ramsey. I bet he's never stopped seeing her. This has been going on for years, if you ask me.'

Maxine clenched her teeth, stood up and looked at her friends. 'Let's do this. But let's do it right. When we get inside the boozer, I don't want to run in all guns blazing. Give me a few minutes to decide what I want to do.'

'Yes, it's your shout, we will do whatever you want to.' Lesley squeezed her hand.

The four women finished their drinks and made their way to the pub across the road. Maxine walked behind her friends, Katie leading them to the back of the pub where they could see Ian, his arm draped round Donna Ramsey. Maxine stood with her back to the wall, and she couldn't take her eyes from her husband and his other woman. She could see him laughing, touchy feely, all over her like a rash. Maxine whispered in Lesley's ear and smiled. Lesley left the group and headed to where the karaoke was. Katie passed the drinks about and the friends waited, watching. Lesley was already taking her earrings out and clipping her hair back in case things got messy. Donna Ramsey was a gobby cow and she knew she would not just sit there when it all kicked off.

The fake name Lesley had given on the karaoke slip was shouted out by the DJ and Maxine took a route through the pub that kept her out of Ian's sight. The girls closed in now, edging closer and closer to Ian's table. Maxine grabbed the mic and waited for the song to start. The opening bars of 'Moving On Up' began pumping out. She had a great voice and the swelling enthusiasm of the crowd drove her on – soon almost the whole pub was behind her, singing and dancing. Maxine snaked her way through the punters and reached Ian's table. At first, he was too busy whispering sweet nothings into Donna's ear to notice her. As she finally locked eyes with Donna, she dragged her wig from her head, and she watched her jaw drop. Then she turned to her husband as the song was finishing and cheering erupted. The girls were in position right behind him and Maxine stood there looking at her targets. She tapped the mic and made sure it was still on. She had the attention of everyone, and she coughed to clear her throat.

'Hi everyone, I hate to spoil your night, but I need to let you know that this pathetic excuse for a man sat here with this sperm bank is actually my husband. He's had me thinking that I'm worthless, paranoid and ready for the knacker's yard, but instead of listening to his bullshit anymore I decided to go and find out the truth for myself. Ian, I want a divorce. I was ready to be broken by this moment. Thought I'd find you with some poor young lass who didn't know any better, but seeing you here with this old tart, a downgrade if you ask me, telling you to take a hike feels fucking fantastic.'

A few other women in the pub starting cheering and shouting from across the room. 'You tell him, love, you're better than that, leave his sorry arse and kick the wanker to the kerb.' Donna was about to stand up when Katie stepped into action and sat her back down with the help of Lesley. Jane picked Ian's pint up and swilled it all over him.

'How dare you, Ian! Maxine has been nothing but good to you and you treat her like this, with her of all people. Donna Ramsey is a bike, and you know it. I hope you're happy, you prick, because my friend deserves someone who treats her well and not like you have been doing.'

Maxine stepped in now. 'You're welcome to him, Donna. I'll pack everything he owns and even drop it at your gaff for you. Oh, and Ian,' she chuckled. 'For the record, I've suspected about this dirty little secret for a long time. It's given me time to move my money and change the locks, so I hope this slapper can provide for you, because you're getting fuck-all from me.' She glared at him, vengeance blazing in her eyes. 'What, lost your tongue, Ian? Shouldn't have been sticking it down this one's throat. Or maybe you think you can slap me around like you're fond of, and I'll take you back? Well jog on – I've woken up and it feels great.'

Chapter Twenty-Two

Maxine opened her eyes slowly and looked at the empty spot next to her where her husband would usually lie. In the three days since the showdown, all her bravery had left her. Her hand reached over and slowly stroked the pillow where Ian's head once lay. Her eyes flooded with tears, and she gulped as she tried to remain calm. The girls had stayed with her until late on the night it all went down, and she'd had to tell them to leave in the early hours. Since then, she had got through each day on autopilot, putting on a brave face for work, coming back to a dark and empty house and trying to cope with the void inside. She was full of contradictions – she missed Ian so hard it hurt, yet she knew she was mourning the idea of him rather than the sad reality of who he really was. No, all she wanted was to be alone in peace and quiet to go over everything that had happened, replay it in her mind and find some sort of calm.

Maxine placed her hand on her chest now, a pain deep inside her heart, a stabbing sharp pain. So, this was heartbreak then, a feeling of emptiness, no motivation, nothing to get out of bed for. She'd filled her days playing love songs, looking at old photographs, memories. Maxine looked over at her mobile phone and could see all the messages and missed calls from her husband and her friends. She picked it up and launched it at the bedroom wall. 'Fuck you, Ian, fuck you!' she screamed. There was no pill for this, no quick fix, it was only time that would heal her broken heart. Some people never get over a broken heart though, she thought. They never loved again, too scared to ever come back to the place where they felt all this pain. Heartbreak changes a person, she knew that now. Would she ever trust again, would she always doubt others and herself? As much as she hated Ian, she hated herself for having been fooled for so long and for this sinking feeling that she wasn't good enough and that, if she'd been different, better, sexier, he wouldn't have cheated. Her brain was playing tricks on her, she told herself. Forget his shagging around – she should have walked away the moment he laid a hand on her. But shoulds and woulds were easy to say, and harder to make true.

Four days passed, and none of the girls had had a call or text back from Maxine. Katie and Lesley and Jane were getting worried and now they all turned up at her house to try and help. Jane reached under the plant pot and smiled at the others when she found a silver key there. Maxine had always had a spare key and she was glad Ian hadn't tried looking for it. Jane slid the key into the door and the others followed her. Katie picked up the heap of mail which suggested Maxine hadn't even put her head outside for days.

'Maxine?' Lesley shouted. There was no answer downstairs. After they had checked the living room and the kitchen, the three of them headed up the stairs with caution.

Lesley opened the bedroom door. There was a figure lying in the bed and they could see only the top of Maxine's head. The bedroom looked like pure carnage. Photographs ripped and scattered about the floor, mountains of clothes piled high, all cut up and destroyed. Lesley sat on the edge of the bed and gently patted Maxine; her voice soft. 'Max, love, come on, it's only us.'

Jane opened the curtains, and the daylight came streaming inside the room. Maxine groaned as the cover was removed from her head. Katie stood at the other side of the bed.

'Chin up, my girl. We're all here with you now. No man is worth your tears, trust me.'

Maxine tried to sit up in the bed, her eyes were still half closed. Lesley passed her a drink of water. Jane plonked down on the floor and stared up at Maxine: she was a shell of her former self, sallow skin, dark sunken eyes.

'I'll go and make you something to eat, maybe a bit of soup.' Lesley left the bedroom.

Katie started to move the clothes from the floor. She picked up a photograph that had been shredded. 'Maxine, can I bin all this?'

Maxine's voice was low, barely enough strength to answer her. 'Get rid of anything that bastard owned. I want it all gone, everything.'

Katie found a discarded bin-liner and set about cleaning the room up until Lesley returned with a tray. She sat down next to Maxine and encouraged her friend. 'Come on, girl, eat something. After this you can go and get a shower and try and sort yourself out. I'm not being funny, but it smells like something's died in here.'

Maxine pushed the silver spoon away. 'Did this all really happen? Talk about bad dreams…'

Lesley sighed. 'It did, my darling, but it's over now and you can start rebuilding your life as from today. The worst has passed. No more tears.'

Katie walked over to the bed, and scooped the mail up from the bedside cabinet and passed it to Maxine. 'Here, open these, see if it takes your mind off things. I can see there's a holiday brochure in there – maybe that's what you need.'

As she dropped the post on the bed, a gold envelope slid from among the flyers and bills. As soon as she saw it, Lesley stopped. She never said a word, she just hovered at the edge of the bed, watching every move Maxine made. The card was opened and silver hearts fell from it onto the duvet. Maxine read out loud.

'Secrets, secrets. Which one of your friends is keeping a secret from you? Friendship is like paper. Once it's torn, it can never be truly fixed.'

Maxine sat up straight in the bed. She shot a look at Lesley and then Jane and then Katie. Her bottom lip trembled, and she dropped the card so it lay open on her chest.

Lesley quickly picked it up. 'What the fuck is someone playing at? Why would Kimberley be out to get you, or even know where you live?'

Maxine closed her eyes. 'One of my friends is keeping a secret from me. What the hell is that supposed to mean?'

Lesley stood staring out of the window. 'Someone out there is out to ruin us.'

Maxine was frowning. 'If this is Kimberley, does she think I don't know about the child you had? Why wouldn't they send this to John, not me? We know everything about each other, we don't have secrets.'

Katie stood with hands on her hips and shot a quick look at Lesley. 'It's all bullshit. Whoever is playing silly buggers needs to sort their head out. I say we ignore the letters and see what happens. I can bet your life that nothing more will come of it.'

Maxine looked around her bedroom after it had been cleaned, and shook her head. Jane sat with her now and reached over to hold her warm hand in hers. 'I know you don't think it right now, but you will get better. What doesn't kill you makes you stronger and all that. So, dry them bleeding tears and let's call this day one.'

'I feel humiliated, everyone will know what's happened. My husband is a dirty dick and he's been caught playing away from home.'

Katie climbed in next to Maxine and snuggled into her. 'Ian will fall to pieces without you, Maxine. On my life, give it a week or so and that plonker will be camped outside your door begging you to come back. Our next mission is to make you feel strong enough not to listen to him.'

Jane grinned. 'This is where I come in. You need a makeover Max and that's my job to sort you out. I'm going to book you in at the salon for a hair colour change and a new style. You've looked the same for years and it's time to step out of your comfort zone and try something new. A nice dark red would suit you.'

Katie agreed and started pulling her fingers through her own hair. 'I could do with a restyle too. Why don't we all do it? It might just be what we need to liven us all up again. I'm game for it, if you lot are?'

Jane rolled her eyes. No doubt she'd be paying for Katie as she was on the bones of her arse and still out of work. Lesley agreed and started to look on her phone for inspiration. There was no way she would be going for any mad colours, maybe a few highlights and a few inches off her hair would be enough for her.

Jane's mobile started ringing and she jumped up and left the room to answer it.

When she came back in, she looked anxious. 'Francis wants to meet up later tonight. Can I tell Tommy I'm staying with you, Max, to give you some moral support? I hate to tangle you up in all my shit, but he already thinks I've been acting strange lately.'

'Just this once,' Maxine sighed. 'You need to sort this out, Jane. Are you forgetting that you're pregnant? This problem will not go away by itself. In fact, the longer you leave it, the worse it gets.'

'I know, I know. Every night I'm awake thinking about it. This could be my one and only chance to be a mother. I know I'm not sure who the father is, but, come on, more than likely the baby is Francis's. I'm going to mention children to him tonight and see what he says. I owe him that much.'

'What about Tommy in all of this?' Maxine replied. 'You need to work out your priorities. You've got a wedding booked in a few weeks.'

'I need to make my mind up and fast,' Jane answered.

Maxine looked unconvinced. 'It would be best to call it off now rather than wait until the wedding day, wouldn't it? Come on, we can all see that you're not ready for marriage. A ring on a finger doesn't solve it all, you know. Look at me, for God's sake.'

Jane sat chewing on her fingernails. 'I can't believe I've done this to myself – only I can sort this. Just let me do it at my pace. If it all goes tits up, then I will have nobody to blame but myself.'

'You're going to have to go at the pace of biology, J. Once you start showing, it might be too late to make up your mind.' Lesley was more brusque than usual, and changed the subject fast. 'Right, first things first. Let's book in at the salon and sort ourselves out.'

Katie nodded. 'You don't have to ask me twice. I need a bleeding miracle to sort my life out at the moment. I've heard they need bar staff at The Magpie so I'm going to try there. I mean, come on, how hard could that be? I've watched people pour enough pints, surely I can master it, and it will get me out each night instead of sat in that pit of mine staring at the walls. And, to add insult to injury, our Jade has said she's moving out. At least I've still got you lot.'

Lesley managed a smile at that. 'Come on, look at us all. Jane is preggers, Katie has no job, Maxine has just found her husband cheating. And me, well, I've got a step-daughter with a vendetta against me, but we've come through worse, so straighten your faces and let's get back in the game. It ain't over til it's over, right?'

The driver of the Merc drove past the salon watching the gaggle of women go in, arms around each other, laughing. They were like butterflies – beautiful but easily broken. It was almost a shame that he had to hurt them. Almost.

Chapter Twenty-Three

The salon was busy and the four girls were sat in the reception area waiting to get called. Jane had known it was their busy day, but they would always make room for her and her friends. Plus, she loved the chat. If you wanted to find out anything, then this was the place to be. It was gossip heaven. Stacey, the salon manager, had been here for years, and once anyone sat in her chair she didn't stop talking, even to take a breath. This was more than a hairdresser's, this was a place for therapy, staff and clients all putting the world to rights and giving their advice.

Stacey walked over to the girls and smiled, showing off her pearly white teeth. She was a good-looking woman, and you could tell she'd had work done to keep it that way. The word was that she'd had her boobs done and a tummy tuck last year, but she insisted it was because she was always at the gym. Since when did going to the gym make your bust go up three cup sizes? Jane knew she'd been under the knife, but she never called her out on it.

Stacey ran the place like a military operation, turned a tidy profit and never minded Jane playing the owner card.

Stacey eyed up the friends. 'Maxine, I'm going to start with you first. Jane's told me you're going for a whole new look?' Stacey took her to the chair. 'Come on, girl, I'm going to work my magic on you and that bastard will be sorry he ever strayed.' Stacey lifted Max's hair up and sighed: split ends, lifeless hair, colour that had faded. 'Right, don't get scared, but I'm thinking that we go with a completely new colour. I'm thinking a nice honey blonde, it will suit your skin tone. I'm going to suggest some extensions too, that will give you fullness and length. Proper beach-babe look. In fact, what about a spray tan too? Jenny is in today and she has a lovely new tan in. It's not very dark and it looks so nice, just like you've stepped off the lounger.'

Maxine was up for anything. A new hairstyle, a new life, a new man, anything to take away the pain she was feeling deep in her heart. 'Stacey, just make me look different. We're all going out tomorrow and I want to feel good. If I'm honest, I've felt like an old has-been for a long time. I've let myself go and I know it. I suppose that's what happens when you feel like you've got nothing to look forward to, isn't it?'

'It sure is, lovey. Take it from me, you always have to look after yourself and keep on top of your game. Not for any man, but for yourself. Men are bleeding cheeky, you know. They put weight on, don't exercise or nothing, yet they expect us to be tip-top every day. While they expect women to be getting to the gym, going for facials, waxing, brows – I mean I had one client in here asking if my girls do bleaching where the sun don't shine, if you get me. I'm all for looking your best, but forget vajazzling yourself for a fella when what they've got looks like the last turkey in the shop. No, if you want to feel good, then look good on your terms. So, I heard your Ian was slipping it to Donna Ramsey. No, don't look embarrassed. We hear it all the time, someone's hubby running off with some dolly-bird. Look at Jackie Dolan, her husband was a slob, had nothing about him, and yet he ran off with that blonde tart from the front desk at the builder's yard. She was only after his money of course, but he didn't know that at the time. He left Jackie without a second thought, just packed up and moved in with the slapper. Jackie was a broken woman, and it took months before she was alright. Don't get me wrong, she's back with her husband now, but she went to hell and back while he was gone.'

Maxine sat up straight in her seat, eyes open wide, voice low. 'So, she forgave her husband?'

Stacey looked at her reflection in the mirror. 'Yes, well not straight away. He was begging her to have him back, telling her he'd made a massive mistake. Flowers and chocolates he sent her for weeks, always sitting outside her house waiting to talk to her.'

Maxine clenched her teeth. 'I won't be forgiving Ian, never in a month of Sundays. He's made his bed and now he can lie in it. I just knew he was up to no good, you know. Gaslighting, they call it, and that's what was happening to me. I thought I was going insane, imagining things, seeing things that were not there, when all along I was right. On my life, Stacey, I thought I was losing the plot. Some days I didn't know if I was coming or going. I'll never forgive him for that, ever.'

'You should get your brothers to give him a good arse-kicking. Who does he think he is treating you like that? Your Tony is a nutter and he'll put him on the missing list, given the chance.'

'I thought about it, Stacey, don't think for one minute that I haven't, but what would that do? Nothing, really. Anyway, I want Ian to know I can finish him off myself. I've got ideas if he even tries coming near me again. Show him I'm not his timid little woman anymore, that's what I plan to do.'

'There you go, that's the spirit, girl. Once I've finished with you, you will be like a new woman.'

'I hope so Stacey, I bloody hope so.'

The hairdresser started to apply the colour to Maxine's hair, and Jane and Katie and Lesley were all in their own chairs now.

The door opened and a cold gust of wind came in causing everyone to turn around. Melissa Myers. Jane eyeballed the girls. This was trouble for sure – Melissa had resented them since school and, after not seeing her for years, to see her twice in as many weeks made Jane nervy. Every time this woman was in the same room as them, she kicked off and couldn't keep her big trap shut.

She clocked them straight away and slowly sat down in the waiting area. Jane covered her mouth and whispered over to Lesley. 'Here's trouble.'

'Tell me about it. How long are we giving her before she opens that big mouth of hers?'

Melissa's stylist sat her right opposite the girls. As soon as she was seated, she shot a look at each and every one of the four friends. Here it was, they didn't have to wait long. 'I hear your fella has been sleeping with that Donna Ramsey, Maxine? I always knew Ian was a dickhead. Shame you didn't listen when everyone told you the first time around.'

Maxine bit down hard on her bottom lip and she was about to reply when Katie defended her. 'Keep your smart remarks to yourself. Who's given you the rights to judge anyone when you've had a string of fellas who treated you like shit? At least Maxine has carted hers, unlike yourself when Jerry Donald cheated on you.' Katie grinned: game, set and match, she thought.

Melissa went bright red but then played her trump card. 'Well, you lot would know about cheating. I see Jane is still wearing her engagement ring, yet she has a new fella on the go; don't tell me this dirty cow didn't let on that I clocked her at the Midland with her bit on the side? I've still got to tell Tommy when I see him what his trollop of a girlfriend is getting up to when he's not with her.'

Katie was first to reply, thinking on her feet. 'You must think we came down in the last shower. Jane, she's on about the meeting you had with the wedding planner. Melissa, you go right ahead and have a chat with Tommy, because he will laugh right in your face. Do yourself a favour and keep your beak out of other people's business. At least get your facts right first. On my life, get over us all, will you? The years have gone by, and you still can't let it go. Get a grip, woman, and move on.'

Melissa was fuming. She ignored Katie's comment and started to speak with her stylist, her cheeks blazing red.

By the end of the afternoon, Maxine looked completely different. Stacey was right: the new colour really suited her. The extensions made her hair look luscious and the curly blow she'd had finished the look. She looked healthier than she had for years – oiled and tanned and like she'd been on a cruise. Maxine looked at herself in the mirror and had to check it was really her staring back. Where had she been hiding all these years? The corners of her mouth started to rise. The new hairstyle had knocked ten years from her. Jane was still lying back having her Russian lashes done, and Katie was having her eyebrows tinted, but Lesley could admire her new look. There was a lightness to Maxine's voice the friends hadn't heard in years.

'I just want to say thank you. Without you lot I would have wallowed away in self-pity for years. I know it's only early days, but I feel better already. I'll never let no man treat me like this again. I know my worth and I won't let that prick stamp me down anymore because I was too scared he would leave me. I know you all think I should have got rid of Ian years ago, but I wasn't strong enough back then. I feared being on my own, not having him with me. But I knew I had to face it one day or another. Times will be hard for me to start with but I'm going to take it day by day. I going to find me again. I think I've been lost, girls, very lost in fact.'

Katie was tearing up. She understood that feeling of being alone, no one to lean on. She reached over and held her friend's hand. 'You're a survivor, Maxine. Take it day by day, queen, one step at a time. You'll have good days and bad days, but trust me when I tell you that one morning you will wake up and you will realise that happiness starts with you, not no bleeding man. Self-love is the best kind of love a woman can have.'

A few of the other clients looked over and smiled. Everyone, in fact, apart from Melissa Myers who was sitting under the heater.

When the girls walked out of the salon, Melissa watched them leave. She smirked at her reflection in the mirror and whispered, 'Watch out, bitches, watch who has the last laugh.'

Chapter Twenty-Four

Jane sat in the corner booth in the city-centre restaurant she'd chosen. She'd texted Tommy to say she was going straight from the salon to meet the wedding planner, and hoped that Frankie could make it. She knew she looked her best – she'd new nails on as well as the fresh set of lashes – but she felt sick as a dog.

When she saw Francis stride in, her pulse raced. But not from lust like usual. She could recognise the cold grip of nerves – like a band tightening around her chest. She tried to steady her breathing.

Frankie sat down, spreading his legs to fit his muscly thighs under the table. He clicked his fingers to summon a waitress and ordered Champagne without even asking Jane what she wanted.

'What are we celebrating, Frankie?' Jane asked, terrified he somehow knew what she was going to tell him.

'I've just had a nice little business deal work out,' he replied. 'It involves you, actually, so I thought I'd treat you to a bottle of Bollinger to celebrate.'

The waitress came back, filled two flutes and left the bottle in a cooler next to them.

'Well, I've got some news that involves you, too,' said Jane, knowing she had to bite the bullet.

'So, go on, spit it out,' said Francis, pushing one glass towards her.

Jane didn't pick the flute up, afraid her shaking hands would give the game away. She could feel time slowing down. She wanted to breathe in every second – these were the last moments she could keep the secret to herself.

'I'm pregnant, Frankie.' There, she'd ripped the plaster off and said it. 'And I think it's yours.'

The silence was louder than any gunshot.

'Fucking hell. You daft cow.' Frankie's words weren't what any pregnant woman wanted to hear. 'What do you mean, pregnant? We've barely been back from Benny long enough for you to know. Are you sure?'

'I've done millions of tests, Frankie.' Jane reached to touch his arm and Francis yanked it away. 'And I've been puking up and everything smells wrong. I know I'm tubbed, trust me.'

'Trust you? When you were shagging me on your hen do?' There was a cruel edge to Frankie's voice now.

'Don't be like that,' said Jane. 'I know it wasn't how any relationship should start, but we both felt something special, didn't we? That night on the beach, under the moonlight?'

Francis was looking into the middle distance, as if he was working something out. Jane pressed on. 'We've not even talked about our future, let alone whether we saw nippers in it, I know. But I'm thirty-eight, Francis. Tommy and I have never got pregnant, so this could be it for me.'

'What do you mean by that? Is it too late to go to a clinic and get it sorted?' Frankie looked unimpressed.

'I don't know, Frankie, I don't know anything anymore.' Jane blinked back tears.

'Well, you might as well know what my little deal was, in that case.' Frankie pushed his sleeves up. 'You know that favour you did me? Bringing home that bag I forgot in Spain?'

Jane nodded. 'I wasn't quite straight with you. It was full of steroids. My boss who owns the club out there has a nice little sideline in supply. A bloke like me going through customs? Well, let's just say I draw attention. But a bunch of pissed-up girls on a hen do? They're ten a penny. I bet no one even gave you lot a second look.' Frankie laughed.

Jane had flushed hot then ice-cold. 'Are you telling me you used me as a fucking drug mule? I could have been banged up for bringing your sodding bag back?'

'Keep your hair on, darling. You didn't get caught, did you? And they're legal, anyway. Maybe just not quite in the quantity in that bag. But I knew you'd be grand – you'd talk your way out of anything.'

Jane's mind was whirling. She couldn't make it make sense.

'So, are you telling me this was all an act? You were just looking for a bird to con?' She felt sick.

'I'm not saying I didn't enjoy the sex. Right little tiger in the sack, you are. But all that moonlight bullshit? Come on, who actually says that stuff and means it?'

Jane was lost for words. She'd come here to drop a bombshell and she was the one left reeling. She tried to pull herself together. 'So, the baby? I wasn't planning on raising a kid with a fucking drug dealer for a dad…'

'Well, that's convenient,' drawled Francis. 'Cos I wasn't planning on having kids at all. Look, you made me a packet on those pills you brought back. I'll pay for you to get a termination. I'll even not tell Tommy boy, if you keep schtum about what I've told you.' He reached into his pocket and slid a roll of notes over.

Jane was tempted to throw them back in his face. But instead she picked up her Champagne and threw it at him. As she stood up and walked out as fast as she could, she could feel her world crumbling around her.

Chapter Twenty-Five

Katie stood playing with the cuffs of her sleeve as Ged, the landlord of The Magpie, came out front to see her. She'd put her best blouse on today, showing a bit of cleavage, and a tight pair of skinny jeans with her red heels to impress him. She hoped he would give her the job just on her boobs alone. Katie hated being interviewed; she always said the wrong thing or didn't know the answer. Ged was old-school, though, mid-fifties, and he didn't strike her as the type to ask for references. He gave the impression of being a man who'd enjoyed his life as a barman, someone born to run a pub. With his wide girth, he looked like an egg on legs. But he oozed confidence and was straight to the point. 'Howdy, Katie, sorry I've been ages. I had to nip downstairs and change the barrel, right pain in the arse, it is. Anyway, let's grab you a drink and we can go and sit down, have a bit of a chat and you can tell me some more about yourself.'

Katie smiled at him, fluttering her eyelashes, flirting with him in the hope that he would give her a trial shift. If she didn't get some cash soon, there'd be nothing left on the gas and lecky. She'd already turned the fridge off – no point paying for that when she couldn't afford to put anything in it. She dialled up her flirting to maximum and walked over to a corner table once she'd told Ged what she would like to drink. She'd asked for a soft drink. It was before twelve o'clock and she wanted to make a good impression. Ged waddled over to her and thumped her drink down on the table. He stank of stale fags and old beer. But Katie supposed that went with the territory. She sipped a mouthful of her drink and sat back in her chair, playing. Already she could see his eyes on her chest. Bingo eyes, she thought, eyes down.

'So, Katie, have you done any bar work before?'

She'd rehearsed all this so was quick to reply. 'Not really, but I've been on the tills for so long I'm great with people – plus I've drank in enough boozers to know what makes a good bar staff. I learn quick and I'm reliable.'

Ged rubbed at his thigh and looked around the pub. 'You can imagine we get chocker in here at night, especially if we have got a gig on. Even if you've got no experience, I suppose I could train you up and see how you get on. It would mean working very closely together – long nights. Do you think you can handle that? If so, when can you start?'

Katie was going out on the razz tonight with the girls since they were all glammed up after the salon, and there was no way she was missing a free piss-up with Jane and the gang. She tilted her head to the side and pretended she was thinking. 'I can start on Monday, if that is any good to you?'

Ged ran his tongue over his tobacco-stained teeth. 'Bloody hell, I was hoping you would say you could start tonight.'

'I wish I could, lovey, but I've got something on that I can't cancel.'

'So, let's say you come in an hour earlier on Monday and I can give you a bit of one-on-one training. I'm looking for someone who works every night of the week, are you alright with that? Because I don't want you saying you can do it and then further down the line start pissing me about.'

'I can work as long and hard as you need.' Katie held his gaze.

Ged reached over and shook her hand, holding on a moment too long to be comfortable. 'I have one rule here, darling. I need to tell you that you don't date any of the punters who come in here. Alison who worked here last was a swine for it. I've had women coming in here looking for her after she'd been caught out sleeping with their husbands. Plus, it's not good mixing business with pleasure, is it?'

Katie pulled her shoulders back and let go of his hand. Her voice was firm, and she seemed offended by his comment. 'Ged, I'm no trollop. I'm very particular about the men I date, so you won't have to worry about me having relationships with your punters.'

'I'm not saying you would, I just had to put it out there that it's not good for business. Go ahead and flirt with them, by all means, but keep your knickers on, that's all I'm asking.' He chuckled to himself as he slurped on his pint of bitter. 'So, welcome to the team, and I'll see you on Monday at eleven o'clock. Oh, for the record, what you hear in the pub stays in the pub. I don't want you repeating anything you hear outside these four walls. The men here come to escape their balls-and-chains at home, and they will probably end up chewing your ear off with all their problems, so not only will you be a barmaid, but you will also become a counsellor. On my life, the things people tell you when they've had a few scoops is unreal. It will make your toes curl, some of the stories you hear.'

Katie stood and put her jacket back on. She smiled at Ged. 'See you on Monday. I'm looking forward to it.'

Stopping off at home to change, Katie opened the front door and stood over the pile of brown envelopes that were lying on the doormat. Bills, bills and more bloody bills. She supposed she should be glad that it was still bills rather than the bailiffs. She bent down and scooped them up with one hand as she headed into the kitchen. Jade had moved some of her things out already, and today she said she would call for the last few bits she had left there. The place looked half empty – she hadn't realised how much of the little things that made a house a home belonged to Jade, not her. She was already missing her, not to mention the handouts Jade gave her when she was skint. She felt awful, as if she'd driven her daughter out, failed to provide the stability she craved. She knew she'd raised Jade right, to stand on her own two feet and not take any shit from anyone. She supposed, although she was disappointed in herself, she should be proud of her daughter for getting out. But it left Katie back where she always was: on her own again.

Katie flicked the kettle on and sat down at the pine kitchen table. This table had witnessed so much in the past: celebrations, confessions, tears, the lot. Jade had grown up around this table. Even when she'd been broke and gone hungry herself, she'd always put food on the table for Jade. This was where she used to do her homework, where she would colour in and make all the sparkling cards for Christmas, where they sat and had tea and toast to cheer her up after her first teenage boyfriend turned out to be a rat. It was where they had Christmas dinners and hangover brekkies. Katie closed her eyes as a flashback of her daughter laughing and singing filled her mind. Katie started to open the letters one by one: get it over and done with. One day, she imagined not being driven to a panic attack by the sight of a bill. But she dropped all the brown envelopes when she spotted a gold one in their midst.

Her breathe caught in her chest as she started to open the letter. The silver hearts she was expecting fell onto the table and she was thunderstruck as she read the words inside.

'Secrets, secrets. It's better to have no friends than to have a fake friend who lies to you. The clock is ticking, bitch.'

Katie dropped the card and pushed it across the table away from her like it was diseased. She stared at it, trying to work out it what it meant. She wasn't one for crosswords and puzzles. What did they mean: was it accusing her of lying? Who the hell was sending these cards and what did they know? More to the point, what did they want? Katie was savvy enough to know someone going to all this trouble wasn't just doing it to stir: they were looking for something.

She tapped her fingers on the table. She grabbed her phone and rang Lesley. 'I've got a gold card too now. It came this morning. What the hell is happening, Lesley? Because it's freaking me out. I think I'm going to have a seizure or something, my heart is like a speeding train and my head hurts. We need to find out who's sending these and take them down. I know I said to ignore them, but why the hell am I getting one too?'

Lesley was trying to calm Katie down, but she stood up now, pacing the room. 'Who the hell is doing it? If it's Kimberley, then we need to go and see her. I'm not scared of some kid. Put me in front of her and I'll scratch her eyes out. What does she think she knows? More to the point, if she thinks she's Wagatha Christie for finding out you had a kid when you were a teenager, why hasn't she told John and been done with it? And why bother the rest of us?'

Katie stayed on the phone for a few more minutes arranging where to meet tonight, then ended the call. She read the card over and over again. What did they mean by 'the clock is ticking'?

Katie, Lesley and Maxine got to the bar first and were huddled round, looking at Katie's card, waiting for Jane to show. None of them were in the mood for a big night out, but none of them wanted to be alone. Each with their own skeleton in the closet. Katie shot a look over to the door as Jane walked in. She was about to wave her card at her when she saw the look on her face. A woman on a mission.

'How did it go with Frankie? Did you tell him about the baby?' Lesley asked.

'You won't fucking believe this, girls. I've been had. He's stitched me up like a kipper. He's—'

Katie butted in. 'Did he run a mile when you told him about the baby?'

Jane laughed, bitterly. 'If it was just that, I'd have expected it. No, it turns out this bun in the oven isn't the only thing of his I brought back from Alicante. You know that bag? Turns out it was stuffed with steroids. He was giving it all that about his business – clubs, property, a port-fucking-folio of interests, he told me. Nah, he's basically just a drug dealer in a nice suit.'

'Jesus, Jane. I'm surprised you didn't faint on the spot.' Maxine looked horrified. 'You could have been banged up – we all could.'

'Fuck me sideways,' said Katie, never one to mince her words. 'Bet you're glad you didn't ditch Tommy for that druggie now, aren't you?'

Jane leant over, resting her head on her arm. 'I don't know, girls. You could call it a lucky escape, but I'd started to think about having this baby. He wants me to get rid and I just don't know. What am I meant to do now – tell Tommy it's his?'

'Plenty of people do it,' said Lesley. 'I read somewhere that at least five percent of people's parents aren't the people they've been told.'

'Yes, but with all these DNA tests these days you've got to be careful, J,' Maxine piped up. 'Are you sure you want to have that hanging over your head? Tommy's a lot of things, but he's not stupid. What if it pops out looking like Frankie? And could you keep a secret that long?'

At the mention of secrets, Katie remembered about her card. 'I was just showing this to the girls when you walked in. I've had an envelope too today – look. There is only you left to receive a card, then it's a full house. What do you think they want from us? They've not asked for any money or anything, have they? They haven't even said what they think they know, just bleeding riddles, stuff that plays with your mind, thinking what they might know.'

Jane slammed her flat palm on the table. Her eyes were wide open as if the penny had just dropped. 'What if it's not Kimberley? What if it's someone who's got an axe to grind with us all? I bet it's Melissa ruddy Myers. She's been out to get us since school. She would love to cause trouble for any of us. She's a vindictive bitch with a long memory and we all know what she would do to get one over on us. Do you remember when we lied to our parents and went to that rave?'

Katie was nodding. 'Yes, Melissa grassed us up because she never got an invite.'

Lesley piped up now. 'And what about when she cancelled my birthday party when I was twenty-one? I'll never forgive her for that, and I know it was her because her friend told someone I know.'

Jane ran her finger around her glass and nodded. 'I nicked Pauly Turner from her, didn't I, just before I met Tommy, and she always said she would pay me back. It could well be her.'

'I've got to admit,' said Maxine, 'It's suspicious that she seems to have gone out of her way to avoid us and yet at the salon she sat there for hours like she was queen of the world.'

Katie started to relax. Melissa was sneaky, but she wasn't scary. If she wanted to start all this funny business, then let her, she would eat her for breakfast. Maybe things were looking up. 'I got the job at the pub, girls. I start on Monday, even though the cheeky git told me that I'm not allowed to sleep with any punters or to gossip about what I hear in the boozer. What's all that about? You know me, one of the main reasons I wanted the job in the first place was to see if I can meet a decent bloke. I've been on all the dating sites and the men are perverts, asking for pics of your bits before they've even asked your name. Honestly, it's not like I'm looking for someone to shower me with expensive gifts and exotic bloody holidays. The way I've been going, I'm lucky if a man buys me a kebab at the end of the night.'

'That's great news, Katie,' Lesley said.

Maxine smiled at Katie too. 'The tide could be finally turning for you. Hopefully this job will put you back on your feet and sort your finances out as well as your love life.'

Jane realised Maxine made a good point. Until now, Jane had always paid for the lion's share of her friends' nights out and weekends away. Jane looked down at her diamond ring. It wasn't only her heart that was on the line – her bank balance was at risk too. 'The wedding is so near, and I don't want to put Tommy through any pain if I decide I don't want to marry him. I know Tommy inside and out and he is a decent man. I'll never want for anything with him. Is it fair to make him bring up another's man kid?'

Lesley raised her eyebrows. 'You know what I think – you should stick with Tommy. You've had your fling, got it out your system before you got married, and you've realised for all his flash talk he was just a pill-pusher. It shows you didn't really know him. Better you found out now.'

Jane still looked tormented. 'I can't believe I swallowed all his lies about falling for me. I thought it was strange that he never really talked about his family or even his friends. Imagine if he's got a wife and kids or a girlfriend somewhere.'

'Whether he's got kids or not isn't the problem here – it's whether you're having one. I don't know how many times I need to tell you to get that sorted.' Katie darted her eyes at Jane's stomach.

Lesley had a pained expression. 'You all know giving a baby away was the toughest thing I've ever done. I can only tell you to look into your heart. Think long and hard about it, Jane. It will change your life, if you decide to keep it. You and Tommy could make amazing parents to that kid. But only you know if you can take the pressure of knowing you'll always have that secret from Tommy, always be waiting on the truth coming out.'

'If the shock of today has taught me anything, it's that I need to protect myself – my heart, my money, my future. Frankie conned me good and proper. But I can't let my heart rule my head again. Tomorrow I'm going to the accountant's. I need to know what would happen if Tommy kicked me out. If he ever finds out, I couldn't expect him to do anything else. Could I raise a baby on my own? I will have a decision by tomorrow night. Tommy is out on a local stag night with some of the lads from work and, since I can't drink, I was thinking we could have a bit of a pamper night. None of us got time for that today. I can book one of the beauticians for a home visit, if you all fancy it?'

Katie didn't need asking twice. Anything free and she was up for it, but before she could reply, she pointed at the door. 'Oh my God, look who's just walked in, Jake Pritchard. I told you we'd been texting.'

The girls looked over towards the bar and there he was, the lad they all knew from school, or at least, the man he'd grown into.

Jane was gobsmacked. 'Bleeding hell, Katie, he's changed. Decent, he is.'

'I did tell you, but you all ignored me. He's been messaging me for ages but, if I'm being honest, I only answer when I'm bored.'

Lesley chuckled. 'Get over there, girl, and see what he's saying. Bring him over here so we can talk to him too. Maxine, his mate looks a bit of dish too.'

Maxine went bright red and flicked her hair over her shoulder. 'I don't know if I'm ready for another man yet. I'm not over Ian.'

Jane scoffed. 'You know the saying. The fastest way to get over a man is to get under another one. Go talk to him, practise your flirting. I thought you was going to be a yes-girl from now on? Don't be going back on all the things you said to us.'

'I'm not, but I feel that I need a bit more time.'

'Sod that,' Katie blurted out. 'Live for the moment.'

Katie stood up and winked at her friends. 'Time waits for no man. Or woman. In for a penny, in for a pound. Off I go.'

The girls burst out laughing and watched the pro in action. Katie sashayed over to Jake and tapped him on his shoulder. As soon as he saw her, his face lit up.

Maxine watched. 'I know she's had a hard time recently, but what she lacks in wealth she makes up for in confidence. How does she do it?'

Jane nodded. 'She's always been a chance-taker, has our Katie. Nothing ventured, nothing gained. So, she might feel that she's lost more than she's won, but at least she doesn't let life stop her trying. I think we could all take a leaf out of her book and be a bit more confident. Katie was right about one thing. Time is short, whether we know it or not.'

Chapter Twenty-Six

Tommy sprawled across the bed with a white towel wrapped around his waist. Jane walked in and drank him in. He was trim, tanned and she wondered why she'd ever let Frankie turn her head. She felt conscious and breathed in as she climbed onto the bed next to him. 'I'm absolutely knackered, you know. This wedding is taking it out of me. I've got no appetite and I've not been sleeping properly.'

'Tell me about it. You've been tossing and turning every bloody night, waking me up.'

She studied her man and lay her head on his warm chest. 'We will be happy, won't we?'

Tommy could hear in her voice that she was emotional, and he lifted her head up to look her in the eyes. 'Of course, we will be happy, babes. As long as we stick to our rules, we will be the happiest couple ever. You know they're the holy bible of good relationships.'

Jane stared up at the ceiling. 'I know the rules, Tommy. Bloody hell, I made them with you. Trust each other, never tell lies, and always talk about anything that is bothering us.' It sounded simple – but she'd smashed them all in the last month.

Tommy nodded and turned so he could look her directly in the eyes. 'So, is there anything that is bothering you that you want to talk about?'

Jane knew this was her chance, but the words dried in her mouth. 'No, I'm just a bit stressed with this wedding. It's all the planning. Once we're married, normal services will resume.'

'Glad to hear it.' Tommy's gaze lingered on, as if he was working something out.

Jane couldn't stand being stared at, so she jumped up from the bed and went to straighten her hair. 'The girls will be here soon, so I better move my arse. Letty is still here, and I've told her to start ironing all your holiday stuff. At least then, I can pack your case ready for the honeymoon. Another job from my list.'

'Yeah, tell her not to pack my shorts yet because I'm buying some new ones. I've had those ones for time, and I reckon I deserve some new clobber. Had a nice little deal land at work, too, so we're flush.'

'That's great. I need to grab a few new bikinis too. I hate wearing the same one twice. Perhaps we can nip to the town centre one night and grab what we need.' Jane walked out of the bedroom and headed straight into the bathroom. Her heart was beating, and it was like reality had just hit her bang in the face.

She felt awful lying to Tommy. How would she manage lying about a baby to him for the rest of their lives? She wasn't ready to have a baby on these terms, who the hell was she trying to kid? She could barely look at him, never mind tell him she was having a miracle baby. No, she was going to book in at the clinic. Then, she'd put all her energy into mending things with Tommy and, when they were both ready, if Tommy was struggling to give her a baby, then they would find the best fertility doctor out there and pay for treatment to help them conceive with no lies or cover stories.

Jane looked at her body in the bathroom mirror and examined every inch. She didn't look pregnant: it didn't feel real. The girls were right; it was a holiday fling, and she'd come to her senses just in time. She walked out of the bathroom, and saw Letty carrying a bundle of clothes into the spare bedroom where she did the ironing. 'Letty, pet. Tommy said don't iron any shorts for him yet. He's getting new ones.'

Letty turned and smiled back at Jane. 'Yes, no problems. Let me know when you want your clothes ironing, and I will make a start on them too. I'm going to stay late tonight to get this lot finished, if that's alright with you, then come in late tomorrow?'

'Of course it is. Me and the girls are having a pamper night so you crack on and do what you need to.'

Jane heard the doorbell and walked down the stairs. This must be Gina the beautician, come early to set her things up.

Katie lay on the beauty bed, enjoying every moment of her facial, although even this moment of supposed relaxation and serenity wasn't enough to button Katie's lip. Even while her skin was being steamed and smoothed, she was still talking.

'Jake is taking me out tomorrow night. Jane, can he come to the wedding with me as my plus one? I swear to you now, he could be the one. We don't stop laughing together and he's such a gentleman. I've never had a man treat me this well before. Apparently, he's been into me since school.'

Maxine was waiting for her turn, and staring at her phone while she did. 'Look, Ian has been belling my phone out all day. Last night he was at the house just parked up in the car, trying to speak to me. I told him if he sets one foot near my house then I'll ring my brothers and have him removed. On my life, the text messages he's been sending me are like bleeding novels. He said Donna never meant anything to him and I'm the only woman he's ever loved. I don't believe a word the prick says to me anymore. He said he's at his mam's, sleeping on the sofa. Fine by me.'

'You tell him,' Katie agreed as she sat up from the bed. 'You're onto pastures new and the only time you should ever look back is to see how far you have come.' Katie was on form tonight.

'The only thing I've really missed is his share of the rent and all that,' Maxine said. 'I'll have some more perfumes tomorrow, Jane, so if you want any give me a shout. I've worked out that, if I get a couple of perfumes a week and sell them, they should help cover some of the bills.'

Lesley hated that Maxine was light-fingered and shook her head. 'Max, if you get caught you could end up being prosecuted. Don't chance it anymore. Get another job in the evenings.'

Maxine shook her head. 'When would I have time? It would have to be a night shift and I'd be knackered working every evening.'

'When times are hard you have to do what you have to do,' said Katie. 'Welcome to my world, Maxine. Beggars can't be choosers.' Katie lay back down and closed her eyes.

There was a tap at the door and Letty walked in. 'I'm off now, Jane. I forgot to give you these earlier. Have a nice night, ladies.' She handed over a couple of parcels and packets, then waved goodbye to the women.

Jane looked down at the deliveries and there it was, nestled between her online-shopping parcels: the gold envelope she realised now she'd been waiting for. She lifted it up and showed it to the girls. 'Well, well. I knew it wouldn't be long before I got one.'

Katie sat up from her facial again and Jane waved at the beautician. 'Gina, you can go and have a smoke break if you want.'

The beautician didn't need asking twice. 'I sure do. I'll nip in the garden, if you don't mind.'

Once she was gone, Jane tore open the letter. The silver hearts fell from it just like with the others. Jane opened the card fully and read.

'Secrets, secrets. A mistake is something that happens accidentally. Cheating and lying are not accidents, they are choices, bitch.'

'What is this all about? Does somebody know about Francis and the baby or what? I told you, it's Melissa Myers sending all these cards. Come on, she saw me in the hotel. She's not daft and she would not have bought the story we gave her. I bet she's been following me. Come to think of it, I swear I've seen a black Merc around a lot.'

Katie chewed on her fingernails. 'Somebody thinks they know something, for sure. Look at the cards, they all refer to a secret.'

Jane took a deep breath. 'Well, whatever they think they know is probably old news. If it's Melissa bloody Myers then she's got nothing but a random meeting. Anyway, I'm phoning the clinic first thing in the morning to get a termination booked. I've decided.'

Maxine jumped in and she was angry. 'But it can't just be about you and Tommy. Mine said one of my friends was lying to me: what's that all about? I trust you all with my life, so I think this is all a load of bullshit. If they had evidence, they'd be threatening us. I think this is only guesswork – Kimberley or Melissa stirring a load of crap. Come on, back me on this. I know we've got secrets from other people – but we don't hide anything from each other, do we?'

Lesley was quiet. She knew the signs pointed to her being the one with the secrets. But confessing would break Maxine's heart and break the circle of friends. Perhaps that was what these cards were all about? Someone envied their friendship and wanted to smash it into a million dagger-like pieces.

Chapter Twenty-Seven

At The Magpie, Katie felt like she'd worked behind the bar forever. Ged was singing her praises. 'You're a natural, you are, love,' he said as he came and stood by her side. She was getting great tips too. Maybe her low-cut blouse was helping with that, but she didn't care as long as she was making some money. Katie had a way with the punters, talking to them all, laughing and joking, making them feel like she cared about each and every one of them. One old bloke, who had introduced himself as Simon, had been propping the bar up all night long and every time he saw that Katie wasn't busy he would beckon her over for a chat. He told her he'd lost his wife the year before and she could see it in his eyes that he was heartbroken. Katie got Simon another shot of brandy and placed it next to him. 'Make this your last one, Si. You can barely stand up and I'll get in trouble from Ged if I serve you any more. You've fell from your seat twice already.'

'Oh, you'll get the measure of Ged. His bark is worse than his bite. He knows what I'm like. I'm only drowning my sorrows, I won't cause any bother. It doesn't go away; heartache is there twenty-four hours a day. Grief is a silent killer, you know. My Judy was my life and what am I supposed to do without her?'

Katie leaned over the bar. 'I can't imagine how it feels to lose someone you've shared your life with for that long, but I do know what heartache is, Simon. I've loved and lost, too. My mam died about five years ago and I've never felt pain like it. It's a numbness, an emptiness in your heart, isn't it? You don't ever forget them, but you learn to live with the loss. Come on, your Judy will be looking down at you now thinking, what the hell is he doing getting drunk like this all the time, won't she?'

He lifted his eyes up to the ceiling. 'She sure will be. She'd be right at me, telling me to sort myself out, she would. She was a lovely soul and had the biggest heart ever. When we first met, I knew she was going to be my wife. Honest, I felt it in my heart. It was love at first sight.'

Katie smiled. Maybe that was what she and Jake were feeling. It's just that their first sight had been over twenty years ago at school. He'd already told her he'd fancied her even back then. He'd gone as far as telling her that on the prom night he was all ready to come over and declare his undying love for her. But just as he found the courage to come, he spotted her snogging the face off Paul Tyson. Katie remembered. Prom night was the night that loads of the girls lost their virginity, and Katie was no different: she led Paul Tyson to a quiet cupboard and had sex with him.

It hadn't been all hearts and flowers, but she was glad she'd got it out of the way. Lesley had sex too that night, but she'd never revealed who had taken her virginity, even to this day – said she was ashamed and that she'd rather forget it. When she told her mates she was pregnant and still only sixteen, the friends had taken to guessing. Maxine and Katie figured maybe it was the PE teacher who she had a crush on – she'd keep schtum if she thought she was protecting him from getting fired.

Katie wondered now if she'd missed out on love for the last twenty years – she could have been married to Jake for all this time if she hadn't decided to drop her drawers for Paul Tyson. 'Simon, can I ask you something?' she asked now. 'What did you look for in a wife, what was it about your Judy you loved?'

'Don't get me started, I could go on all night. But, if you want to know, what I noticed was that she was a real lady. She was good-mannered. Not a potty mouth like so many folk you hear today – always loud and brash and shouting the odds.'

Katie inhaled deeply. She was the woman old Simon was describing. Maybe she could calm it down, be more ladylike, treat Jake nicely instead of effing and jeffing around him, ready to kick off.

'I'll tell you what really matters,' Simon continued. 'It's the little things that count. We didn't just tell each other we loved one another – we showed it. A cup of tea at the end of a long day, never going to bed on an argument, letting someone know they're the centre of your world. Now that's love, isn't it?'

These were wise words from this old-timer, ones she would take on board. Before she could ask for more, Ged was at her side and he patted her bum as he spoke. 'A few people at the other end of the bar need serving, Katie.'

Katie remembered his lecture on morals with the clients. Why then did this creep think they didn't apply to staff? She breathed in as she passed him, but he didn't move an inch, making her slide past him to reach the waiting drinkers.

As the last few customers left the boozer, Katie poured herself a large pink gin. She'd been rushed off her feet these last few hours and, as soon as she sat down, she kicked her shoes off and rubbed her feet. First day of work completed and she'd earned some money at last.

Ged sighed 'Punters, eh? I much prefer my pub when they've all gone home.'

'We'd be stuck without them, though,' said Katie.

'Yes, but it's nicer just you and me, Katie, don't you think? Oh, did you not get me a drink?'

Katie blushed. 'Sorry. I wasn't sure if you were having one.'

'What, a pretty woman in my company and I'm not going to have a drink with her? Come on, Katie, pull the other one.'

Katie thought Ged was going to pour himself something, but instead he sat back and watched as Katie served him. She quickly checked her watch then pulled her sleeve down over it. It was nearly one o'clock in the morning. Jake had been messaging her all night long and he was eager to see her when she was free next. She'd tried not to let her new boss see her on her phone, so she was looking forward to getting home and sending some messages back. But Ged plonked down next to Katie and looked like he was settling in for a chat.

'You have done well here tonight, Katie. I didn't think you would hack it. And I'm glad I ignored some of the comments from the men here, because you're lovely.'

Katie nearly choked on her drink and eyeballed Ged. 'Comments like what?'

Ged smirked at her and placed his large, heavy hand on her thigh. 'Come on, Katie, you've got a name around here for being a bit of a goer.'

'Goer! Cheeky bastards. Who are they to say that about me when they don't even know me? Don't get me wrong, I've had a few relationships, but I'm not a slapper. In fact, I have a boyfriend now and I've not got eyes for anyone else. Brad Pitt could walk in, order a shandy and I'd not bat an eyelid. So do me a favour and tell these so-called men that they can do one. I'm very particular about the guys that I date.'

Ged necked the rest of his drink. He stood up. 'I'll get us another drink, shall I?' Katie declined the offer and started to put her shoes back on. It had taken the shine off the night, knowing she was being gossiped about. How dare people speak like that about her behind her back? Ged placed his fresh drink on the table and gripped her by the waist. 'Don't be going yet. The night is still young, and we could have a good time here. Come on, Katie, we all know you love a bit of slap and tickle.'

Katie tried to walk away, but his grip was tight and she panicked as she used all her strength to push him away.

'Ged, piss off, will you. I work here and that's it. What makes you think you can touch me like this? You're out of order.'

Ged was at her again, gripping her tighter, the heat of his hands on the bare skin at her waist where her top was rucked up, then he was kissing her neck, biting at it. 'You love it. Come on, relax and have a good time.'

Katie was flung to the floor and Ged was on top of her trying to get his pants down. 'Get off me, you dirty bastard. I swear, Ged, I'll ring the dibble on you. Take your dirty fucking hands from me now!

Ged was a dead weight on top of her and she felt like she was suffocating underneath him. With any strength she had left in her body, she flailed about and finally swung her knee into his crotch. Ged screamed out in pain and rolled from her, holding himself between his legs and yelling she'd maimed him. Katie was up from the floor in an instant, already panicking how she would be able to get out of the pub. She'd seen him lock up and put the bolts on the door, and he was already up on his knees yelling curses at her. She ran at Ged and booted him right in the stomach. He rolled back over, winded. There was no way this big lummocks was getting up for a minute now. She only needed enough time to slip the bolts. 'You big dirty sleaze, who do you think you are? Do you treat all your bar staff like this? I'm a mother, I don't want guys like you out in the world my daughter's growing up in. I won't let you get away with this. So you can expect a knock on the door from the police. Attempted rape, this is.' Katie grabbed her handbag and the key from the table and sprinted to the front doors. Her hands were shaking as she twisted the key, heart pounding inside her ribcage.

It was pitch-black outside as she let the heavy pub doors slam behind her. It felt like a dark black cloak had been spread across the sky. Rain was hammering the pavements. Katie was crying her eyes out as she headed down the road, letting the rain mingle with her tears. She wasn't stopping for love nor money. The traffic was quiet and there wasn't a soul about. She didn't know if it should make her relieved or afraid. Her feet pounded the pavement, and she ran from the pub feeling better for every metre she put between her and that place. 'Bastard, bastard,' she sobbed quietly.

Katie had been running for over ten minutes and she was gagging for breath when she finally stopped in a bus shelter. She dropped her head into her hands. Her body was shaking, and her sweat felt cold on her skin as shock gripped her all over. She had been in enough scrapes – blokes catcalling her, swinging a punch or two in fights, even fighting off a mugger once – but she'd never experienced anything like this in her life before. If she told a man no, then that was it, it should have been enough. Was this her own fault, she asked herself now, had she given him the wrong signals, was her blouse too low, was she asking for it? No, that kind of thinking had gone out with the ark. Ged wasn't going to make her feel guilty or tarnished just because he put his greasy, unwanted hands on her.

Katie held her head up and looked at the silver moon in the night sky. A big bulky tear steamed down her cheek. She reached inside her handbag and rang Maxine, her hands still shaking. Her friend would still be awake at this hour, she bet. Since Ian had left, Maxine had told them she was having difficulties sleeping, always awake in the midnight hour. Katie stuttered as Maxine answered her call almost straight away. 'Katie, calm down, what's happened?'

Katie was still sobbing and she couldn't get her words out properly. 'Please come and pick me up, Max. I'm on Oldham Road near the petrol station. Hurry up, Maxine, please, come quick.' Katie ended the call and searched in her bag for her vape. Once it was in her hands, she sucked and sucked on it until she could get control of the sobs that had been coming in waves. She knew she should have been on the blower to the police, reporting everything the landlord had done to her: this was sexual assault, plain and simple. But she needed a friendly face first, someone to steady her while she decided what to do next.

Maxine pulled up on the edge of the road as she spotted Katie at the bus stop. She honked her horn and sat forward in her seat. What the hell had gone on? Her head was doing overtime. Katie ran to the passenger door and yanked it open. Once she was inside, she slammed the door shut behind her, checking over her shoulder. 'Drive, Maxine, just drive and get me as far from this place as possible.'

Maxine shot a look at her friend and knew not to speak. She clocked that buttons were missing from her blouse and her make-up was smeared. She reached over and patted Katie's knee. 'You're safe now, love, you're safe.'

Katie gave her a small nod, her body shaking from head to toe. 'I'll tell you when we get home. Please just drive, just drive.'

Safely inside Maxine's house, with the door locked behind them, Katie chugged hard on her vape, hands still trembling. 'He said all the men call me a goer, Maxine.'

'Who did?'

'Ged the fucking landlord, that's who. He's just tried raping me. His hands all over me, touching me, kissing me.'

Maxine snarled. 'Fuck off, you mean the owner of The Magpie?'

'Yes, him. He locked up and thought he would stand a chance with me, the pervy sweaty bastard. I can't go back there ever now. I'm debating ringing the police on him.'

'Debating! Bloody ring them and have him arrested. What he's done to you is not right. How tapped in the head is he to think he can treat you like this and get away with it? And, if he's tried it on you, I bet you're not the first.'

Katie's voice was low as she replied, 'Do you think it's my fault? Look at the way I'm dressed.'

Maxine dragged Katie's face up to look at her. 'Are you for real, girl? It doesn't matter if you were dressed in your bra and knickers, no man has the right to touch you unless you say so. No means fucking no.'

'He was so strong, Maxine. I thought I was never going to get him off me. If I hadn't found the strength to knee him, he would have raped me for sure. He was trying to get his pants down.'

'I'm ringing the police, Katie. That pervert wants locking up.'

Maxine started to look for her mobile phone when Katie lunged to stop her. 'No! Leave it. I don't want anybody to know about this. It'll be in papers if I take him to court. People will judge me, say it's my own fault. And what about Jake? Just when I've found someone who's decent this happens. No, put the phone away and sit back down. I'll be fine soon. It's only the shock of it right now. I want to think things through. I might call the cop shop in the morning. But I'm back to square one now, though, aren't I? No bloody job, no money.'

Maxine cuddled her tightly in her arms. 'You poor thing, what a thing to face when you were just trying to do your job. You've been through a terrible ordeal that no woman should ever have to go through.'

Katie pulled away from Maxine and looked her directly in her eyes. 'I may be a wreck right now, but I'll be fine. There is more than one way to deal with people like Ged. I want him to know what it feels like when someone bigger and stronger than you comes at you. First thing in the morning, I want you to get in touch with your Tony and tell him what has happened. You know the score. If they want paying, then I will pay them, but I want that pervert to feel as scared as I did tonight.'

Chapter Twenty-Eight

Maxine quickly checked her text messages when she was on her break in work. Clare, her line manager, was on the prowl, she was forever coming into the canteen checking on the workers. She forbade any staff looking at their phones on the shopfloor, so she was glad to get an update. She had spoken with her brothers the day before and now the deed was done.

Just after closing last night, her brothers had gone to The Magpie and dealt with Ged. The pub would not be open for a few days at least, windows smashed, optics shattered, barstools launched across the room, apparently. Maxine's brothers were ruthless, and they wouldn't have simply given him a talking to. No, they would have kicked his arse good and proper for groping a woman who didn't want to be touched. Maxine texted Katie and told her not to worry anymore. The score was settled and Ged would think twice before he man-handled any other woman who had told him no. Maxine sat down and sipped her coffee.

Why did she have no problem sending in the heavies to save a friend, but she hadn't been able to do it for herself once and for all? Shame could be as powerful as fear, she realised now. She determined that she'd never let it control and silence her again.

She only had ten minutes left of her lunch break and then it was back to the shopfloor, dealing with customers who couldn't make their minds up. How hard could it be to pick a bottle of perfume? It wasn't like they were buying a house. She could tell the window-shoppers from the serious buyers, had learnt to focus her time on the shoppers that might lead to her commission bonus being better that month. The worst customers were those who treated the whole thing like they were professionals – wafting their hands around, claiming to smell cedar or wet moss in a perfume Maxine knew damn well was made in a factory, next to the washing up liquids and loo cleaners. They were the ones who asked for the coffee beans to sniff before they smelt another fragrance, trying to protect their delicate noses. Then there were the men who were buying perfumes for their bits on the side. Maxine could tell them a mile off: always edgy, wanted to be in and out of the store as quickly as possible before they were spotted. If they were clever, they always bought two of the same – one for their wives and one for their mistress – that way neither could accuse the rat of smelling of another woman. Maybe Ian had been to another store and bought a fragrance for Donna. Her blood boiled thinking about it. It killed her to think of Donna wearing the same perfumes she did, smelling like her while she did the dirty. She grimaced – she needed to rid her mind of this picture she had formed in her mind, before she went berserk. She scrolled through her photographs and stared at images of her and her husband in better days. She looked at a snap of when they first met. How young did they both look? She had a dodgy perm, and her fringe was massive; even the way they were dressed made her cringe. She felt sorrow grip her body as she looked at more photographs. This wasn't helping. Why was she torturing herself this way? She should have deleted the lot of them. Somebody came into the room behind her, and she quickly placed her phone back in her bag.

'Are you alright, Clare?' Maxine asked her line manager. Her boss shook her head as two security men entered too.

Clare coughed to clear her throat before she spoke. 'Maxine, can you take your belongings and go with these two gentlemen, please? This is a routine search as I've had several anonymous calls telling me members of my staff are stealing from the store.'

Maxine's windpipe closed up, restricting her breathing, her cheeks felt hot. 'Yes, no worries. I'll just finish my cuppa and I'll be with you. I am on my break still, you know.'

Clare's voice was raised as she stepped closer to her employee. 'No, Maxine, you need to go now. If everything is fine, then I will give you the time back later.'

Maxine was in a panic, she'd not long concealed two perfumes in her large handbag. Her heart was thumping, and she made no eye contact. She slowly picked her handbag up and grumbled at her boss. 'Where do you get off treating people like criminals? I've got rights, you know. I bet you love this.'

Her manager held a hand up at Maxine. 'I don't want to hear any abuse, Maxine. A lot of workers are getting searched today, so I'm not singling you out. It's all above board and head office know about it.'

'I don't want those goons putting their hands all over me. I'd rather quit. You can shove your job up your arse. I'm going to leave and, as for being searched, you can piss off. What kind of a person do you take me for, anyway?'

The security guards stepped closer to Maxine and the larger of the men spoke. 'It will take a few minutes of your time. If you have nothing to hide, then it shouldn't be a problem, should it? One way or another you won't be leaving here today unless we have carried out a search on you. You're still on company premises and we've had a legitimate tip-off.'

Maxine dumped her handbag on the table and started to pull out random objects and throw them down. 'See, nothing in here but bits of make-up and a hairbrush.' Maxine side-eyed the guards. She'd stashed the perfumes deep in her bag where the lining was ripped. 'What do you want me to do – open up my toiletries bag?' Maxine waved a purse full of pads at the men.

The guard stepped to the table and held his hand out. 'No, that's fine, but can I double-check the main bag?' He didn't give her time to reply, but snatched the bag and pulled it towards him. Maxine stood with both her hands on her hips, hoping they'd just do the kind of cursory check you got at concerts or theatres. 'Well, this will be getting reported to the top. Do they know this is how employees are treated?'

Clare was silent, staring at the handbag. One by one, the perfumes were pulled from inside. All eyes were on Maxine now. She stuttered, her face beetroot, 'I don't know where they have bleeding come from. Somebody must have put them there. On my life, I didn't know they were there. This is a set-up, for sure. Come on, you've never liked me, I bet you stashed them there.'

Her manager was calm as she watched Maxine start to pace around the room in a panic. 'I'll leave her here with you, gentlemen. I'll go and inform the police.'

Maxine shouted out. 'The police, for what? This is a big mistake. Someone is out to get me. You know me, go on, tell them I'm a trustworthy person and I've worked here for years.'

Her manager started to back out of the room, a look of disgust in her eyes as she shook her head.

Maxine had been escorted out of work by the two officers who had come for her. They let her keep her dignity by taking her out from a side door instead of using the main door. Maxine was crying, though she'd given up on pleading her innocence. As soon as she got into the police station, though, she calmed down. It was as if she could pretend it wasn't real. *Twenty-Four Hours in Custody* was one of Maxine's favourite television programmes and she now realised she'd learnt a lot from it. She never thought in a month of Sundays that one day she'd be here like the people she'd watched on the box, but now she found she knew her rights and was demanding to make a phone call.

She tried to imagine it was all just for tv, that it wasn't her life. She didn't protest as all her property was taken from her and she was escorted to a small cell with just a toilet and a small blue mattress. She was relieved that the police officer who was dealing with her was quite sympathetic. 'It's quiet in here for now, love. Hopefully we can have you in and out after you have been interviewed, before all the nutters come in at night. That's something nobody needs to see, let me tell you. Shouting, screaming, booting doors, enough to make your toes curl.'

Maxine hesitated walking to the cell. She froze as she got to the door – if she said anything to this officer, would it count against her? 'Somebody planted those perfumes in my bag, I said that to my boss.'

The officer raised his eyebrows high and sighed. 'Listen, if I had a pound for everyone who come in here telling me they were innocent, I would be a rich man. I'm only doing my job. I don't make the decisions, I just follow the orders. If you want my honest opinion, you don't look like one of those people that work for the organised gangs, the ones who steal to order. If you're only a petty thief, you'll be in and out – we haven't got the resources to bang up every small-time crook.'

Maxine was trying to reply but the officer's words were ringing in her ears. A petty thief? A small-time crook? Was that who she was now? She thought about how, only this morning, she'd pledged never to feel shame again. It turned out it hit differently when you were ashamed of your own actions, rather than someone else's. She wanted to grab the copper by the collar and tell him she was a good person really, going through a bad patch, making bad choices, but he looked at her blankly, opened the door fully and waited for her to step inside.

'How long will I be here for? When will they interview me? I still haven't made my phone call. I need to let my friend know I'm here. Can somebody phone her, please?' Her words fell on deaf ears. The large iron door slammed shut behind her, shaking the room. Maxine stood pummelling her rounded fist into the back of the door. 'Did you hear me? I need to let somebody know where I am.' Her legs buckled underneath her as she slid slowly down the closed door. Her head fell into her hands and her shoulders shook as she cried. There it was – just when she thought she'd been at her lowest and loneliest after leaving Ian, she'd found a new low, and she'd brought it on herself. 'Help me, please, somebody help me,' she snivelled.

It must have been at least four hours after Maxine had been arrested that somebody finally came to her door and opened it. She was sat on the edge of the bed and alert. 'It's freezing in this place. Am I going home now or what?'

The female officer led her out of her cell and down a small corridor. She opened the door to a room and told her to go and sit down. A duty solicitor had been appointed for her, the officer told her, and he was due there at any second. Maxine sat down and looked around the room, tapping her fingers on the wooden table.

The interview didn't last very long, half an hour at most. Maxine had decided while she was waiting that she'd better stick to her story and deny any knowledge of the stolen goods. Surely, they didn't have proof it was her. Okay, it was her bag but the bottles could have been planted. The interview was coming to an end and Maxine asked a question. 'My line manager said there was an anonymous phone call reporting theft in my workplace, is that correct?'

The interviewing officer read through his notes and confirmed this was true.

'Can I ask if this was a female or a male who reported it?' Her solicitor intervened and stopped any further conversation. 'Maxine, we can talk about this later, but for now do you understand everything that has been said and know the charges you are facing?'

'Of course I do. I'm innocent until proven guilty, aren't I? So do your job and get me out of this place.'

The officers left the room and Maxine couldn't wait to talk to her solicitor. 'How long will they keep me in here? I've had nothing to eat and I'm freezing in that cell.'

'It shouldn't be long now. The officers will speak to the Crown Prosecution Service, and they will make a decision on what and if you are being charged with anything.' The solicitor started to close his briefcase and stood up. 'I'll tell them to hurry up if they can. Once you have been charged, I will know more, and I'll be in touch with you.'

He shook her hand and left the room. Maxine's eyes welled up at that human contact. How could she tell her family and friends where she had been and that she was a thief? It was mortifying. But something was lying heavy on her mind. Who had made the phone call to her work? Was this the same person who had sent her the gold envelope or what? One thing for sure was that somebody out there was out to get her and her friends. The girls needed to do something and fast before that somebody played their next ace.

It was Katie who came to pick Maxine up. As soon as she walked out of the police station, she hugged her tightly. 'Bleeding hell, Max, this is not what you need right now. How many times have we told you to knock it on the head? There are other ways to get money, and remember you need to be on at Ian to help with the bills too.'

Maxine started walking to the car. Raging inside, she was. 'I know, but I just got used to the money, didn't I? It gave me little extras – helped pay for my holidays, clothes, nights out – and once I'd kerbed Ian, it saved me from going cap in hand to him. And you know what it's like round here, everyone's doing it. You can't walk into a pub without someone offering you some bargain – doesn't matter if it's a pair of Nikes or a fillet steak, there's always stuff falling off the back of lorries. I think that's why I thought I'd get away with it – it wasn't hurting anyone, and no one else seems to get nicked.'

Katie opened the car door and Maxine jumped into the passenger side. Once they were both inside, Katie flicked the engine over and turned the heating on full. 'I couldn't believe it when you rang me and told me what had happened. It's not your finest hour, I know, but it's also not like you have stolen millions of pounds, is it? You will probably get a fine at court and a slap on the wrist. Half the kids on our estate have been caught on CCTV robbing from the newsies and they just get barred from the store.'

Maxine turned and faced Katie. 'It's not like that. Somebody rang in and said I was stealing. Obviously, it was anonymous, but I've got my ideas about it.'

Katie whistled. 'What a grass. Who would do something like that and, more to the point, who knew you were taking stuff?'

'My point exactly. It could be Ian or the same person who has been sending those gold cards. I've sold perfumes to quite a few people in the pubs, but I can't see them dobbing me in, can you? They're usually glad I'm selling the real deal, not selling them the knock-off stuff that smells like cat's piddle.'

Katie shook her head. 'You're right. I bet it's Ian. He knows you rely on selling a few bottles here and there, and when he realised you weren't going to take him back, I bet he got the green-eyed monster and stuck you in it. What a Judas.'

'I know Ian is a joke of a man, but would he really stoop that low and have me lose my job and be arrested?' Maxine looked thoughtful. 'He must know I've not reported him for domestic violence yet, and surely he'll think that, if he shops me, I'll tell them about what he did. I've got pictures I took on my phone, messages.'

'Yeah, it's a risky move, isn't it. At least, you're out. Now we can get to the bottom of it all. I can stay over, if you want. There is nothing worse than dealing with stuff on your own.'

'Thanks, Katie, you're right. I don't want to be alone tonight. My head is all over the place, thinking all sorts.'

Katie pulled off into the traffic. She wanted to support her friend, but it was also true that she didn't want to go home tonight to her empty house – her gas had run out and she was potless, no money to even warm her home. Katie knew if she didn't find work soon, she would be evicted because she couldn't pay the rent. Maybe she could sell the car, she thought? But it was leased and she owed more on it. They'd likely take that too next month when she missed a payment. She sat waiting in the traffic at the lights and looked at the row of shops on her left-hand side. 'Look at that place, the agency. They are always advertising for cleaners in their window. I might call in tomorrow and see if they have any hours going.'

Maxine stretched so she could see. 'You and me both, Katie. I'm unemployed now too. Who's going to hire me if I've got a conviction for theft? As if I needed this to happen when I'm going through what I'm going through. I'd better bloody get a job before the courts hang me out to dry.'

Katie started to drive as the lights changed. 'Welcome to my world, Max. I take one step forward and two steps back in anything I do. The only thing that seems to be going well at the moment is me and Jake, but I won't hold my breath; no doubt he will piss off soon, just like all the others have.'

'Stop being so hard on yourself, Katie. You've just had bad luck with men in the past. Look at me, I've been with the same man for years and he's pissed off with that scrubber, Donna. I wish he would have done this at the start of our marriage. At least then I would have been young enough to start again. Do you know how hard it is to be on your own after splitting up with somebody you've spent over twenty years with? Nothing feels right. It's like I've lost a limb. Even doing the big shop is strange. I made two cups of tea the other day. It's everything, just knowing somebody is at home with you calms you down. What's my life going to be now, Katie? One-night-stands and the odd date? Come on, let's face it, who wants a woman my age when all those glammed-up young things are out there hunting for an older man with money?'

Katie burst out laughing. 'Wow, try and be a bit positive. Yes, life will be hard at first, but you will get used to it. At least you're not getting cheated on and slapped around. Come on, do you want to jump straight into a relationship again, or are you down for some fun, no strings attached?'

Maxine let out a large, laboured breath and held her head back. 'My life is just going from bad to worse at the moment. I look different but on the inside I'm still the same old me. I like routine, I don't like change.'

'Well, change is going to happen, and you will have to get used to it, fact. It's just the fear of the unknown, Max. I promise you, give it a few months and you will love the single life.'

'I hope so, Katie. Ian's still texting and phoning me all the time, and the other night I was that weak that I was going to tell him to come back home. I mean, people work through their problems, don't they?'

Katie pulled up outside Maxine's house. 'If you ever, ever, get that urge again, just think of seeing him with his tongue halfway down Donna Ramsey's throat. He's a born cheat, Max, he's not changing his spots now.'

Chapter Twenty-Nine

Jane stared at the huge wall clock that decorated one wall in her living room. She would have done anything to stop the ticking hands and pause time. Every tick, tick, tick brought her nearer to events she was dreading. Even surrounded by her friends, she felt so alone. They'd planned to go round to Maxine's to cheer her up after her run-in with the police, but when Tommy had said he was going to work that night – apparently, he had a meeting with some big boss who could put a lot of work his way – the girls met at Jane's as usual. All the friends were sat down together but, instead of their usual chat and shrieks of laughter, the room was quiet. They were all thinking about their own problems and pondering the unspoken question – who was it who was out to get them?

As usual, Katie decided she would be the one to lighten the mood. She passed Maxine her mobile phone. 'Max, look, I set you up on this dating app. It's easy, you have three swipes so, if you like the look of them, you can get talking to them and arrange a date.'

Maxine nearly choked on her drink. 'Me on a date? Stop it. I'm nowhere near ready for a date. I need to get my head sorted, let alone my body. I'll have to go on a diet first, tone up. Anyway, who's going to want to date a convict like me?'

'You're always looking on the negative. Come here and have a look. See what you think.'

Maxine sat next to Katie and watched the screen as Katie zoomed in on the profile pics. 'Ew, you can't be serious, he's got a monobrow and looks like he's never seen a toothbrush. Look at the state of his teeth. Don't swipe him. In fact, is there a block button?'

Katie grinned at Maxine's wide-open eyes as she looked at the next profile picture. Tall, dark, handsome, same age as she was, lived nearby, he was ticking all her boxes. 'Oh, he's fit. I wouldn't kick him out of bed, for sure.' Before Maxine could say another word, Katie swiped the profile so the man could send her a message.

Maxine squawked. She got on the floor and started to do a few sit-ups. The girls roared laughing as they watched her.

Katie shouted out, 'He's messaged you already, Max! Should I open it?'

Maxine rolled on her side to get up from the floor. 'No, wait for me, wait.'

The girls gathered around the phone and stared at the screen. Maxine opened the message – a picture, not a text. She examined the photograph, turning the phone one way and then the other, not sure what it was at first. Once she knew, she dropped the phone and jumped up out of her seat. Lesley covered her mouth with both hands and Jane bit down hard on her lips so she wouldn't laugh. Katie just couldn't hold it in and burst out laughing. The man had sent a dick pic asking if she wanted to come for a ride. 'The dirty bastard. Why would he send me a pic of his tackle when he doesn't even know me?'

Katie was used to the dating apps and took it all in her stride. 'That's tame compared to some of the stuff I've had sent me. That's the only thing with these dating sites: you have to sift out the weirdos who are just on there for the kicks of sending women mucky pics. I've seen a lot of men on here who are married, too. Honest, Johnny Tartan from the Two Hundred estate is on all the dating apps. He's got a bloody wife and about four kids, but his profile says he's single and he's a fireman. He's a lazy fucker who's not worked a day in his life – he probably wouldn't even get off his arse to escape a burning building, let alone put out a fire. He's on the sick too – scrounging his way through life. I didn't have the heart to tell his Mrs I'd seen him on there. But, come on, someone will tell her eventually and let's see how he talks his way out of that one. Most guys who get caught cheating on it say someone's made a fake profile of them using their photographs. Believe that and you'll believe anything.'

Maxine was howling laughing as she picked up the phone to look at the snap again. 'Katie, how many men would you say you have slept with? You lot know I've only ever slept with Ian, and I can't imagine stripping off in front of anyone else. How do you do it – you know, pulling a stranger? You've probably had more fellas than I've had hot dinners.'

Lesley rolled her eyes, knowing Katie would lie and not admit to half of them.

'Cheeky. No, it's not a lot, no more than twenty.'

Jane spluttered on her wine and couldn't hold her tongue. 'You liar, Katie! You slept with twenty blokes before you were eighteen.'

Katie was up in arms defending herself. 'No way. Okay, about twenty-five but no more than thirty,' she chuckled.

There was loud knocking at the front door and Jane sat up straight. 'Lesley, go and see who it is, will you? Tell them I'm not well, if it's one of the neighbours.'

Lesley left the room and the others carried on talking.

Lesley rushed back into the room and the colour had drained from her face. 'You better come outside and see this.' The girls looked puzzled. 'I said get up and come and see our cars. The neighbour's just seen someone running off after they'd done it.'

Jane was up, tying her hair back with a bobble. Maxine went out first followed by Katie and then Jane and Lesley. They all rushed out to the garden and down the path to the road where they had parked. Who would do something like this? On all the girls' cars had been spray-painted the same words. Secrets, secrets.

Maxine was gobsmacked. Katie ran over to her car. Jane went to her own car and kicked the tyre. 'Who the fuck is doing this to us? Someone ring the police, because this is criminal damage. How dare anyone do this to our cars! I swear to God, if I get my hands on them, I'll do them in. Quick, Lesley, ring the police. I'll ring Tommy and see if he can get a few of the lads around here to search the area.'

Katie came to Jane's side and spoke in a low voice. 'Are you sure you want Tommy involved? Because the first thing he's going to ask is why someone is writing these words on all our motors. We can't pass this off as random. Think about it, we need to deal with this ourselves. Surely you know somebody who can come and take the cars away now and get it sorted?'

Maxine was by her side now too. 'I can't afford to have this removed. I've just lost my job and so has Katie.'

As per usual, Jane said she would foot the bill. Lesley was walking up and down the road and she'd found a spray can tossed in the bushes. Her heart was pounding; she realised things were getting serious now. Yes, she could cope with a card landing on her doormat, but this was on another level. The police needed informing about all of this, for sure, before somebody got hurt.

Jane watched as her car was towed away down the road. It was late in the evening now and each of them was in shock at what had just happened. They went back into the house and sat down on the sofas. Jane was furiously tapping at her phone. 'Why now? If it had been last week, we'd have had the Ring doorbell working and have half a chance of seeing it who it was. But Tommy took it down at the weekend, said the gutters were leaking into it.'

Maxine piped up. 'I bet it was Ian. He's probably followed me here and done this to get back at me. He's tapped in the head, he is.'

Lesley shook her head. 'Nope, this is the same as the cards and I don't see Ian going shopping for gold envelopes and silver hearts. It's got a woman's touch all over this – it puts Kimberley back in the frame. She knew I was coming here tonight. She'd called round to try and sweet talk her father again and I left them to it. I bet she's come here with her nutty friends and got them to help her.'

Katie scratched her head. 'It might be Ged. Maxine, he knows your brothers, and he will know that they know me. Maybe it's him.'

Jane slammed her palm down on the arm of the sofa. 'Use your loaf, Katie. It's not Ged. We barely knew the bloke when all this started. But it could still be Melissa Myers. You saw the look in her eye the other day when we were all together, she hates every single one of us with a passion. This has got her written all over it. She probably thinks she can mess with us all just because she saw me one time with Frankie. But why hasn't she already told Tommy, if she wants to hurt me? She could cancel the wedding like that.'

Katie walked over to the large front window and stared out into the night. 'Someone's out there laughing at us, and I don't like it. We need a plan. I say we go and see Melissa Myers, and Kimberley, and ask them outright. We'll tell them we know what they are doing and see what they say.'

'I'm not going anywhere near Angela and Kimberley. I wouldn't be able to keep my hands off them,' Lesley muttered. 'I say we report it – this is the first time they've actually caused some damage. As I see it, we don't have a clue who's doing this, do we? It's all guess work. We need to be extra vigilant and think about making it official with the police.'

'And what will that achieve? Bloody nothing,' Jane replied. 'They don't even come out when a house gets burgled anymore, so they'll do sod all about some graffiti on a couple of cars. They're not sending out Sherlock Holmes on the say-so of us women. No, if we want this sorting, we do it ourselves. The only thing we need to do is make sure none of us breathes a word. Cross your hearts and hope to die, it stays between us, because if anybody got wind of this, it could ruin us.'

Katie nodded. 'Especially you, Jane, because you're the one who's been really racking up the secrets recently. I know we all got cards but none of us have much to lose. I think we got cards because we're hiding your secret.'

Jane narrowed her eyes. 'Oh, go on, blame me for this, why don't you? I know for a fact you've all got something to hide – even if you don't admit it. Yes, I've fucked up, but at least I'm open about it with you lot. You three, you'd better take a long hard look at yourselves and ask if you really know the women in this room.'

Chapter Thirty

There were only three days left before the wedding and Jane was run ragged, but she couldn't slow down and rest. She was forever on the phone checking everything had been taken care of. It hadn't helped that they'd lost a whole evening of planning and sorting when they'd had to get their cars sorted. Katie had come up trumps – someone she'd had a fling with was saved in her phone as 'Kane – Car Guy' and, after Jane had put a fair wad of cash his way, the cars had been returned the next day. The girls pretended they'd had them valeted. But it meant that now Jane was further behind than ever. She was checking their playlist, waiting to hear if the florist had found the orange blossom she'd ordered, and wondering what she'd use for her 'something borrowed' and 'something blue'. She still wore her mum's wedding ring on a chain around her neck, and she was going to tie it onto her bouquet as her 'something old'. The only good thing about being rushed off her feet was it gave her less time to brood on the roiling guilt that lurked in the pit of her stomach all the time. She hoped getting hitched would put her doubts and shame to bed – but she couldn't be sure. So instead, she powered on through her To Do list.

Tommy meanwhile was lying on the sofa; he'd not moved all day. 'Having a chill day', he'd told her. On a rare day off work he usually just crashed out – either that or spent it in bed with Jane. He watched his fiancée. 'Jane, do you really need to be doing all this fussing about? Who needs chair covers and wedding favours? Surely, it's only a dress and a suit, some flowers for the church, a bit of grub and disco after. Honestly, no one cares about all the rest. If you got off the phone for more than two minutes, you could come over here and attend to your wifely duties. We haven't had sex for over a week now. Surely, you're still not on the rag?'

Jane sighed. 'Tom, sex is the last thing on my mind with everything going on. When this wedding is over, you can have as much action as you want.'

Tommy looked unimpressed. 'What's that saying about the bird in the hand and the bush?' He made a grab for Jane, but she dodged and threw a cushion at him. 'Babes, please bear with me. Everything will be back to normal soon, I promise you. We have both been busy; I thought the same about you. I know you work hard, but you've been in the gyms or head office dawn til dusk some days.'

'Maybe because you blow me out all the time. I might be getting sick of waiting about until you say you're ready. You should be glad I'm throwing myself into work rather than the arms of another woman...'

Jane knew he was right, and the guilt set in. She stared deep into his big blue eyes. How could she have risked everything for Frankie? 'Like I said, normal services will resume soon and we will be back on track.' She lay down next to him, cuddling him and smelling his skin. Tommy always smelt fresh, like clean laundry. 'Tom, do you think we will ever have children? I know you said wait til after the wedding, but it's something we need to address sooner or later.'

Tommy looked uncomfortable. 'There is no way I'm going having tests and them telling me what I already suspect. I'm a Jaffa. No man wants to admit that. Do you know how that would make me feel, knowing that I could never give you kids? I wouldn't feel like a real man anymore. It would do me in. I'd rather not know than see it in black and white.'

'Tom, don't be stupid. Lots of men have trouble downstairs, you're not on your own. We could go private; nobody would ever know, only me and you.'

'I don't want to even think about this. Why are you bringing it up now, just before we get married?' He pushed her away from him and jumped up, standing over her. 'That's what's been wrong with you, isn't it? Go on, say it. You've been having second thoughts about marrying me because I might not be able to give you a baby. Go on, spit it out, I can take the truth.'

Jane stood up. 'Why are you saying things like that? I've barely mentioned it before because I know you hate talking about it. I needed to ask the question, but it makes no difference to me if you can't have kids. I love you all the world and back again, and if we have to adopt or go surrogate, then that's fine.'

Jane led him back to the sofa and kissed the top of his head. 'Babes, just breathe. I love you, every inch of you, and we will never talk about this again. Like you have always said, if it happens, it happens.' She held his warm hand in hers. 'Right, enough misery. We are getting married in a few days. Let's stop being sad and stop worrying about shit before it happens. It is what it is, and this time next week we will be lying on a beach somewhere enjoying our honeymoon.'

Tommy picked her up and swung her around, his problems subsiding. 'Go and get ready – I'm taking my fiancée out for dinner. I'm starving,' he chuckled, back to his usual self.

Katie walked down the main road looking for the agency she'd seen that was looking for cleaners. She'd asked Maxine to come with her, but she refused, telling her she wasn't ready for work yet in case they asked for a criminal records check. She'd said her head was mashed with everything that was going on and needed time to decide what to do next. Time Katie couldn't afford. She only had about a day more on her electric before she'd be sitting in the dark as well as the cold. She looked at the sign above the shop: *Make your world All Perfect with AP Cleaners*. This was it. She straightened her wind-swept hair and took a deep breath before she stepped inside. She needed this job more than anything; she had only a couple of hundred quid left in her bank to last her the rest of the month. Universal Credit had paid her this to help her tide things over until she found work, and she had to get this job. Jade was coming around tonight to see her. She was bringing her new man to meet her, and she couldn't bear it if the power went out while her daughter was over. Katie wasn't looking forward to meeting Jade's boyfriend, if the truth was known. What was the point in playing happy families, acting like she was this happy-go-lucky woman, when in fact she was brassic, lonely and the victim of some kind of revenge feud?

Katie put on her best brave face and smiled at the receptionist as she walked towards the counter. 'I saw your notice in the window that you are looking for cleaners? I would like to apply, if that's alright. I'm looking for full-time hours, do you have that?'

The young woman smiled back at Katie. 'Yes, we have hours to suit. Firstly, can I ask you to fill out an application form and then we can take it from there. I'll print an application off for you, and you can sit down here to complete it or take it home and bring it back when it's done.'

'I'll stay and complete it, if that's alright?' Katie had no time to waste.

The woman went on her computer. 'I'll just print it out, take a seat.' Katie was starting to relax now. That hadn't been so bad, had it? The woman hadn't laughed at her or asked for experience or told her they had no vacancies. And, unlike at The Magpie, she wasn't at risk of being pawed. She looked around the room while she was waiting. It was a nice set-up here, lots of bright colours, pictures hung on the walls, nice décor.

Katie completed her application form and read through it one last time. She'd exaggerated a little on it, put down a few more qualifications than she really had, and she'd used all her best lines: told them she was trustworthy, could work as part of a team or on her own initiative, the usual crap she wrote when she was applying for a job. She put the lid back on the black biro, stood up and walked back to the counter. 'There you go, all completed.'

The receptionist took the application from her and read through it quickly. Katie stood watching her, nervous that she'd made a mistake on it or something. 'That's all fine. If you're not rushing, I can see if the manager has time to interview you?'

Katie had wanted it to move quickly, but she hadn't expected it to be this fast. 'Erm, yes, that will be great.'

The receptionist went into another room, holding the application in her hand. Katie wondered what they were going to ask – she hoped she would not have to do a demonstration? The receptionist was back, smiling, showing her pearly white teeth. 'Go through, the manager will see you now.'

Katie walked down the small corridor and was met by another door. She inhaled deeply and mumbled, 'Come on, Katie, you've got this. This could be your lucky day.' She knocked gently on the door and listened carefully for an answer.

'Come in,' a voice shouted from the other side of the door. Katie entered the room and could see a woman with her back turned to her.

'Take a seat, I will be with you in a second, I'm just looking for some envelopes,' the woman said.

Katie sat down, nervous now about what questions she might be asked. She was a good cleaner – kept her own home spick and span – but if they asked anything about health and safety, or wanted to know why she left her last job, she'd be stuffed.

The woman turned around, walked back to her desk and sat down. Katie looked directly at her and blinked. Was she seeing things or what? Was it Angela Potter sat right in front of her?

Angela smiled, recognising Lesley's friend. 'So, you're looking for work?'

Katie stuttered an answer, still not sure if she should stay here or not. She had the friend code to follow, and Angela was Lesley's arch enemy, so this was never going to work, was it? But she needed dough so badly. She knew what she had to do. She stood up. 'I was looking for work but not here with you. I didn't know this was your company.'

Angela chuckled and rolled her black biro around in her fingers. 'Just for the record, I wouldn't have given you a job anyway. Any friend of Lesley's is no friend of mine. She's a life-wrecking bitch, and the way she's treated my daughter is horrid.'

Katie tried for once to keep her cool. There was no way she was getting into a slanging match with this cow.

'Lesley is my friend and she's a lovely person, unlike you and your daughter. You can shove your job right up your arse.'

Katie walked to the door with Angela calling after her, 'One day, that wench will be back out on the street where she belongs. John has never stopped loving me, I can tell.'

Katie turned around and spoke through clenched teeth, her knuckles turning white as her fingers curled into two tight balls at her sides. 'You're delusional. There is something not right in your head, woman. John left you because you were a cheating skank. You left your kids with him so you could go out at night getting laid. Don't think I don't know about you, because I do.'

Angela came out from behind her desk and stood facing Katie now. 'Is that what your gullible mate told you? Don't make me laugh. He was the one who got caught with his pants down first, not me. Ask him about the receptionist. Yeah, go on. Dolly Mason she was called. Ask him about the late nights he used to work with her and what I caught him doing when I turned up one night unannounced. When I cheated, I was only giving him a taste of his own medicine.'

Katie was stuck for words for a few seconds. 'It means nothing to me. John loves Lesley and you need to get over it. Just let them be happy instead of always being there in the background causing bloody mayhem. You look like you're on to a good thing here – so leave them alone.' Katie twisted the gold door handle. Before she left, she turned around and snarled at Angela. 'And just for the record, love, Lesley is one of my best friends and, if you have beef with her, then you have beef with me. And, sweetheart, you don't want beef with me, because I'm not patient and peaceful like Lesley is. I will ruin you if you take me on. If you don't believe me, then test me.'

Angela was raging but she couldn't get her words out before Katie left the room.

Katie slammed the door shut and stormed into the reception area. She eyeballed the receptionist. 'I wouldn't work for that old hag if my life depended on it.' She stalked out of the building and headed back down the main road. There went her last chance of finding a job around here.

Chapter Thirty-One

Maxine lay in bed, restless. All night long she'd been tossing and turning. Her head was going to explode if she carried on like this, picturing herself in prison, Ian laughing at her. She gave up and sat upright. Sleep was a million miles away from her tonight and she came to terms with the fact that this was going to be a long night. She reached over and looked at her phone. Two o'clock in the morning. The hours past midnight were long and cold and she'd seen far too many of them recently. She picked up her book again and had another go at reading the novel she'd been trying to read for days. None of the words seemed to be sinking in, though, no sentences making any sense. It was a good book, one of her favourite authors, but she had no appetite for love stories anymore. The books always gave people a happy ending but, after recent events, she no longer believed in them. Love was a con, in her eyes now. She swore she would never fall in love again. She put her book back down and then froze as she heard a noise outside the bedroom. She tiptoed out of bed and held her ear to the door, listening carefully. Nothing. It was probably her mind playing tricks on her again. Ever since Ian had gone, she found it hard to settle each night, always jumping up at any noise she heard. There had been reports of break-ins and a carjacking in the area lately, and she felt like an easy target for any thieves now she was living on her own. She pulled the duvet almost over her head, trying to muffle her ears, and snuggled down. But the noises came again, floorboards creaking.

'Hello?' she shouted. There was no reply. Maxine felt sick. She clutched her phone, ready to dial 999. The bedroom door was opening slowly. What were they going to do? She had no jewellery worth nicking, nothing of any value at all. Maxine shouted out again. 'I've rang the police so, whoever you are, you better get out of here right now.'

The door opened fully, and Ian stood looking at her. There was a look in his eyes that told her he meant business. The look she'd seen before when he'd slapped her around for back-chatting him. 'This is what you have driven me to, breaking into my own fucking house. I've asked to speak to you time and time again and you are ignoring me like I've never existed. Listen to what I have to say, then I will go. *If* you're civil to me.'

Maxine wanted to scream, wanted to run, but she felt paralysed. 'Get out of here.' She managed to find the words. 'I swear to you, if you don't leave, I will have you arrested, you crank. How on earth did you get in here?'

Ian walked further into the bedroom and sat on the edge of the bed. 'Calm down, woman, what's all the shouting about? And ring the police if you want. This house belongs to me too, or are you forgetting that? You might have changed the locks, but you didn't change where you put your spare key, you daft cow, so I've not broken in.'

'I want you gone. You have nothing to say that I want to hear. Go and see if bleeding Donna Ramsey will listen to you, because your lies are wasted on me, let me tell you. No more the fool am I, Ian. I've finally seen you for the lying, conniving bastard you really are. I'm so over you, done with every dirty lying bone in your body.'

'Maxine, we were in a bad place, had been for a long time. Come on, you weren't interested in me anymore. I'm a man with needs. If you'd made more effort, I wouldn't have gone looking elsewhere.'

She poked her finger right in his face. 'You're a dirty twat who couldn't keep it in his pants, that's who you are. Go on, how many more have there been? Because this wasn't the first time, was it?'

Ian shook his head and looked away from her. 'That's all in your mind. I always said you were paranoid. Look, I married you when we were young. All the girls wanted me, back in the day, and I chose you. That must prove something to you.'

'Oh, don't do me any favours, Ian. You married me because my dad had a few quid and you knew he would put a little deposit down on this place, knew he'd help start you out in business. You just wait until my brothers hear about this. You'll be a dead man walking, trust me, so do yourself a favour and piss off before you make it any worse for yourself.'

For the first time that night, Ian listened. Clearly, the threat of violence was all that worked with him. 'Give me a break, Max. We've had a lot of good years. I've given you a nice life. The least you can do is overlook a few little slips. Tell you what: we can go on holiday, if you want, a nice break, just me and you?'

'Piss off. I wouldn't go to the toilet with you. Do you really think in that daft head of yours that a holiday will fix everything?'

'Well, how about this? It's Jane's wedding soon and I want us to go as a couple. If we have a good time that day, then we could try something else.'

Maxine laughed. 'You won't be coming to no bloody wedding. Jane is my friend, and she hates your guts after what you've done to me.'

'Tommy is my friend and I will be going to the wedding. He's paying for it all, so sod Jane, I'm not arsed what she says.'

'You have no respect for anyone, Ian. You should be hiding under a rock somewhere, ashamed of what you have done. But no, look at you, still trying to pass the blame. I want you gone now.'

'I'm going nowhere until I've said what I have to say.'

'I think you've said enough. Was it you who rang my works and told them I was having perfumes away? Because well done you. I've lost my job now because of you.'

Ian looked blank. 'What the hell are you babbling on about? I didn't make any phone call.'

Maxine teared up and started to tell him about her ordeal.

'Bleeding hell, Max. I'm sorry, sorry that I wasn't here supporting you. I've been a selfish prick. I didn't realise what I had until it was gone. Will you let me stay? Just for tonight? Can I just lie next to you? I swear I won't touch you. I only want to be near you. I would do anything to make this all go away, Max. Honest, you say it, and I'll do it.'

Maxine sat back in the bed. Ian had been her world since she could remember. Seeing him and hearing his words tonight cut her deep inside. Did she really want to move on? *Could* she move on and be with another man? She didn't think she could. It was all a big act in front of her friends, pretending she was up for dates and the single life when in fact she was still mourning the end of her marriage. It felt so easy to let him lie there. Believe his apologies. Maybe, she thought, it was true: better the devil you know.

Chapter Thirty-Two

One day to go until the wedding and everybody was working overtime. Everything was being double-checked, companies being rang to check there were no problems, outfits being ironed. Tommy and his best man, Gav, had booked into a hotel and left the girls to it.

Jane stopped for a moment and sat chugging on her vape, with Katie by her side sucking on hers too. Lesley and Maxine had gone out to pick up a takeaway and had been gone for twenty minutes.

Katie looked at Jane. 'I'm glad I've got you on your own. This has been doing my head in all day. I need to tell somebody and get it off my chest.'

Jane could tell by Katie's face that something was lying heavy on her mind. 'Are you alright, Katie?'

'No, love, I'm not. I found something out yesterday and I know I need to say something, but I need to run it by you first.'

'Go on then, what is it?'

Katie sat playing with her sleeve cuff, then looked directly at Jane. 'I went to apply for a cleaning job yesterday and the bloody firm ended up being Angela Potter's cleaning company. I nearly died a thousand deaths when I found out it was her who was interviewing me. Fuming, I was. I told her she could shove her job up her arse and that I would never work for her, ever. I said Lesley was my friend and that I had loyalty towards my friends.'

'I'm proud of you, babe. It would have been dead easy for you to take a job, especially because you're skint.'

'I know, but I kept thinking about those letters – and that it must be her daughter sending them – and it didn't sit right with me. Anyway, we got into an argument, and she started to slag us all off. What she told me next made me feel sick inside.'

'Why, what did she say?'

Katie closed her eyes. 'She told me that John had always been a player and, before Lesley, he had a bit of a thing with a young receptionist who worked for him. I hate to say it, Jane, but I had a gut feeling that she was telling the truth. I give her some abuse back when she laid into Lesley, but she said she only started seeing other men after she found out her husband had been sleeping around. She hates us all, detests every single one of us. I really think it's Kimberley sending the cards.'

Jane picked up her vape again and took another drag. 'So, do we tell Lesley or what? Because I would want to know something like this, wouldn't you?'

Katie thought about it. 'It would break her in two. All it will do is mess with her head. Imagine knowing something like this after what's happened. No, let's keep tight-lipped about this.'

'I'm with you,' said Jane. 'We'll keep an eye on things and, if we see any dodgy dealings, we'll tell Lesley straight away. It could all be fantasy.'

Katie felt relieved, the burden on her shoulders lifting. 'That's a great idea. I'll watch him tomorrow at the wedding. If he's lying about anything, I will be able to see right through him.'

Maxine and Lesley returned, and soon the girls all sat around the table. Jane pulled off a large slice of pizza and rammed it into her mouth. She'd not had a bite to eat since throwing up her breakfast.

Maxine was picking at her food and not really eating. She took a sip from her wine glass and coughed to clear her throat. 'If we're not keeping secrets, then I might as well come clean: Ian was at the house last night. I woke up and he was at the end of my bed.'

Lesley threw her hands in the air. 'The weirdo! I hope you rang the police on him, had the prick arrested?'

Maxine looked down at the table. What she was about to say would shock her friends and she was hesitant. 'He said he wants to take me away on holiday, fix what he has broken. I told him about losing my job, about waiting to see what happens on the shoplifting charge. He said he's realised how badly he's treated me and wants to make amends.'

Katie let out a sarcastic laugh. 'How can he fix what he's done? He can't un-shag Donna Ramsey, can he?'

Maxine looked up briefly, hated that she had to be reminded about her husband's infidelity. Jane, keenly aware of what she might say to Tommy if he found out about her affair, was more cautious, ignoring Katie's words and urging Maxine to continue.

'He said we can try again, start dating each other, going for meals like we did in the good old days. That's if I don't get banged up for theft.'

Katie squeezed her friend's hand. 'They won't send you down for a first offence like this, Max. You need to tell them the strain you were under – just left an abusive husband, previous good character, all that. It's not like you're a criminal mastermind, is it? The jails are full of really nasty pieces of work at the moment – drugs dealers, armed robbers, sex offenders – you don't belong there. Sure, you did something daft, but I think, when the magistrate takes one look at your haunted face, they'll know you will never step out of line again. The most dangerous thing you're likely to do isn't going back on the rob – it's letting that waster of a husband back into your home.'

'Rein it in, Katie,' Jane said. She knew she was the only one on Maxine's side when it came to deciding if Ian could change his ways, and was ready to back her friend in listening to her heart. After all, wouldn't she want Tommy to do the same?

But Lesley chimed in, 'Forget about the cheating, Max. You have to make up your own mind on that. What bothers me more is how he treats you generally. I know you've never told us as much, but I swear he's laid hands on you. We're only thinking about you, Maxine. That man humiliates and belittles you. In fact, the way he's spoken to you for years has made my blood boil. He shows you no respect whatsoever and he's lucky I've not punched his lights out.'

'He said he will change; I have to give him the benefit of the doubt, don't I? He's never admitted anything has been his fault in the past, ever. This could be him turning over a new leaf.'

Katie wasn't buying it, and it was clear from her tone of voice that she thought Maxine was making a big mistake. 'You've not even been on a date with anyone else yet. Don't jump back in too quickly until you've seen how a real man treats you. It doesn't have to be serious. Have some fun like he did and set the record straight. Why should you have to lie there each night with him in your bed, knowing he's slept with somebody else? No, go and sleep with another man and see if the grass is greener. At least go on a date before you go rushing back to him.'

'I haven't gone rushing back, I'm telling you where we are at. Katie, I'm not like you. I can't just go and sleep with some random guy. I'm shy.'

'You weren't shy when you were on holiday. You were out from under his shadow, eyeing up all the talent in Benidorm. You even let that fella kiss you.'

'Exactly. *He* kissed *me*, and I pulled away. I wasn't going looking. It meant nothing. For me, if I sleep with someone, it has to mean something. I'd be putting my heart on the line – and at the moment it's still full of Ian. You know what it's like when you can't get someone out of your head, don't you?'

'I know what we're talking about, Maxine, I'm not daft. I'm only saying let him sweat. Variety is the spice of life, after all.'

Jane could see these two would never agree and she jumped in before Maxine could reply. 'Girls, give it a rest, will you? I'm getting married tomorrow, and I don't need us lot arguing and falling out. Maxine, do what's best for you and we will support whatever you decide, but if you think Ian shows one single sign of getting mean or aggressive, you tell us immediately.'

Maxine smiled over at Katie. 'I will, Jane, and thank you.'

There was knocking at the front door. Jane went to the front window and could see a man holding something in his hands. She rushed out of the living room to open the front door. The man passed her a box and started to walk down the garden path. Everything she'd ordered for tomorrow had already arrived. She shouted after him, 'Excuse me, is there anything to sign? Who's it from?'

The man was already out of the gate and called back to her, 'I don't know, I just do my job and deliver the orders.'

Jane stood on the front doorstep for a moment, watching him go, before she went back inside and closed the front door after her. In the living room, she placed the yellow box on the table and looked at the girls. 'Oh, I bet it's from Tommy, a little gift before we get married. He's so thoughtful, isn't he?' She flipped the lid from the box and her eyes opened wide. The girls stood around and peered in, too.

There was a huge cake in the box, with lashings of white icing and the words 'Secrets, Secrets' written across the top in red icing. Jane slammed the lid on the cake box and stood back from it, still staring at the delivery.

'Who the fuck is sending things like this to me? Especially the day before I get married.' She looked for an order slip or a message. She found a card tucked in at the side and read it out.

'You can't have your cake and eat it. Just you wait and see.'

Lesley folded her arms tightly. 'I knew we should have done something about this. Look at us now. The night before the wedding is meant to be fun and here we are, looking over our shoulders, wondering who's coming for us.'

Katie opened the cake box again, looking for any details about where it had come from, anything that could lead them to finding out who was behind this. There was a small white sticker on the back of the box with details of the shop it had come from. Katie googled the address on her phone. 'It's off Rochdale Road, near the Harpurhey Asda. It's somebody local then, to go there and order a cake, isn't it? Hold on, I'll phone the number and see if I can find out anything else. I doubt they can tell me, though. It's all data protection, isn't it. And I bet they're shut for the day now.'

'Just try and see,' Maxine blurted out.

They sat around Katie as she rang the number, but it was no use. 'Voicemail,' she mouthed at her friends, but she stayed on the line. She was using her telephone voice and, in all fairness, she sounded posh as she left a message.

'At least it's a start. I bet the police could go in and ask the questions. They would have to answer then, wouldn't they?' said Lesley.

'I don't think the police will have the full force out over a cake being sent, though, will they,' Jane replied. 'Get it out of my house. Please, someone take it and launch it in the bin. It's giving me anxiety just looking at it.'

Katie scooped it up and left the room.

Lesley was spooked: chucking out the cake wouldn't change the message. 'It's always the same words they use, Jane. *Secrets, secrets*. I wish they would just say what they think they know and get this over with. It could be you or me in the frame – unless Katie or Max have something they're not letting on about.'

Jane pulled the fluffy grey blanket from the corner of the sofa and wrapped it around her body, but it did nothing to stop the chill spreading through her veins. 'This is what they want us to start doing – doubting each other, suspecting our best mates. We play it by ear and wait until they get in touch again or get bored. If it's Kim, she's probably got the attention span of a gnat. Hopefully, whoever it is will make mistakes along the way and, as soon as they do, we'll be waiting to land on them like a ton of bricks. I'm not letting it get to me. Honest to God, I've got bigger things to worry about than some schoolgirl feud or your nutcase stepdaughter. I've got a big day ahead of me tomorrow, and after that I'm jetting off on my honeymoon, so they can piss off. They're not spoiling my wedding day.'

Lesley wasn't as able as Jane to just push it all to the back of her mind. She couldn't help but ask questions of everyone in her life. Who knew what? Who was out to get her? But Jane had been like this since they were kids –

never one to brood on things, she lived her life able to lose herself in the moment.

Now she tried to change the mood and flicked some music on. She stood up, shook her body and started dancing and singing along to a Whitney Houston track. When Abba's 'I Do, I Do, I Do, I Do, I Do' followed, she grabbed her friends' hands and formed a circle, swaying one way then another. The mood seemed to be lifting until Abba faded out only to be replaced by 'Suspicious Minds'. The friends dropped their hands, each of them feeling the rising fear inside that all their secrets were about to spill over.

But the show had to go on. Despite the gnawing anxiety the friends felt, from the outside they looked like a picture-perfect bride squad. The girls had matching pyjamas on, and they were taking selfies and putting themselves all over social media. The hairdressers and make-up artist would be there early in the morning, and the girls were staying over. It was late now and, knowing sleep wouldn't come easy, they went to bed.

Jane lay in her bed and looked over at her wedding dress hung up on the other side of the room. In the gloom, with only the glow of the streetlight on it, it looked ominous – ghostly, even. But then the headlights of a passing car would hit it and the diamanté would shimmer like silver stars in the night sky. This time tomorrow night she would be a married woman. Her stomach churned at the thought of it. Was it excitement? Or was it that anxious feeling she'd had since she'd come back from her holidays?

Katie was next to her in the bed, having hopped happily into Tommy's usual spot, and was still awake too. 'It's all going to be alright, Jane. You will make a beautiful bride and you will live happily ever after. You've got "lucky cow" written all over you – you're Teflon, one of those people who seems to know how to dance through life not letting things get you down. It's women like me who don't ever get the dream. I thought Jake might have been my dream guy but, now I've slept with him, I've barely heard from him apart from a couple of excuses. I might give men up and stay single. If I concentrate only on myself, then what have I got to lose? I'm just unlucky in love.'

Jane reached over and smoothed a piece of hair that was in Katie's face. 'Don't give up on love. You deserve to be happy and who knows who you might meet at the wedding tomorrow? Tommy has lots of dishy mates who might take your fancy. And anyway, if I had a quid for every time you'd told me you were giving up on men, I'd be richer than the king.'

'No, I mean it this time: count me out. I'm thinking of something our Jade told me. She said if I put as much effort into a career as I do with men then I would be beyond successful. She's right, you know. All the men I've slept with have brought me nothing but trouble. I'm just a fool in love and always think the next man will be different. I've got no man, no money, and it pisses me off knowing that I don't even have a career to fall back on. You've all got something to show for life, but me, I'll always be just Katie who scrapes by.'

'Stop talking like that, Katie. Get it out of your head that you're not successful. You've done something more amazing than the rest of us – you've raised an incredible daughter. That means more than any number on a bank balance. Anyway, I get a lot from Tommy. And Lesley and Maxine got money from their partners over the years. I think love is just around the corner for you. You have to keep the faith.'

Katie smiled. Jane had been a good friend and, even now on the eve of her wedding, still had time to give her a boost. 'You're going to be the most beautiful bride ever tomorrow, Jane. Tommy will be gobsmacked when he sees you walking down that aisle.'

'He'd better be; the dress cost more than the bloody honeymoon. I'm going to sell it as soon as I come back from holiday. This wedding has cost an arm and a leg. Looking back, maybe we should have just gone abroad and had a few friends with us while we tied the knot. It would have been much easier, less stressful and cheaper. And we'd have been safe from busybodies sending stupid notes and wasting their money on cakes and spray paint. Or we could have eloped…'

'It's done now, so enjoy every moment of it. Memories are part of the glue in a good relationship, and what a memory this will be for you both.'

Jane closed her eyes and started to drift off to sleep. 'You're right, Katie. I'm going to remember my wedding day for the rest of my life,' she whispered dreamily.

PART FOUR

Dawn broke in fiery reds and oranges streaking the morning sky like a warning. It was early but they couldn't sleep any longer. The day was finally here. No more secrets.

Love hurts? Well, the truth was going to hurt a whole lot more.

Chapter Thirty-Three

The front room looked like a beauty parlour, make-up all scattered about the tables, hairdryers, curlers, the lot. Jane sat in the large black leather chair, having her make-up done. Her hair had already been pin-curled and she was still wearing her cream silk dressing gown. Katie, Lesley and Maxine were in the queue for the make-up artist, sitting in a cloud of setting spray and perfume.

Letty came in holding a big spray of flowers in her arms. 'Jane, these have just come for you.' She walked over to the bride-to-be and passed them to her. 'Give me a shout if you need anything, I'm just going upstairs to do the beds.'

Jane sat forward in her chair, smelt the flowers, reached inside the luxurious roses and found a small white card. Tommy loved cream roses and he'd sent her some spectacular ones in the past. It reminded her of all the good years they'd had. Her French-manicured nails slid under the envelope flap to open it. She pulled out the card.

Lesley clocked something was wrong and walked over to her. 'I'll put them in water.'

Jane passed her the card and waved the make-up artist back over to continue.

Lesley read the card and flushed red. No love note, no 'see you in church' message.

'Secrets, secrets, bitch.
Roses are white, roses are red.
When the truth comes out, you'll wish you were dead.'

Her legs were shaking as she walked over to Katie to show her the words that were written on the card. Maxine couldn't wait for her turn; she jumped from her seat, snatched the card out of Lesley's hand and read it. The hairdresser and make-up artist were watching them now. They could sense that something was wrong.

Katie tried to cover. 'Oh, Tommy is such a romantic guy. *I can't wait to be your husband,* he's written.'

The hairdresser smiled. 'That's so nice. I wish my man was romantic like him. My guy won't even give a door a bang, a tight-arse he is. Always penny-pinching.'

The girls all started laughing, relieved to break the tension.

But Lesley was quiet, and she kept looking over at Maxine, mouthing, 'What the fuck?'

Still, there was no time to discuss anything now. The wedding cars would be here soon to pick them all up. Jane was finished with her make-up, and everyone clustered around telling her she looked amazing.

'You look like you belong on the front cover of a magazine,' said Maxine, in awe of her friend's ability to put on a brave face. No flicker of doubt or worry showed through the airbrush-smooth make-up and the carefully pinned hair. The hairdresser and the make-up artist came to her side and wished her all the luck in the world. Then Katie walked them to the front door.

Jane stood in front of the long mirror in the hallway, and it was only then, looking at herself, that a wave of emotion took over her entire body. At first it felt like nerves – natural on a wedding day, Jane said to herself. Then she felt a hot sweat break out, prickling across her corseted back. Her pulse was loud now, a drumbeat in her ear, and then a clenching feeling spread across her chest. She'd had panic attacks before, had hidden them from Tommy in case he thought she was weak, but although she recognised the signs, she felt powerless to do anything about it.

Lesley was first to act. 'Maxine, quick, get her a cold drink of water. Take deep breaths, Jane, big breaths and blow them out slowly.' She made Jane match her own breathing – long, slow inhalations and exhalations until her delicate hand had stopped trembling.

Jane finally found her words. 'What the fuck, girls? What if this isn't it, what if it's just a warm up and someone tries to spoil the wedding today? Why send me bleeding flowers? What are they going to do next? I'm dreading the ceremony now. Is it too late to tell Tommy we should elope?'

The girls were looking at each other but nobody had the answer. All of them were dreading what could be said in church but, whatever was ahead, it was too late to turn back now.

'Come on, girl,' Katie said. 'We're having this wedding, and we'll get through the day and, once you and Tommy are wed, it's a new start for you both. You've got more important things to think about than some daft cow playing silly buggers sending you flowers. Think of how proud your mum would be to see you looking like this. Don't let anyone take that from you.'

At that, Jane sobbed. 'You're right, K. My mam would have loved this. I'm just glad you lot are here – since she died, you've been like family to me. I mean, a girl should have her father walking her down the aisle today but mine's been AWOL for years. We wouldn't know each other if we passed in the street. I know I'm lucky I've got a brother to do it, and he's come over from Leeds to be at my side today, but it should be my dad, shouldn't it? Our Liam is sound enough, but he's been gone from Manny for nearly thirty years now. He barely knows Tommy, doesn't really know me any more – I was a kid when he left home. I wonder if all this is why I almost screwed everything up with Tommy – like I had to break it before he did. I never knew what any marriage really looked like from the inside, let alone a happy one.'

None of them replied, they just let her talk. 'I think it's there, like a bruise on the inside, knowing that everyone leaves me in the end – Dad, Liam, Mam. Even my sister. Tracy doesn't come back from Spain from one year to the next. I thought she would have made the effort to come to the hen do, but if she was too busy for that I suppose I'm not that shocked she said she'd couldn't come today. No, our Liam will do me proud enough walking me down the aisle. It's not like Tommy's got much family left either, so at least both sides of the church will be the same. What's it they say – friends are the family you choose yourself?' Jane stopped talking and had a few sips of cold water. She inhaled deeply and gritted her teeth tightly. 'Jeez, listen to me. I sound like a card factory. No, enough blether. If someone wants to try and ruin my day, then let them. I'm ready for them. Watch this space. If anybody attempts to split me and Tommy up, I'll throttle them. They will wish they never messed with me to start with. Meltdown over, girls. I just needed a quick cry. Good job my make-up hasn't smudged, because I would have had to call the girls back. Right, get your frocks on, ladies, it's show time.'

As the three friends walked back downstairs, for a moment all their worries faded away. They looked amazing in their bridesmaid outfits. Pale yellow slim-line dresses, delicate silver jewellery and a flash of a silver shoe. Their tans complemented the colour of the dresses, and the sight of them was like a ray of sunshine from between the clouds. In the living room, they stood with arms around each other, posing and taking selfies as they waited for Jane to come back down.

Katie was gazing out of the window with the excuse of looking out for the wedding cars. But, in reality, she was making sure nobody was lurking in the bushes. Finally, the motors came into view and she saw Liam getting out of one. Jane glided into the room as if she was walking on air. They all looked at her and grinned.

Katie was the first to speak. 'That dress is out of this world. After you've worn it today, can I please try it on? Because, let's be honest, it isn't likely I'll ever be wearing one of my own.'

'Of course you will, Katie,' Maxine said.

Liam walked straight into the front room and froze on the spot when he saw his little sister stood in front of him wearing her wedding dress. He looked up at the ceiling and made the sign of the cross. 'She looks gorgeous, Mam. I know you're looking down on us today and I know you'll be by our side when she says "I do".'

The girls agreed and started to pick up their flowers, yellow and white with silky ribbons tied around them.

'Right, Jane, we'll see you at the church,' Katie said.

They each hugged Jane and left to get into the second car.

Jane smiled over at her brother. 'This is it – no turning back now.'

Liam helped pick up her flowers and made sure her dress didn't get trapped as she walked out of the door. Letty smiled. 'You look amazing. Have a great day. I hope it all goes well. This place will be spick and span by the time you're back.'

Jane didn't reply, just gave a tight smile. Her nerves were kicking in now and she couldn't wait to get the ceremony over with. Liam helped her into the car as some of the neighbours who were out clapped to show support. She waved at them through the window as she drove past them, feeling like Cinderella going to the ball. She only hoped the rats wouldn't appear before midnight.

The drive to the church seemed to be endless. Jane was too nervous to talk and instead watched the Manchester streets glide by. The traffic was slow and she couldn't work out if she wanted time to speed up or stay frozen in this moment forever. She knew they were running late but, if today went smoothly, she and Tommy would have all the time in the world.

The wedding bells started chiming as Jane's car arrived at the church. Jane could see her bridesmaids through the car window and that helped calm her. She dipped her head low for a moment so nobody could see her and sucked hard on her vape for a last few blasts.

Liam laughed. 'Always the rebel, aren't you, sister?'

She blew the grey smoke from the side of her mouth and wafted it from her face. 'Yep, I'm still breaking the rules, Liam. Some things never change, do they?'

'Correct. Come on, you. Let's get you hitched.'

The car door opened, and Lesley and Maxine and Katie were right there waiting for her like they said they would.

Katie was at her side. 'The church is packed out. I'm not going to lie, I've clocked a few dishy men in there,' she giggled.

Jane laughed. The moment was here now, just a short walk to the church doors and she'd leave her old life, even her old name, behind.

The organist played the Wedding March and the bridesmaids went walking in first. The girls scanned the guests – for friends, for lovers, for enemies. But there was nothing unusual to spot in the sea of smiling faces.

All heads turned to look as Jane made her entrance. Tommy was stood at the front of the church in his navy suit and, despite his smile, anyone could see the nerves kicking in, his fingers tapping out a beat against his leg.

Jane was at his side now and he looked over at her and smiled. 'You look amazing, babes. I'm glad you finally turned up; I thought you were going to leave me here by myself, jilted.'

'I would never do that. I love you too much,' she whispered.

And so it began. The priest started the service, the solemn traditional words bringing tears to a few eyes, followed by laughter as the priest spoke about the couple, how they met, memories they had shared.

Katie nudged Maxine as the part came that all four friends were dreading.

'Should anyone present know of any reason that this couple should not be joined in holy matrimony, speak now…' – the priest seemed to leave an excruciatingly long pause – '…or forever hold your peace.'

Lesley closed her eyes and, as Jane shot a sidelong glance at her, she could see the grip on her friend's hymn book tighten, and she too held her breath, expecting somebody to shout from behind them.

Not a peep. Maxine exhaled and rolled her eyes at Katie and Lesley, whispering, 'See, all that worrying for nothing. We can relax now.'

The bridesmaids were all smiles and Katie eyed up some bloke a few seats down from her.

'I now pronounce you husband and wife.'

Cheering broke out from the guests as Tommy kissed his bride for the first time as a married couple.

The bells pealed as they walked out of the church together, photographer snapping away in front of them. Tommy held Jane's hand tightly and squeezed it. 'You're mine now, babes. Let's get this reception started – it's going to be a night to remember.'

Chapter Thirty-Four

The reception was in full swing. Gavin, Tommy's best man, had just read out his speech. Tommy had stuck to the traditional thank-yous, giving out lockets to the bridesmaids as keepsakes, while Jane had said all the way along she didn't want to give a speech. Instead, it had fallen to Lesley to speak.

She was nervous and for days now, on top of everything else she had been juggling, every spare moment she'd been thinking about this daft bloody speech. She had told herself, 'For crying out loud, it's only talking in front of people, how hard can it be?' But, in her heart of hearts, she admitted that she'd half thought they'd never make it to the wedding day, never thought she'd actually be giving a speech. She quickly had a swig of her wine and searched for her notes. Everyone clapped as she stood up and she felt her cheeks glowing already. She wanted the ground to swallow her up.

Katie was tipsy at the side of her and she shouted, 'Go on, my girl, smash it.'

Lesley coughed to clear her throat. Her voice was shaky to start with. 'Ladies and gentlemen, my speech is not going to be long. I just want to say a few words as I know Jane would have loved her mum here today. I've been lucky enough to grow up with Jane – sorry: *Mrs Braxton* – and have seen her grow from a quiet child to a strong woman. She's kind, generous, and always there to listen to anyone who needs a bit of friendly advice. We have been through thick and thin together, always there to support each other and pick each other up when we've fallen or lost our way.' She shot a look over at the groom. 'Tommy, you're such a lucky man to be able to call this woman your wife. We will have to share her, because you can't have her all to yourself. I wish you both all the luck and happiness in the world and hope you have many wonderful years together. Can you please raise your glasses to the bride and groom!'

There was whooping and clapping, and Jane could tell by Lesley's face that she was glad it was over. Now all the friends could start to relax. The meal was served and, as the day turned into evening, the DJ arrived in the corner, getting ready to play all the crowd-pleasers.

As everyone got up from their tables, a man from the venue tapped Jane on her shoulder. 'I've had a note about a little extra that's been arranged for you and Tommy before your first dance.'

Jane leant into Tommy and laughed out loud. 'Oh, you lot, I knew this night would be full of surprises.'

She was led, along with her husband and the bridal party, to a small room off the main hall. A screen was set up in front of them and, as the friends settled, the lights dimmed. Katie and Maxine looked blank, as did Tommy, who sounded keener on hitting the bar than sitting through more soppy memories. 'Come on, I've got a party to attend. I've not even had a proper dance yet.'

A slideshow started rolling and photographs of Jane and Tommy filled the screen. Pictures of them both on holiday leant a glow to the room, photographs from nights out and birthday celebrations. Jane snuggled into Tommy. 'Aw, look at us, babes, that was ages ago. Where did you find all these photographs? I've not seen them in years.'

Tommy raised his eyebrows; he didn't have a clue what she was talking about. Another slide filled the screen and, as the small crowd focussed on it, silence fell. There was no more laughing. Tommy pushed Jane away from him and stared deep into her eyes.

'Who the fuck is that?'

Jane panicked, looking at the photograph of her and Francis that had stopped everyone in their tracks. More photographs followed and it became clear that somebody had followed Jane when she'd first met Francis, and taken photographs of them both all night long. She cringed as a photograph appeared of her on the beach, kissing Frankie. She dreaded to think what was coming next.

But Tommy had yanked the wire from the screen, and now spun round, nose to nose with her. 'Don't even try to deny whatever that is, Jane. It's not old, and it's not innocent. They are the clothes you wore when we went out the other night, and that is your hand down another man's trousers. Start talking, Jane, start fucking talking because this better be good.'

Katie and Maxine pulled Tommy away from her and scanned the room to work out who had done this. The big black heavy curtain behind the screen twitched slightly before a silhouette appeared from behind it and came to stand at the front of the room. Lesley squeezed her eyelids and ran to the switches to get some light into the room.

The woman stood tall and smiled. 'Secrets, secrets.'

'Letty, what the hell are you doing here?' Jane yelled.

Letty stepped forward and smiled at them all. 'I know. Surprised, eh? I thought it was time that we spoke about these secrets you've all been keeping.'

John looked puzzled as he stared at Lesley.

Ian whispered into Maxine's ear, 'What the hell is going on here?'

She snarled at him, 'Be quiet, will you, and let her say what she has to.'

Katie was ready to kick off, but Tommy dragged her back. 'Let her speak. Let her tell us what she knows about you all.'

Letty sat down on the chair she'd pulled out from behind the screen and crossed her legs demurely. She looked so different out of the tracksuit she usually wore to work. She had on a knee-length black dress and her shoulder-length hair was loose with soft curls.

Tommy was bubbling with anger. 'Come on, then, say what you have to so I can get the fuck out of here away from this slut.'

Jane was crying already. Her survival instinct told her there was no coming back from this: the evidence was right there in front of them for everyone to see.

Letty began to shed some light. 'So, Tommy, I'll tell *you* what I know first,' she smiled. 'Jane went on her hen party in Spain, and you were kind enough to get them a VIP spot at one of the best nightclubs in Benidorm. There she met a man called Francis. You've seen on the screen what happened. But what happened in Benidorm didn't stay in Benidorm. Maybe she can fill you in on all the details you need to know. She owes it you to tell the truth, doesn't she?'

Jane was trying to run at Letty, but Tommy dragged her back. 'Sit down, bitch, and listen to this. How could you lie to me, treat me like this?'

Maxine knew this wasn't going to end well and there were questions she wanted answering before a brawl broke out. 'Are you the one who's been sending the cards?'

Letty nodded. 'A nice touch, I thought. Especially after Jane had sent me round to all your houses, it was easy to learn everything I needed to know.'

Maxine was straight back at her. 'So, what are my friends not telling me? Go on, fill me in, if you know something. I'm not proud to admit it, but we all knew what happened on the hen.'

Letty stood and walked over to Katie, eyeballing her, looking her up and down like she was spoilt goods. Katie lifted her eyes to meet hers. 'What the hell are you looking at me for?'

'Katie slept with your Ian. I heard her talking to Lesley about it. They've kept this from you for years, Maxine. A drunken knee-trembler, Katie called it. It was the first thing that made me realise you might all be as bad as Jane.'

Maxine looked at Katie and then Ian. She bit down hard on her lips and clenched her fists. She was ready to explode, not sure if she wanted to punch her husband first or her friend.

But Letty had more to tell. 'And I need to bring my friend in to tell the rest of the story, because without her none of this would have been possible.'

The black curtain moved again and in walked Angela Potter.

Angela smiled over at Lesley and John. Lesley sat on the edge of her seat, gripping the edges of the chair like she was holding on for dear life.

'You may be wondering what my part was in this.'

Tommy was losing patience and wanted out of here as soon as possible. 'Hurry the fuck up. Just tell me what's what, then I'm getting my solicitor on the phone and getting today annulled and you lot out of my life.'

'Calm down, Tommy boy. I'm getting to the best bit.' Angela licked her lips and flicked her hair over her shoulder. 'I met Letty a few years ago when she came to me for a job. She'd just moved to Manchester, and she was struggling to make ends meet. I gave her a job and that's when we got to know each other better. She's a very hard worker. She told me that she'd come to Manchester to try and find her mother. You see, Letty was adopted when she was a baby. I thought about how I'd feel if I'd had to give Kimberley up, and I wanted to help. I took the information that I had and spent hours searching hospital records and speaking with social services. I employed somebody to help in the end, because it was getting me nowhere fast. Anyway, bingo, I found her mother. Neither me nor Letty could believe it at first. I think you don't mind me speaking for you here, Letty, but your emotions were all over the place. I remember you saying you didn't even know if you wanted to meet her. The records showed that a fifteen-year-old girl had given her away when she was born because she couldn't look after her. I think a few of us here know exactly who that woman is. Once I found out who her mother was, I knew I could get Letty to help me too, in return for all the time and money I'd spent searching for her mother. So, when Jane rang my company for a cleaner, I knew Letty was the one for the job. She could be my ears, tell me what was going on and keep me in the loop. You're probably asking yourselves who Letty's mother is, aren't you? Well,' she paused and smiled. 'Lesley, meet your daughter Letty.'

John twisted his head and looked at his wife. 'Is this true? Why have you never told me about this before? I thought I knew everything about you.'

Lesley was choking, her words stuck in her throat. She knew this secret was only the key to another. She was desperate to reach out and embrace her daughter, but she knew there was a question she was bound to ask that would shatter the last remnants of their world.

Letty came to Lesley. 'So, Mother, do I have a father, or is that something you are going to deprive me of too?'

Lesley had frozen, flashbacks from her past flooding her mind. 'I wanted to know how you were so badly, wanted to know you were alright. I gave you up not because I didn't love you, but because I did. I was a young girl. I had no money to feed you. My parents would have disowned me. I had no choice. And… and I couldn't ask the father for help. My friends will tell you the same – they stood by me throughout the pregnancy, through the hardest day of my life signing the adoption papers. But, even in all those long months, I never told them who your father was.'

Letty looked unimpressed. 'I've had years of wondering who my parents are, visualising you and what you might look like. I ask only one thing from you, and I will never contact you again. My father's name. At least you owe that much to me.'

Maxine and Katie and Jane all looked at each other. Lesley looked around the room and decided there was no point nursing this secret any longer. Everybody's eyes were on her, not a sound from the gathering – they'd come for a wedding and got a drama instead.

Lesley's voice was trembling, her friends could hardly hear her. 'It was the school prom and we'd all had too much to drink. We were leaving school, and it was a big celebration. I was steaming, everybody was.' She snivelled and wiped her eyes with a bit of white crumpled tissue she pulled from her clutch bag. 'I felt sick and went outside for some fresh air. I thought I was alone, but I wasn't. I was being sick, and he rubbed my back and held my hair back. He even sat with me until the dizziness had subsided.' Her voice got louder now, desperate. 'He initiated it. I would never have kissed him in a million years. I knew he was taken, forbidden fruit. I'm so sorry, this has haunted me for years.' Lesley broke down and dropped her head into her hands, head shaking as she continued. 'He kissed me and led me to quiet place. He told me we had to hide away from the teachers until I had sobered up, otherwise we would be in big trouble. One thing led to another, and we ended up having sex. I had never had sex before. I don't think I even knew what he was doing until he was inside me. He was my first. How could I tell anyone that I was taken advantage of? Who'd have believed me, a drunk fifteen-year-old? I felt so dirty, I didn't want anyone to know – I wanted to pretend my first time was all romantic, so I blocked it out. I didn't want you to find me like this. I didn't want you find your father like this, to know that he—'

Letty stared at her. 'Just tell me his name. That's all I want, a name.'

Lesley shook her head and covered her face with both hands. 'Maxine, I'm so sorry. I've never told anyone who the father was before. It's,' – she paused and swallowed hard, ragging her hands through her hair – 'Letty is Ian's child.'

Maxine screamed out like an injured animal. Ian looked like he was frozen, and Letty tried to take in what she'd just heard.

Maxine stumbled her way to the exit. 'Open the fucking door. I want out of here. Is there anyone in this room who hasn't slept with my so-called husband? Get me the hell out of here, now.'

Angela opened the door with a smile. Her deed was done here today, and she stood there serenely looking at the remaining three friends. She raised her voice. 'Feel the pain like I had to. Feel it deep in your hearts while your world falls apart right in front of you and there is nothing you can do about it. Your secrets are out, now live with them.' She turned on her heel, and was gone. Letty followed her and Tommy not long after. Katie and Jane and Lesley stood there, shellshocked.

Ten minutes later, in a reception side room, Jane's black mascara was streaming down her face. She'd sent Liam out there to see if he could find Tommy, but there was no sign. Lesley, usually the practical one, was virtually in a trance, staring in front her, not uttering a word. Even Katie, who could usually be relied on to find the funny side of any situation, was simply sat shaking her head.

Eventually she was stirred by an alert on her phone. 'I've rang a taxi, and we can all leave from the side door there. I've had a word with the manager and he's going to tell the guests that you and Tommy had to leave because of a family emergency. There is no point in ending the party, is there, if it's all been paid for?'

Jane sucked in a large breath. 'Just get me home and out of this bleeding dress. This isn't over. No way is that Letty getting away with this. How conniving is she? I mean, her problem was with you, Lesley, not with us, so why ruin us all?'

Lesley turned her head, devastation written all over her face. 'How has it come to this? I've thought about her every day of my life since I last held her, but I was too scared to face the truth. It was easier to keep it a secret than to know I've created a monster by letting her turn to Angela not me. It's over – everything is over now. John and me? He won't have me back, and I don't know how I go about healing things with Letty. My life is in ruins.'

'Join the club,' said Jane. 'You're right – why did I ever think Tommy wouldn't find out about Frankie? Why did I sleep with Frankie in the first place? I've always felt that, if I kept moving, I could outrun everything – my past, heartbreak, bad decisions. But no more, no more running. I've only been keeping this a secret for a few weeks – Katie, on my life, I don't know how you did it for so many years.'

'I'm just gobsmacked you slept with that rat, too, Lesley. I thought it was only me. I was so ashamed of my night with him but, I can see now, he used that. He knew he'd shamed you into silence once, years back, and the arrogant prick thought he was untouchable. But how did you bear all that alone?' Katie looked baffled.

'Maxine loved Ian from an early age, you know that – she idolised him. Meant she could never see his flaws,' Lesley said quietly. 'She'd only been seeing him a few weeks by prom night, but she was already smitten with him, infatuated, I think. I could never have hurt her like that by saying her beloved boyfriend had stuck it in me when I was too drunk to know what was going on. Once

I found out I was pregnant, I knew I could never keep the child or tell anyone about Ian. You girls helped me through one of the hardest times of my life back then and I just wanted it over so I could move on with my life. If I had told Ian that I was pregnant, could you have imagined Maxine and everybody else? I would have been slagged off by everyone who knew me, including you lot. It was easier to say nothing. And, if you say nothing for long enough, eventually, even when you want to speak, you can't. Oh, my baby girl, what have I done?'

Jane was drying her eyes now. 'Well, sometimes the truth is better left unsaid.'

There was a short silence, then Katie said, 'I don't know about that. We've all been carrying this weight around with us. Regrets are as toxic as secrets. I wish I could change what I did, but I can't. I don't know if Maxine will ever speak to me or you again, Lesley, you know that, don't you? Especially now he's got a daughter that none of us knew about. That will break Maxine in two because Ian has always been the one who didn't want any children. But if you can take anything from today, at least we've all had to put down those weights we've been carrying. We've had to let go of our secrets.'

The manager popped his head inside the room. 'Your taxi is here, ladies.'

Jane hitched her dress up and bent her head low; she didn't want anybody to see her like this. Lesley and Katie followed her.

The taxi pulled up outside Jane's house. Tommy's car was there, and she could see black bags piled high on the back seat of it. Katie clocked them too. 'Do you think it's a good idea you coming here? Maybe you should wait until he has gone and then come back. Jane, he was raging, and I didn't like the look in his eyes when he was speaking to you. He's hurt. Maybe let him calm down first.'

'No, I have to face this. You two are here with me, so he won't do anything in front of you both. I've hidden from the truth for too long.' Jane pushed the front door open with the palm of her hand. It wasn't locked and she could hear noises coming from upstairs. Katie and Lesley went into the front room and sat down. Jane went straight upstairs.

Tommy was in the bedroom, emptying drawers, pulling clothes from the wardrobe. He clocked her at the door and carried on with what he was doing. Jane edged into the room and sat on the bed. 'I'm not going to ask you to forgive me, Tommy. But I do want you to know it was a mistake. It was a stupid holiday romance that got out of hand. You're the one I love. I know you won't take me back, but I need you to know I love you.'

He turned his head slowly and smirked at her. 'Damaged goods, you are. Everything we had has gone. I wouldn't touch you with a barge pole now.'

'Tommy, is there any part of you that still loves me? We could even still go on our honeymoon and try and sort this out. Cheating on you was the stupidest thing I've ever done. And you might as well know, he was nothing compared to you – in fact, he was a waster, a drug-pusher.'

'What do you mean, what kind of drugs?'

'What does it matter, Tommy? But he used me, I'll tell you that. Seduced me and used me as a drugs mule. I could have been slung in prison.'

'Would have served you right – two-timing slut,' Tommy laughed, a cruel smile on his face.

He rammed some more clothes into the bin-liners and tied them up. He stood over Jane and looked down at her. 'I had a feeling you were shagging about, you know. I could feel something had changed, but you lied to me and told me I had nothing to worry about. Our rules, Jane, you broke our rules and there is no going back from there. I'm leaving you and I'll tell you now, I will never be coming back. Anything that I leave, I will get someone to come back for, so have it ready.'

Jane pleaded with him. 'Please, Tommy, let's talk again when you have calmed down. We're married now, we have made promises to each other.'

'Promises mean nothing to you, clearly,' Tommy growled as he carried on packing his clothes up.

Jane sat on the bed crying, tears streaming down her face. 'I was a fool, I know that now. We could have been so happy, Tommy. You will be the biggest regret in my life. And, if we're coming clean, then there's something else you need to know—'

Before she could finish, Jane heard noises outside the bedroom. She lifted her head slowly and watched as the door swung open. Letty was stood there.

Jane sprang from the bed like boiled water had been poured all over her. 'What the fuck are you doing here?

Haven't you done enough? I never want to see you in this house again.'

Letty walked over to Jane and opened her palm to reveal a silver key. 'I've come to bring your key back. You got caught up in all this, but I've got no sympathy. I owed Angela a lot. She helped me find my mother and, when she sent me to your house and I found out that it wasn't just your friends keeping secrets, I knew it wasn't right. Tommy is a lovely man, and you should have never treated him like that. And what about me? I worked hard every day for you, and you never really appreciated any of it. You took it for granted that people would always run about after you. All the mess you left for me, all the evenings and weekends you pissed off and left Tommy to fend for himself. Do you not think that you should have been spending time with him, the man you love, instead of jetting off with your friends sleeping with every Tom, Dick and Harry?'

Jane snatched the key from her hand and flung it on the bed. 'Since when has my relationship had anything to do with you? You're a cleaner, nothing more and nothing less. What, are you jealous?'

Letty smiled at Jane and shot a look over at Tommy. 'I'll go and wait in the car. Make sure you get the case I packed for you with all your holiday clothes in it. We only have a few hours before we have to be at the airport.'

Jane digested what she had said with a sour expression. 'Did you just say *we*?'

Tommy smiled too now. He walked to Letty's side, draped his hand around her neck and kissed her cheek.

'She sure did. Letty is coming with me on honeymoon. You don't think, once she told me about you, that I sat here crying about it, did you?'

Jane's jaw dropped. 'Are you saying you two are together?'

Letty said, 'Jane, your man was lonely. I was the one looking after him while you were away doing God knows what. I cooked and cleaned for him and, for months now, I've been doing more for him than you have. And yes, as I don't like secrets as much as you seem to, we have been sleeping with each other. And since you've been putting it about too, you can't give Tommy any grief. Abuse it and lose it, that's what I say.'

Jane glared at Letty and screamed, 'You vindictive, two-faced cow! Don't think this'll last. You're young enough to be his daughter!'

Tommy didn't seem phased by it all. He picked up his black sports bag and hooked it over his shoulder. 'Come on, Letty. Sun, sea and sex await us. Two weeks on the beach to look forward to. It was a good job I changed the names on the holiday, wasn't it?'

As he opened the door, Lesley and Katie almost fell through it.

Letty straightened her hair and squared her shoulders.

Katie was confused. 'What's going on?'

Jane could hardly breathe, her words getting stuck in her mouth, time slowing down as she processed everything. 'Those two are together. He's been shagging her all along.'

Lesley turned to Letty, trying to digest everything, looking deep in her eyes. This was her daughter and her best friend's husband. What a mess.

Katie shook her head and walked to Jane's side, escorting her back to the bed. 'Sit down, Jane. If Tommy is shagging that tart, then good luck to him. Girls like her don't have men for long. She's just wrecked all our lives, yet she's stood there like butter wouldn't melt in her mouth. I'm sorry, Lesley, I know she's your daughter, but she's been got to by Angela.'

Jane listened to every word Katie said and found her inner strength at last. There were no more tears now. She stood up and let out a laboured breath. 'Katie's right, Tommy. You two won't last. I've hurt you and I apologise for that but, come on, two wrongs don't make a right, do they?'

Tommy didn't even give her a backward glance.

Lesley ran after Letty as she followed her man out to his car. 'Letty, please, just wait a minute.'

Letty stopped and waited for Lesley to catch up with her. 'What do you want?'

Lesley stuttered, not really sure of what she was saying next. 'I know you don't want to hear this, but you have to remember I was younger than you are now when I had you. I've never forgot you. Every day, I've thought about you and where you might be. Circumstances have stopped me looking for you. I thought about it loads of times, but I gave you up, left you. Why would you ever want to see me?'

'I thought about you every day too. I felt I never belonged with my adoptive parents. Don't get me wrong, they were lovely people, but I always knew I had my own mother and father somewhere out there in the world. I used to dream that one day you would come knocking on my door and take me back.'

Lesley was broken now, tears pouring from her eyes. 'I wish I could have. My parents were strict and, once they knew I was having a baby, they sent me away until you were born. They made me sign the adoption papers and they took you away from me. I was never allowed to speak about you again. You took a piece of my heart with you that day. I spent ten days with you after you were born, and I named you Casey. I used to sit and hold you every minute of every day while you were with me. The day they took you will haunt me forever. I told them I had changed my mind, I was keeping you, but they never listened and took you anyway. Maybe one day, we can have some kind of a relationship and get to know each other properly?'

Letty shook her head and looked the other way. 'I don't think so. My heart can't stand any more disappointments. I've seen you now and I know who my father is. If I change my mind, I will get in touch. I don't know what I expected when I found you, but this was not how I planned for us to meet. I got caught up in Angela's schemes and I couldn't get out. I want peace in my life now. Seeing you and knowing what happened has helped me find that. Right now, I just want some sun and some peace – and Tommy can give me both.'

Lesley choked up and nodded. 'I'm sorry.'

Chapter Thirty-Five

Jane was cleaning the front room. With no cleaner to help her, she had been putting off facing the chaos left from the morning of the wedding. It had been three days now since it had all come out, but there were still wilting rose petals on the floor. Their 'Bride Squad' robes were left slung over the sofa and scattered about were half-drunk flutes of Prosecco that had gone as flat as the wedding day itself. Jane knew her neighbours and even the wider estate were taking about it. The gossipers were having a field day. She hadn't been out yet and there was something therapeutic about wiping away the mess and chaos of that day. She looked at the living room after she'd finished. She was an independent woman now and, if this ordeal had taught her anything, it had taught her never to rely on a man again. She'd spent the last few days going over the accounts for the salon, working out what her future looked like now. She was going to have to rely on herself from here on. But she also knew that she needed to repair the fault lines between her friends. They'd been at her side before Tommy came on the scene, and she wanted the four of them to still stand proud now he was gone.

Lesley honked her horn outside the house. Jane looked out of the window quickly and grabbed her house keys and her coat. She brought a couple of bottles of wine with her too. She locked up and walked out of the gate. She could see a few women from her street talking not far from her and it was obvious they were discussing her messed-up life. She smirked and shouted over to them, 'Do you ladies know anybody who wants to buy a wedding dress?' She sniggered as she watched the women shake their heads. There you go, let them talk about that now for a few days.

Katie was in the passenger seat. 'I don't know how you've persuaded Maxine to see you, Jane. I mean, what if she's only agreed to it so she can punch our lights out?'

'Us girls need to stick together. Granted we've made some bad bloody decisions, but I told Max life isn't about not making mistakes, it's about how you move on from them. Talking of which, how're things at your house, Lesley?'

'I'm sleeping in the spare room. It's been tough, but you're right – it's better to face my past and the truth about Letty, and work out what comes next, than it was keeping it all locked up inside. John and I've agreed we're going to call it quits, and I thought it would break us, but we have both stayed civil. Weirdly, I think we feel like we've got more in common now – we both have daughters who need our love and support and a way of getting out from Angela's shadow.'

Jane sighed. 'That woman has a lot to answer for, hasn't she? I want revenge, I'm not going to lie.'

Katie agreed. 'She must have a weakness. I'm right behind you when the time comes to get our own back.'

Lesley shook her head as she pulled off onto the main road. 'I feel more chilled than I have done in decades. Sure, I don't like the woman, but life's for living, not for vendettas. The only thing I will say is that I don't think she's a good influence on Letty or Kimberley. For that reason, you might want to have a look at what's in the carrier bag on the seat next to you, Jane.'

'You dark horse!' said Jane as she pulled out sheafs of paperwork. 'What's all this?'

Lesley smiled enigmatically. 'I was up in the loft, looking for my memory box from when Casey, sorry, Letty, was born, and I found all of Angela's accounts books from the business she ran when her and John were married. It looks like she's been dodging tax. I'm not saying she's doing it now, but in the past she has. A quick phone call to the tax office should sort that out.'

Jane nodded slowly. 'That's a start, I suppose. But I'm not like you, Les. I was thinking something more dramatic – like those bleeding cards Letty kept sending.'

Maxine saw the car pull up, and paced up and down the front room, agitated, sucking hard on her vape. Jane walked in first and hugged her. Katie and Lesley stood together near the door and neither of them moved a muscle. Jane pulled the bottles of wine out of the bag and plonked them on the table. 'Get some glasses, Maxine. We can all have a drink before we start to sort out this unholy mess.' She passed her one of the bottles of fizz. 'Let's start with the good stuff. Celebrate us all being free of our baggage.'

Maxine eyeballed Lesley and Katie and went into the kitchen. Katie nudged Lesley and whispered, 'She's going to kick off. Did you see the look she gave us?'

Lesley went and sat down on the chair near the door. That meant Maxine would have to sit on the sofa between Katie and Jane. Maxine came back into the room holding four glasses pinched in her fingers. Once she placed them on the table, Jane popped the cork and started to fill the glasses.

'Do I have to ask where Ian is?' Jane enquired.

Maxine shuddered. 'I don't know, and I don't care. He hasn't dared show his face since the wedding. I've had a lot of thinking time these last few days and, while I'm furious you lot didn't come clean before, I think it's the only thing he could have done to turn that switch off in me forever. Something about knowing he's been doing the dirty on me since we first started dating as kids has finally made me realise there was nothing to fight for, no happy days to get back to. He's been a snake since day one.'

Lesley grasped her wine glass. She wanted to get this over with as soon as possible. Her voice was quiet. 'Maxine, are you ready to hear what I have to say?'

Maxine nodded and Lesley began. 'Maxine, I think the world of you and wish I had told you before. I don't know whether it was assault or abuse, but I never consented. I don't think I knew what rape was, and I certainly didn't want to use that word once I found out I was pregnant. And I know you probably want to hear me say I wish that night had never happened, and in so many ways I do, but I can't ever wish Letty away. Even with all the pain she's caused us, I know she was sent to me for a reason and, if I have to spend the rest of my days making things right with her, I will.'

Maxine listened, digesting what she was saying.

Lesley went on. 'When I found out about Katie sleeping with Ian and never told you, you should know that she was all ready to tell you, but I stopped her. You loved Ian and you would never have a word said against him. Be honest here: at that time, if Katie had told you she'd slept with Ian, you would have probably put all the blame on her.'

Katie was relieved Lesley was taking the lead – she'd worded it so well. If Katie had been doing the talking, she would have been more direct and told her Ian was a dirty bastard and he should have kept it in his pants.

Maxine took a drink of her wine and kept the cold glass in her hand, running her finger around the edge of it. 'I know, I know. I've been thinking, and I can understand why you both kept it from me. It still hurts though, and to hear Ian has a daughter when he's always told me he never wanted any kids has hit me hard.'

Katie looked at Maxine. 'I'm sorry too. I was weak – I was in a spiral where I didn't value myself, I was only worth what men saw in me. I know my friendship with you is more important than any date or one night stand.

Anyway, if I don't respect myself, then how can I expect any man to?'

Maxine raised her glass in the air. 'I say bin off men from now on. We only need each other. But we never lie to each other again.'

Jane's face went bright red, and she shook her head. 'Alright, alright. I want to restart our friendship on a fresh note, and I don't want to lie to any of you anymore.'

Lesley and Katie looked puzzled.

Maxine nudged Jane. 'Spit it out, then, what are you lying about? Please don't tell me you've slept with Ian too. Bloody hell, it would be a full house if you have.'

The girls chuckled and watched as Jane stood up.

She put down her untouched glass, and slowly she lifted her jumper up and revealed a small bump. 'I know I said I was booked in the clinic just before the wedding, but I couldn't go through with it. This could be my only chance of a child. I don't need a father around as long as I have you girls by my side. Godmothers rule!'

'Jane, you'd trust me as godmother?' Katie gasped.

Lesley started to smile, as did Maxine. 'This is our chance to do it right. Motherhood – shared. Jane, we'll be with you every step of the way.'

Jane's hormones were all over the place and she burst out crying. 'Thanks, girls. I knew I could rely on you all. So, I thought we could celebrate with a little trip to the sun. My treat, of course. I say we go somewhere hot before I can't fit in my bikinis, and just chill together and repair.

We've all been through a lot lately. The last trip we took ruined me. Hopefully, this one will fix me.'

'Jane, you can't! You need to save your money for the baby.' Lesley looked shocked.

'Okay, you might as well hear part two of the baby-daddy truth-bomb.' Jane took a breath. 'I got a text the other day. From Francis. No, don't say anything. Yes, he'd heard about the wedding, and no, we're not getting together. But I figured, if this chapter of my life is really one without any secrets, then I had to tell him I'd not gone to the clinic.'

'Did he hit the roof?' Katie winced.

'No, quite the opposite. Once I told him I wanted nothing from him – no cash, no commitments, no contact – he was fine. In fact, he told me he'd give me something worth more than any child support.'

Maxine was on tenterhooks. 'Christ, Jane, what did he give you?'

Jane smiled. 'His secret. Which turns out not to be so much *his* secret, as Tommy's. You know that bag of flipping pills he got me to bring back? Steroids and all that rubbish? Turns out my husband-for-a-day, Tommy, isn't the good guy he likes to make out.' The girls leaned in, topping up their glasses. 'The whole reason Tommy sent us to that resort, that club, is because Frankie's boss is his supplier. He's been giving him access to pills for all of Tommy's gyms for years, Frankie tells me. He damn well knew that someone was going to get us to bring the pills back – Tommy didn't care if me, or any of us, got stopped and charged. All he cared about was his cut. But it means he won't be giving me any bother when I ask for my share of the house and our bank accounts.' Jane stopped, letting the truth sink in.

'Christ on a bike,' was all Katie could muster.

'Do you know what? Frankie was right. Knowing this – yes, I felt like a fool when I realised Tommy had been playing me – but it finally explained to me why I felt like something wasn't right, maybe even why I was tempted by Frankie. Tommy never really loved me, and perhaps I never really loved him. It's this baby I'm carrying – this is what love really is.'

The girls hugged. Katie was the first to break away. She wanted to say something to the group. 'If we're making big announcements, I'm enrolling back in college. I'm going to study law and see if I can make something of myself. They say it's never too late to learn, and I really think I would love it.'

'Well done you,' Maxine said. 'Although I wish you'd done it years ago. I've got a date for my hearing and my solicitor is making my head spin. But the good thing is, she says, I've got a high chance of only getting a fine. She agreed with everything you girls said about explaining the abuse Ian's been dishing out for years.'

Lesley hugged her. 'Well, I'm going to get my money from the divorce and then I'm going travelling and, Maxine, once you get your hearing out of the way, I'm hoping you will come with me. I'm going to take three months out and see the world. When I come back, I'm going to hope Letty has calmed down, and got Tommy out of her system. I want to see if she'll let me into her life. It won't be easy, but good things often aren't, are they?'

Maxine didn't need asking twice. 'I've already thought about it. I'm going to sell the house and buy a flat, which means I will have enough money left to live on and come travelling too. I need a fresh start. Here's to no more secrets.'

Chapter Thirty-Six

Katie sat with the phone in her hand. Jane and Lesley and Maxine were all by her side as she made the call to HM Revenue and Customs. 'I would like to report fraud and tax evasion, please. Angela Potter from AP Cleaning Services.'

Once the call was made and all the details were given, Jane opened the card and wrote on it: '*Secrets, secrets*'. She placed the card inside the gold envelope and wrote the address on the front of it. Lesley peeled the stamp and stuck it on the envelope. They smiled at one another and at the envelope lying on the kitchen table. Katie ran a single finger across the front of it and said, with a cunning smile, 'Don't get mad, get even.'

Rumour had it that Ian was living in London somewhere. Maxine had never asked her brothers anything about what they had done to her husband, and maybe it was better that way. As long as he wasn't in her life anymore, she was happy. There would be no more midnight visits to her house, no more attempts to win her back with weasel words. Good riddance.

After they'd sealed the card, it was time for farewells. Lesley and Maxine were heading to the airport. After Maxine's hearing left her with only a fine, she was free to travel. The two friends said goodbye to Katie and Jane. Jane's stomach was huge now and she was due any time soon. Lesley and Maxine had said they'd delay their trip until the baby was born, but Jane was having none of it. Katie was with her anyway, so she wasn't alone. The girls huddled together and said their goodbyes.

Lesley and Maxine walked into the airport and waved one last time at Jane and Katie. The adventure had begun, and this was a new chapter for all the women. Katie put her arm around Jane. 'Remember what we wrote on our pencil cases all those years ago, J? Well, I say nothing changes. True friends are never apart, maybe in distance, but never in the heart.'

EPILOGUE

Katie was sitting in the hospital canteen, reading the paper, waiting for Jane to come out of her midwife's appointment on her due date. She shivered as she looked at a story on the second page – a body washed up on the Spanish coast had finally been identified, a man called Peter Markham. Katie experienced a sudden flash of buried memories from the hen do. A tall guy buying her drinks. The lapping waves darkening and reflecting back the neon signs of the beach bars. A gold bracelet on his wrist. Him pushing her to do more than she wanted. His hands around her neck. Her pushing back. A splash and then nothing more to be seen on the surface of the dark waters. Don't get mad, she thought, get even.

Acknowledgments

Thank you to my husband James and my children Ashley, Blake, Declan and Darcy for always supporting me.

Thank you to all my readers and followers on Facebook, X and Instagram for all your support.

Big thanks to Gen, Meg, Alice and all the team at HarperNorth for always believing in me and my stories and for all the hard work they do.